"MISSILE," MA
"COMING IN F

Grimaldi shoved forward on the cyclic and aimed the Black Hawk for the ground. Their only chance to survive the attack was for him to get the chopper in the dirt and present a tail-on target to the Strellas.

"Another one's coming in from starboard," McCarter warned.

With two missiles zeroing in from different directions, Grimaldi had to stop running and go into missile evasion maneuvers. But he was a second too late. The nose of one of the Strellas grazed the top of the chopper's tail fin and detonated.

"Oh, damn," the Stony Man pilot muttered. "We lost the tail rotor."

Bolan keyed the mike. "Hang on, guys. We're going down."

DON PENDLETON'S

MACK BOLAN®

STONY MAN™

TRIPLE STRIKE

A GOLD EAGLE BOOK FROM

WORLDWIDE®

TORONTO • NEW YORK • LONDON
AMSTERDAM • PARIS • SYDNEY • HAMBURG
STOCKHOLM • ATHENS • TOKYO • MILAN
MADRID • WARSAW • BUDAPEST • AUCKLAND

First edition November 1998

ISBN 0-373-61921-9

Special thanks and acknowledgment to
Michael Kasner for his contribution to this work.

TRIPLE STRIKE

Printed in U.S.A.

TRIPLE STRIKE

CHAPTER ONE

Eastern Bosnia

United States Air Force Major John Hammer was
cruising at twelve thousand feet through the night
skies over eastern Bosnia. Hammer was a third-
generation Air Force pilot. His grandfather had flown
P-51 Mustangs against the Messerschmitts of the
Third Reich, his father had blasted North Vietnamese
convoys on the Ho Chi Minh Trail and Hammer had
gotten his licks in during the Gulf War. He'd been
an Eagle driver back then and had blasted two Iraqi
air force MiG-29s out of the sky on the first day of
the air war.

Now he was flying the world's most advanced spy
plane on a top-secret mission over Bosnia, and he
was digging it. He knew that Bosnia wasn't much of
a war zone, but it was the closest thing to combat
flying there was for an American pilot right now.
And though his subsonic TR-3 Night Owl stealth
plane was a far cry from the Mach 2 F-15 fighters

he had flown in the Gulf, it was the hottest thing in the air in this part of the world this night.

The mission that had dragged him out of his bunk back at Aviano Air Force Base in Italy wasn't all that exciting. Flying a snoop-and-poop wasn't the same as flying MiG CAP with his weapons hot, no matter how classified it was. But it was a real mission, and it was sending him in harm's way again and that was the only thing that counted.

Hammer's eyes swept across the Night Owl's instruments and digital readouts again. His recon data links were on-line and hot, transmitting everything his sensors were picking up to the satellites and ground stations that were tracking him. He hadn't been told exactly what he was looking for, only that it had something to do with a guy with an SAR implant. He had been instructed to fly over an area of several hundred square miles with all of his sensors hot and let the mysterious black boxes in the belly of his bird do their thing. If whoever it was that the brass wanted him to find was down there, he'd find him or her.

Checking his nav screen, he saw that he was approaching the end of this leg of his search pattern and got ready to make his next scheduled turn. It was a moonless night, which made his matte black aircraft invisible to sight, as well as to radar, but at twelve thousand feet, Hammer really didn't have to worry about anyone on the ground seeing him anyway. He was in his own world with only the stars for company.

"Zero Seven Five," the voice of the airborne mission controller orbiting to the west over the Adriatic Sea came over the earphones in his helmet. "This is Blue Bell Control, over."

"Seven Five, go." Hammer felt his adrenaline surge as he clicked in his throat mike. On this kind of mission, the AWACS plane wouldn't be talking to him unless it was important. One of the rules of stealth on this kind of mission was that he didn't use his radio except in an emergency. Radio transmissions could be detected and used to track his flight path the same as radar.

"This is Control," the AWACS answered. "Be advised that we have picked up a bogey heading your way, vector two-eight-niner. Over."

Hammer automatically looked out of the curved canopy as he reached over to switch on his own airborne radar. Per SOP, Night Owl pilots made their recon runs with their radars shut down so enemy aircraft or ground stations couldn't pick up their emissions and track them, either.

"Seven Five. Do you have an ID on him, over?" he asked as his radar screen flickered on.

"That's a negative," Blue Bell answered. "But he's coming on fast, Mach 1.4. Over."

Suddenly Hammer saw a shadow block out the stars in front of him, and he knew he was screwed big-time. Slamming the control stick forward, he put his plane into a steep dive, but it wasn't fast enough. The other pilot apparently saw him at the same time and put his plane into a dive to avoid him, as well.

The two aircraft didn't hit head-on; in fact they barely touched. But as light as it was, the collision tore the vertical stabilizers off of the TR-3, throwing it into a flat spin. Hammer barely had time to reach for the ejection handle to his bang seat before the Night Owl started coming apart around him.

The rocket motor in the bottom of his Lockheed-Martin ejection seat blew him through the closed cockpit canopy, sending him six hundred feet into the air. At the top of its trajectory, the seat automatically separated from the pilot and the spring-loaded parachute deployed.

Fighting to get his parachute canopy under control, Hammer watched his multimillion dollar, high-tech spy plane turn into aerial junk below him. He looked for the other plane, but didn't see anything, not even the blue flame of its exhausts. But if it was flying as fast as the AWACS had said it was, it would be out of sight by now. Alone in the night sky, he fell with only the sound of the wind in the chute's risers for company.

Checking the altimeter on his parachute harness, Hammer saw that he was getting close to the ground. With no moon to illuminate the terrain below him, he decided to take his chances with what fate had given him rather than trying to pick out a safe landing spot. In the dark, everything down there looked the same, so trying to change direction might well take him into something worse than what waited below.

The landing shock took Hammer by surprise and drove the wind out of him. Looking around, he saw that he had landed in a cleared area. He couldn't see much beyond that as he hit the release to drop his parachute harness. He was reaching into the pocket of his flight suit for his survival radio when he felt a blow to the head and everything went black.

Stony Man Farm, Virginia

HAL BROGNOLA, Barbara Price and Yakov Katzenelenbogen were crowded into Aaron Kurtzman's computer room at Stony Man Farm watching the real-time readouts that were being sent from the TR-3's satellite data link. The spy plane was transmitting a full range of infrared video, magnetic imaging, electronic emissions, terrain-mapping radar and everything else in its sizable bag of tricks.

This electronic information was all encoded, and usually only the top-secret arm of the government known as the National Reconnaissance Office received it. In their headquarters outside Washington, D.C., electronic and photographic intelligence from spy satellites and aircraft such as the TR-3 flowed in to be decoded and analyzed.

Stony Man Farm didn't need a multimillion dollar facility and a staff of hundreds to decode and study this classified information. All it needed was Aaron Kurtzman and his small cybernetics staff. He had long since worked out a decoding program for the NRO transmissions and could read the data from the TR-3 as it fed in. The Farm would get the information anyway sooner or later, but Kurtzman wanted to know what was happening now.

"We lost him," Kurtzman said, turning in his wheelchair to look up at Brognola.

"What do you mean, you lost him?" Brognola growled around the stub of the unlit cigar stuck in a corner of his mouth. As part of his duties as special liaison to the White House, the Justice Department official was the director of the Sensitive Operations Group, the official name of the Stony Man Farm team. Whenever the President activated Stony Man for a mission, Brognola traveled from Washington as often as possible to oversee the operation.

"I mean that he's gone," Kurtzman replied. "Vanished. My best guess is that he got shot down."

"But that's impossible. That's a TR-3 Night Owl, the most sophisticated spy plane in the world. It's invisible to radar, infrared and everything else they could think of. It's impossible to shoot it down."

"Impossible or not," Kurtzman stated, "he stopped transmitting suddenly. Unless he's had a catastrophic electrical failure, which is not too likely, he's down somewhere over Bosnia."

Brognola's hand automatically reached for the roll of antacid tablets in his coat pocket.

"Wait a damned minute," Kurtzman almost shouted. "I'm getting something. I'm getting an SAR response from one of the Sky Watch satellites."

"How did that happen?"

"I'm not sure." Kurtzman's fingers flew over his keyboard, locking in the signal. "But I'd say that the TR-3 passed close enough to activate the SAR implant, and it's responding now."

After the near crisis that arose back in 1996 when U.S. Secretary of Commerce Ron Brown died in a plane crash while attempting to land at Dubrovnik, all high-ranking U.S. officials visiting the Bosnian region had been given one of the new military SAR—Search And Rescue—implants.

These were subminiature electronic beacons that would respond to a coded signal that could be sent by a satellite, a search aircraft or by the radios of ground-search teams. Designed to be practically indestructible, the implants had a battery capable of sending the signal continuously for seven days. Since the signal was sent only in response to an activation, the implants could stay "hot" for several weeks, if not months, after their first remote activation.

Hammer's TR-3 had been sent to see if it could activate a SAR implant that had failed to respond to satellite activation. The man who was wearing that implant was down over Bosnia, and the President was anxious to get him back with as little fanfare as possible. Stony Man Farm hadn't been officially tasked with the mission yet, but Brognola knew that it was coming.

"But," Brognola asked, "can you tell which implant is squawking? Wouldn't that Night Owl pilot have been wearing one, as well?"

Kurtzman looked at the electronic code on his screen. "It matches the SAR code we were told to look for."

"It's Richard Lacy, then. He's in Bosnia, right?" Brognola growled around his cigar. He wasn't in the mood to listen to more bad news right now. The disappearance of Richard Lacy on a diplomatic helicopter flight over Bosnia had the Oval Office in an uproar. Not only was the retired State Department official a valued adviser to the White House, but he was also a close friend of the President. Brognola wanted to be able to report that he had been found.

"It's Bosnia, all right," Katz confirmed. "But it's coming from the Muslim section—the part of Bosnia that's not too happy with us right now. In fact, neither we nor NATO have any PROFOR troops in that area anymore."

"Why not?"

"We don't have anyone stationed there because they kept getting shot at, and rather than starting the war again, the UN decided to pull them all out. It's a no-go zone for several hundred miles around that signal location."

"Damn."

"And," Katz continued, "along with Richard

Lacy, we now have the presumed wreckage of a supersecret spy plane and maybe even a pilot down in the area, as well. I think that the President might want to get that back, too. Even wrecked, it's a little too valuable to leave laying around.''

''What's the status of Phoenix Force?'' Brognola asked Barbara Price.

Though she didn't look like anyone's idea of an operations officer, Price was the mission controller for the Stony Man action teams. The Farm was the world's premier intelligence-gathering operation, but simply gathering the data would be meaningless without having the means to act upon it. What made Stony Man different than all the other federal intelligence agencies was that the Farm could call upon Phoenix Force and Able Team to act on the information they developed. They also had the services of a very special man—Mack Bolan.

''They're standing by,'' she answered. ''I alerted them as soon as you called me about this SAR search. I also contacted Mack, and he's available. Grimaldi has a C-141 on ramp alert at Andrews, and I can have them in the air in under two hours. With air-to-air refueling they can be on the ground at the air base in Aviano, Italy, in a little over nine hours.''

''I almost hate to bring this up,'' Katzenelenbogen said, ''but we're going to need to play this one real close to the vest.''

''What do you mean?''

''Well, if we stage out of Aviano, we're going to

be in the middle of a lot of unfriendly, prying eyes. Every UN bozo and his brother will be there as well as the operatives of the so-called Bosnian republics. Even if we try to stay inside the U.S. compound on the base, there are too many people wandering in and out. We won't be able to scratch without someone watching us. And as sensitive as this operation will be, we can't afford that.''

"Do you have a better idea?'' Brognola asked. ''If you'll remember, we don't own a hell of a lot of real estate in that part of the world anymore. We're limited to the number of bases we can use to stage out of.''

"Well, I was thinking of creating a Stony Man annex in the middle of the U.S. part of the Aviano base. That way, at least we can keep the prying eyes on the other side of the fence. I'll set up a CP and comm center and take Able Team with me to run it.''

Brognola turned to Price. ''Do you have Lyons doing anything important right now?''

"They're on stand-down.''

"Okay, I'll talk to the Man and see what he thinks.''

"We need to get this rolling as soon as possible,'' Katz reminded him. ''So we need a decision now.''

As the Stony Man tactical adviser, it was Katz's job to point out the best way to get the job done even when it meant pushing the boss.

"How so?"

"That State Department guy's been on the ground for a couple of days now and the longer he's there, the less chance we'll have to recover him. If they get it in their heads that he's a spy, they're not going to treat him all that well, and since he's an older man, he might not last very long. Any delay at all is too much."

Brognola knew only too well that Katz wasn't exaggerating the danger to Lacy. None of the Bosnian factions was known for its humanity. No matter whose hands Lacy was in, if he was in Bosnia, he was in danger.

"Alert Able Team, too," Brognola replied. "And I'll get the clearance."

"They're already at Andrews with Phoenix."

CHAPTER TWO

Eastern Bosnia

Dragan Asdik waited impatiently for the morning prayers to end so he could talk to the commander of the Iranian freedom fighters who were based out of his castle. Asdik was the lord and master of his valley high in the mountains of Muslim Bosnia and the military commander of the troops in the region. Now that the war for Bosnia wasn't being fought—he knew that it wasn't over, but had just been put on hold—he had been ordered back to his fortress in the mountains to prepare for the next phase of the conflict.

When the words of the last prayer echoed away, a thin man with intense eyes rose and approached him.

"God calls the faithful to prayer five times a day," Major Ari Naslin of the Iranian Ministry of Intelligence and Security reminded the Bosnian.

Asdik gritted his teeth but remained silent. He needed the Iranian troops far more than he needed to speak his mind. In the three-way battle for Bosnia, the Iranian Security Commandos were the unseen trump card waiting to be played. These Islamic freedom fighters, as they liked to style themselves, were a potent weapon that would be brought into full play very soon. And they were a weapon that no one in NATO even knew existed.

The United States–sponsored Dayton Accord, which had been signed in 1995, had been intended to end the war between the Serbs, Croats and Muslims. One of the more prominent issues of the peace agreement concerned the Iranian freedom fighters who had been sent to aid their Bosnian brethren in their fight against the Serbian and Croatian infidels. Under the terms of the agreement, these forces were to be immediately disarmed and returned to Iran.

In apparent compliance with the Dayton Accord, several hundred unarmed, teenage freedom fighters had marched through the streets of Sarajevo on their way to the airport. They had all worn the same kind of uniforms and had carried English and Arabic signs proclaiming that Muslim Bosnia would always remain Muslim. With great media fanfare at the airport, they had boarded chartered jetliners for the trip back to their homeland.

Any experienced military observer watching this carefully orchestrated charade, however, would have immediately noted how young those men were and that none of them appeared to have seen field duty. None of them bore scars, none of them had the thousand-yard stare that marked a veteran of fighting as savage as the Bosnian campaigns had been, and their boots had all been brand-new. In a struggling nation that could barely equip its own forces, why had almost four hundred pairs of new combat boots left Bosnia on the feet of these young men? And that was to say nothing of the uniforms, field belts and other essential gear they had worn. The war was over, yes, but the Muslim Bosnians' resolve to build up their army had been greater than ever, and they needed every scrap of military equipment they could lay their hands on.

When these men boarded the jets and flew away, the Western media observers considered the problem of the Iranian volunteers in Bosnia to be over. Now they could concentrate on other, more-important matters like the persistent rumors of sexual impropriety in some of the villages in the American zone of control. It was being said that young American GIs were trading cigarettes and videos to the local women for sex and alcohol. If these stories were true, they were scandalous and needed to be investigated immediately.

Several days later, older men who were undeniably veterans of the fighting started to disappear from Bosnian army units in twos and threes. Considering the desertion rate in all of the Bosnian forces, however, this wasn't seen as being unusual. Anyone following these men, however, would have wondered why all of them made their way to Asdik's fortress in the mountains.

But no one from the media followed them.

"It is time to talk to the prisoners again," Asdik said. "The Bosnian Agency for Investigation wants a report on them immediately."

Asdik was forced to share his command with the Iranian, and that included sharing whatever information he obtained from the two Americans in the basement cells of his castle.

MAJOR JOHN HAMMER HUNG from ropes holding his arms above his head in his stone cell. "John T. Hammer," he repeated for the tenth time since he had been captured the night before. "Major, United States Air Force. Service number 385-63-9081. I request that you inform the nearest American embassy of my status."

The hulking Bosnian the pilot had nicknamed Godzilla's Little Brother smiled, but it wasn't a pretty sight. "You do not have any 'status,' as you put it, Major Hammer," he said in accented English. "You fell from the sky like a spy, and we do not like spies here."

"I'm not a spy," Hammer said wearily. "I'm an American Air Force pilot assigned to the UN PRO-FOR mission and my plane was damaged in a midair collision. I had to eject to save my life, that's why I parachuted to earth."

"A real pilot would have tried to save his airplane," the Bosnian said with a sneer. "But you abandoned your plane, so you are a spy."

"Look," Hammer said, trying one more time, "if you'll just get hold of the U.S. mission in Sarajevo, they'll tell you who I am."

"Of course they will," Godzilla's Little Brother replied. "They will tell me that you are a pilot, but I know that you are a spy. Do you think that I am a stupid Serb?"

Hammer wisely refrained from telling his tormentor exactly what he thought he was; he wasn't ready to die yet. When the time came that he was ready to check out, however, he would explain it to the big bastard in great detail.

The Bosnian leaned even closer to Hammer, and the pilot held his breath. Godzilla's Little Brother had breath to match his name. "You will confess to being a spy sooner or later, then I will deal with you. We will not shoot you if that is what you are worried about. In fact my government will be glad to release you, but we have to know what you were doing first."

Reaching up, the Bosnian took the rope from the hook and released Hammer's arms. "I will give you a little more time to think about it," he said. "But sooner or later, I will find out what I want to know."

Throughout the interrogation, the man Hammer had nicknamed the Spider on the Wall again stayed out of the way and let the Bosnian handle the questioning. The second man's silence was probably a matter of language, as the two of them spoke to each other in what sounded like Arabic. The Spider looked

Arabic, as well, so he might be an Islamic military adviser. Hammer wasn't a linguist. But he had picked up a little of the language during his Gulf War tour in Saudi Arabia and, during their conversations, he had caught a couple of words he thought he recognized.

As soon as he was alone, Hammer lay on his narrow pallet and waited for the feeling to return to his arms. Each time they hung him up that way, it took longer for him to recover. As he waited, he looked around his cell one more time in case there was something he had missed the first few dozen times he had looked. Unfortunately there was nothing he had missed. Four stone walls without windows, a vaulted ceiling and a thick wooden door. It would take more than a Swiss Army knife to get out of there, and he didn't even have the knife.

Since his earliest days in the Air Force Academy, he had been known as the Jackhammer. Part of that was a play on his name and some was because of the way he had dealt with the traditional hurdles of his plebe year. He had battered his way through his first year at the academy, and the nickname had stuck. But since he hadn't brought a real jackhammer with him, his nickname wasn't going to do him much good. If push came to shove, he could always beat his own brains out against the stone walls to escape. But he was keeping that as a last resort if things got too tough.

So far, though, his jailers hadn't gone beyond

hanging him by his arms while he was being questioned. Though the pain was slowly taking its toll, he could handle it for a while. Compared to what the pilots had suffered in the Hanoi Hilton, it was a cakewalk. He also knew that there was still the off chance that his SAR implant was working and that some other guy was up there in the second Night Owl looking for him.

He wondered what had happened to the guy he had been sent up to look for. Since he had been in the middle of the primary search area when that MiG came out of the night, maybe the guys who were holding him also had the owner of the other SAR implant in the cell next door. What they wanted with either of them was beyond Hammer. He didn't think for a minute that Godzilla really thought that he was a spy. That was a line out of a bad forties movie.

But beyond the fact that his jailers were Bosnian Muslims, he had no idea what political faction they belonged to or what they wanted out of him. Understanding the tangled politics of the region wasn't his strong point. In fact he could barely name the three major ethnic groups, and the various subfactions in those groups were completely beyond him.

Now he wished that he had stayed awake more often in the political-orientation classes back in Italy. All he had been interested in had been the know-your-enemy classes. He had soaked up the details of the weapons he would face, their characteristics, their limitations and the men who would be using them against him. There had been nothing in those classes, though, about midair collisions with stray MiG fighters.

Since he had been blindfolded most of the time after his capture, the pilot hadn't been able to see much when he had been brought to this place. But from what he could tell, he was being held in some kind of old castle or fortress. Considering the history of the region, he wasn't surprised. Before the war, the most recent war that was, there had even been Roman buildings still in use in some of the cities. Turkish castles dotted the landscape, and there were hundreds of old stone structures still inhabited. It was fitting that he was being held in a stone castle: it went with the ancient politics that had brought him here.

DRAGAN ASDIK HAD CUT short his interrogation of the Yankee spy so he could examine the wreckage of the crashed spy plane the man had been flying. He didn't know much about aircraft, and the plane was smashed to pieces, making it difficult to see how it had looked when it had been intact. But even so, he could see that it didn't look like anything he had ever seen before.

"According to my superiors in Tehran," Naslin said as he surveyed the crash site, "the Yankee's airplane is very valuable, even in the condition it is in. They say that it is one of the radar-invisible stealth fighters that bombed Baghdad without being seen and they want to examine it."

When the Bosnian didn't immediately answer, Naslin added, "They say that it will be a sign of your goodwill if you turn it over to them."

The Iranian's words didn't contain a threat, but Asdik knew that the threat was there and that this wasn't the time for him to antagonize his erstwhile allies. The Iranians had proved to be a great help to the Bosnian cause, and he needed them too much. Particularly right now.

The Western media's attention was focused on sex scandals in the PROFOR units and other headline-grabbing gossip. Because of that, little notice was being given to the fact that Serb and Croat leaders in Bosnia were dying in larger numbers than would normally be expected, even by the local standards. They were dying in car crashes, house fires and, in the all-time favorite of the region, ambushes in remote areas. The UN investigations of these incidents always turned up complete blanks. It was true that these deaths all benefited the Bosnian Muslim cause, but there was nothing pointing to Muslim hit squads being responsible for them.

Asdik had to admit that the Iranian commandos were good at what they did. They had been well trained, then they had been tested in battle to weed out the weak and the unlucky. The survivors were some of the best troops he had ever seen, particularly for missions like this. The Western world called them terrorists, but to Asdik they were freedom fighters, and the Bosnian cause needed them right now.

He had no use for a wrecked airplane, though, even one of the famous American stealth fighters. And if the Iranians wanted it, they could have it. For a price, of course. They thought they were the masters of the marketplace, but they had never seen a Bosnian Muslim haggle in a village market. He would give them the Yankee plane, but they would pay for it with even more weapons and ammunition and maybe more of those small but reliable Japanese trucks.

"Tell your leaders that they can have it," Asdik said. "I am glad to do anything I can for the final victory of the revolution. But—". he shrugged "—we are poor here in Bosnia. As you know, we have been cut off from everything that we need to defend ourselves, and the faith, from the incursions of the infidels."

Naslin was a religious fanatic, but he wasn't a stupid man. He had worked with the Bosnians long enough to know that they had been completely corrupted by the West. Rather than willingly work to bring the revolution to further God's regime on earth, they did it only when they were paid. It offended him to have to haggle with them like a woman in the marketplace, but he, too, had his orders and he would obey them.

"You will be paid for it," he said. "I will have my men remove the wreckage and put it in the caves until Tehran can send a plane in to pick it up."

Stony Man Farm, Virginia

HAL BROGNOLA WAS back at the Farm within a few hours. Stony Man was only a ninety-minute helicopter flight from Washington, D.C., so the commute didn't take long. Neither had his meeting with the President. As the leader of the Sensitive Operations Group, he had the Man's ear, particularly when a mission was on. Nonetheless, he was racking up more flight time than a seagull and spent more time in the unmarked courier chopper than he did in his own car.

While he had been gone, the Stony Man team hadn't been idle. Yakov Katzenelenbogen had packed his bags and taken the Stony Man chopper to Andrews Air Force Base to join the action teams for the flight to Italy. By now, they were winging their way across the Atlantic.

Aaron Kurtzman and his cybernetics team had also been hard at work. For Phoenix Force to successfully rescue Richard Lacy, they needed to know as much as they could about the place he was being held.

"What have you been able to come up with on the objective?" Brognola asked Kurtzman.

"Not a lot." Kurtzman's expression was sour. "As usual, we've been handed another can of worms. We don't have anything at all on file on the target area. All we know is that it's a stone fortress several hundred years old that probably dates back to the Turkish conquest of the region."

Brognola wasn't surprised that even Kurtzman's worldwide cybernetic operation hadn't been able to pin this one down. Even though Stony Man had been in business for a long time, the world was a big place and bad guys kept popping up where you least expected them. Someday the entire world would be reconned, the information reduced to cyber-bytes and he would be out of work. Until then, however, he still had to send men in to do the job.

"By the time the teams reach Italy, though," Kurtzman continued on a more optimistic note, "I'll have more information on the target. I'm diverting a Keyhole 12 satellite to make a run over the area. I'll have maps and photos waiting for Phoenix when they land."

"Are you still getting that SAR squawk?"

"Loud and clear."

Brognola suppressed a yawn. He didn't know when Kurtzman slept, or even if he did. Every time he came into the computer room, no matter what the hour, night or day, the man was there behind his keyboard. He couldn't pull that iron-man drill; he had to get some sack time while Phoenix was in the air. "I'm going to grab a nap," he said. "But wake me if anything comes up."

"Will do."

CHAPTER THREE

Aviano, Italy

Aaron Kurtzman was as good as his word. By the time the Lockheed C-141 Starlifter carrying Bolan, Phoenix Force and Able Team touched down at the NATO air base in Aviano, Italy, he had a mission pack prepared and waiting for them. As soon as the plane taxied to its secured ramp area, a courier handed Jack Grimaldi the package.

A small team of men with two, two-and-a-half-ton trucks were also standing by to unload the plane's cargo and carry it to the small building that had been reserved for the Stony Man command post. The work crew had been instructed to do its job without asking questions, but its members were used to having strange cargos fly into the base. Aviano was the operational center for the NATO and UN PROFOR aerial missions being flown in support of the shaky Bosnian peace mission. All sorts of aircraft on all sorts of missions landed there every day.

The Stony Man commandos stayed out of sight on

board the Starlifter while its cargo was off-loaded. As soon as Katz and Able Team left with the CP gear, the USAF ground crews moved in to service and refuel the plane.

While the crew did its thing, Mack Bolan and David McCarter, the Phoenix Force leader, went over the information Kurtzman had sent in the mission pack. The Farm had been able to get them optical and digital shots of the target area, including close-ups of the stone fortress where the SAR signal originated. Several possible drop zones had been marked for the team to choose from. After looking over all of the routes into the target, they made their choice and briefed the other men.

When dark fell two hours later, the C-141 lifted off and banked to the east for the flight across the Adriatic Sea to Bosnia. During the flight, the Stony Man warriors went over their weapons and jump gear one last time. No parachute jump was without its risks. But jumping at night added a certain fillip to the exercise, particularly on a moonless night like the one they were flying into.

The bat-wing parasail chutes the commandos were using were night black, as were their combat clothes, but black wasn't enough when the moon was out. This night, though, no one would be able to see them unless they were smart enough to look for a shadow momentarily blanking out the stars. But that added measure of security worked both ways. With no moon, they would have a more difficult time seeing their drop zone. But considering where they were going, it was a good trade-off.

JACK GRIMALDI WAS cruising at twenty-two thousand feet when the C-141's terrain-following radar told him that he was approaching the drop zone. On the short hop from Aviano, he had handled the flight chores himself—a pilot, copilot and flight engineer all rolled up into one—because McCarter was at the back doing his primary job, leading Phoenix Force.

Reaching out a gloved hand, he throttled back the Starlifter's four TF33-P7 jet engines, and the airspeed abruptly dropped to a little over two hundred miles per hour.

"Striker!" the pilot called back over the intercom. "You guys had better get on your oxygen. We're coming up on the DZ and I'm going to drop the cabin pressure."

"Roger," Bolan called back. "We're ready."

Grimaldi reached down for his own oxygen mask and secured it to the front of his helmet. As soon as the oxygen was flowing, he hit the switch to depressurize the plane. Clouds of vapor instantly formed inside the cargo hold as cold air from the outside replaced the warm air inside the plane, but it quickly dissipated.

"The ramp's going down," Grimaldi warned his passengers.

"Roger," Bolan called back.

As soon as the ramp was down and locked in

place, the six heavily laden commandos walked back to take their places in two lines on the sides of the open ramp. A green light was in plain view on each side. Unlike a stoplight, in this case green meant to stay where you were; a red light would be the signal to jump into the cold night sky.

"Two minutes," Grimaldi shouted.

"Roger, two mikes," T. J. Hawkins replied. As designated jump master for the drop, his job was to see that they hit their DZ, and that meant that they had to exit the aircraft at exactly the right time. Holding up his illuminated watch so he could see it and the jump light at the same time, he counted off the seconds.

"Go! Go! Go!" Hawkins shouted right as the light blinked red.

The first two men in line, Bolan and Rafael Encizo, stepped off the ramp into space. Five seconds later, Gary Manning and McCarter followed them, with Calvin James and Hawkins jumping last.

"We're clear," Hawkins radioed back to Grimaldi as he went into his spread-eagled position for the long free fall.

"Good luck, guys," the pilot answered as he hit the switch to pull up the ramp. As soon as the ramp was up and locked, he repressurized the cabin and took off his oxygen mask. Even at almost six hundred miles per hour, he had a long flight back to Aviano and he might as well be as comfortable as he could.

Switching the radio over to the Aviano CP frequency, he keyed his throat mike. "Burger with fries," he transmitted.

"Roger," he heard Katz reply. "Copy burger with fries."

Advancing his throttles again, Grimaldi put the Starlifter into a gradual 180-degree climbing turn to take him back to Italy. Even with McCarter having sat in to share the piloting duties on the long trip across the Atlantic, he was ready for a little sack time. If the mission went as planned, he'd be piloting a chopper back here to extract the team within twelve hours.

MACK BOLAN LED the other Stony Man warriors in their long HALO free fall through the night sky over Bosnia. High-altitude, low-opening parachute jumps were old hat to all of them, but any time that you were falling through the night sky at 120 miles per hour, you needed to keep your head clear. On any night jump, disorientation was the primary danger and it was only increased when you were free-falling. The other danger was that as fast as they were falling, it would be easy for them to drift past their DZ. To make their assault on the castle within the window of the mission plan, they needed to hit the drop zone exactly on target.

There had been no way for them to mark the DZ this time, so their free-fall navigation was critical. Bolan was using a small inertial guidance system that had been developed for Special Forces teams to keep them on track. Right before exiting the Starlifter, he had plugged the device into a computer jack in the cabin to update it from the plane's on-board navigational computer. The readout it was giving him should be accurate to within a hundred meters.

As the team's jump master, Hawkins was bringing up the rear of the six-man stick. His job was to keep an eye on his altimeter and to try to back up Bolan's navigation. So far, everything was in the green for this phase of the jump. Watching the altimeter wind down, he got ready for the second phase.

"Coming up on the release point," Hawkins radioed his teammates. "On my mark. Five, four, three, two, one, pull!"

Hawkins pulled his D ring, and the shock of the opening canopy drove his crotch straps up into his groin. As many times as he had jumped out of an airplane, he hadn't figured out a way to keep that from happening. If he ever retired from this line of work, he was going to devote the rest of his life to inventing a more user-friendly parachute harness.

Glancing up, he saw that his triangular parasail chute was fully deployed. Now he could go back to concentrating on navigation again. They still had to find that small drop zone in the middle of the mountain forest. Snapping his night-vision goggles over his eyes, he started scanning the darkness below for the DZ.

Since Bolan was in the lead, he spotted the small

clearing first and keyed his throat mike. "We're right on it," he said. "Follow me down."

The clearing was only half the size of a football field, but the parasails made it easy for all of them to hit the mark. Bolan was the first to touch down, landing lightly on his feet and immediately collapsing his chute. The others followed at ten-second intervals.

When Hawkins shucked his harness, he didn't take his chute over to the pile where the others had taken theirs. Carefully he rolled the canopy into a small bundle and secured it to the back of his assault harness. The assault plan called for his using it later.

After setting out security, McCarter removed the satellite radio from his pack. Extending the antenna, he keyed the mike and spoke the code words that would tell Katz that they had arrived in one piece. "Cherry shake."

"Copy, cherry shake."

"They copied," he told Bolan.

"Okay, move out," the Executioner ordered as he glanced at his watch. "We've got a lot of ground to cover."

James took the point position with Hawkins backing him up on slack. With their night-vision goggles in place, the Bosnian forest took on a horror-movie green glow. Nonetheless, it was good enough for them to move through the trees almost as quickly as if it were daylight.

Aviano Air Base, Italy

IN THE AVIANO CP, Yakov Katzenelenbogen put down the radio microphone and looked over at the large-scale map of the area around the Bosnian castle. "They're down," he said. "And for a change, they're on schedule."

"How long will it take them to reach the castle?" Carl Lyons asked.

"An hour and a half, give or take a half hour, depending on what kind of patrols they run into."

"That's putting them there right in the middle of the witching hour."

Katz nodded. As a veteran of more night actions than he liked to remember, he knew that the best time to hit an opponent was between one and four in the morning. That was the time when human biorhythms were at their lowest ebb and guards were the least alert. "That was the plan."

"When's BMNT this time of year?"

Beginning Morning Nautical Twilight was the military's way of talking about the time of morning when there was enough light for an enemy to detect you at a range of a hundred meters. EENT was the other side of the coin, when it became dark enough to need night-vision devices to fight.

"The book says 6:58."

"That should give them enough time to make the snatch and haul out of there."

"The operative word is 'should,'" Katz replied.

"We don't have a lot to go on this time, Intel wise, and they may have to make it up as they go along."

Lyons laughed. "Hell, Katz, we always have to do that. We wouldn't know what to do around here if anything went according to plan."

"Bite your tongue," Katz said. "We don't have much room for error this time, and there's no way to back them up if they step into it."

"We can always call on the UN PROFOR," Hermann "Gadgets" Schwarz said, wearing an innocent expression on his face. His main job at the CP was to keep the satellite links up and running so they could talk to the Farm. "It would only take them two months to make their move. One month to get permission from the Security Council in New York and another one to get their heads out of their anal cavities."

"Right," Katz said dryly. The well-known failure of the United Nations Protection Force in Bosnia was the reason that the President had sent in the Stony Man teams to sort out this situation. Richard Lacy's grandchildren would be in college before the UN would ever get around to doing anything about his release.

"I'll pass the word to the Farm that they've reached the target area." Schwarz reached for the computer keyboard in front of him.

"Do that. Hal needs some sleep, and he won't go to bed until he knows that the guys are down."

"Maybe he'll sleep through the entire operation and leave us alone."

"You wish."

Bosnia

CALVIN JAMES WAS on the point position when the six men broke out of the woods that covered the ridgeline overlooking the fortress in the plain below. The march in hadn't been too difficult. The terrain was rough and the forests thick, but they'd not encountered any enemy patrols and were still on schedule.

"Here it is," James radioed as he went to ground. "We've reached the launch point."

When the rest of the team reached the edge of the cliff, they took up security positions while Hawkins unpacked his parachute again and got back into the harness. When the harness was tight, James and Manning pulled the canopy open to each side and made sure that the risers weren't tangled.

"We're ready," James told McCarter.

The Briton took one last scan of the plains below to make sure that there were no enemy patrols in the vicinity. "It's clear."

Hawkins held the toggles of the parasail in each hand as he walked to within ten yards of the edge of the cliff. Sometimes he really wished that he would keep his mouth shut. Even though he was an experienced parachutist and mountain climber, he had a fear of heights. But then, many jumping junkies did, which was why they stood in the door of C-130s or C-141s and threw their bodies into the void. If you weren't afraid of it, you wouldn't get the rush. But standing on the edge of a cliff in the middle of the night wasn't the same as being in the door as part of a jump stick. Being able to plainly see the jagged rocks below made this up close and personal.

"You ready?" James asked after checking over his jump harness one last time.

Not trusting his voice, Hawkins nodded.

"Go!"

Holding on to the ends of the parasail's wing, James and Manning ran forward with Hawkins to launch him off the edge of the cliff. Hawkins ran like a sprinter wanting to put as much distance as he could between himself and the rock face. With a final leap, he threw himself into the void.

He plummeted like a bird with two broken wings. Above him, the matte black parasail flexed several times, fluttering and threatening to collapse before it finally got enough air moving past it to fully inflate. Then it did what it had been designed to do. It flew.

Catching an updraft coming off the face of the cliff, Hawkins flew the parasail chute like he was in a hang glider. Ever so slowly, he rode the updraft in a wide climbing spiral to gain altitude. He already had several hundred feet to spare, but he wanted to get as much room between him and the top of that castle as he could. The glide ratio for the parasail was good, but for something this crazy to work, every last inch counted.

When he had gained the extra altitude he wanted, Hawkins carefully used the toggle to spill air from the canopy to steer it toward the hulking shape of the fortress below.

He had done some real strange things since he had joined Phoenix Force, but making a one-man parachute assault without an aircraft was a first for Hawkins.

CHAPTER FOUR

In the inky darkness, the pile of stone below looked more like a natural rock formation to Hawkins than anything that was man-made. Snapping his night-vision goggles over his eyes, it became clearer. Now he could plainly see the large tower with its radar antenna and, more importantly, his touchdown point, the large, flat expanse of the roof of the main building.

When his spiraling flight brought him directly over the fortress, Hawkins started spilling air from his chute. As his hard-won altitude bled off, he scanned the rooftop closely but didn't see any guards. Even so, he was careful to come in straight down close to one of the walls.

As soon as his rubber-soled boots touched down, his left hand was stabbing at the quick-release on the harness to free him for action. Snapping up his slung Heckler & Koch MP-5 submachine gun, he stepped away from the deflating canopy and crouched for a moment to get his bearings.

"I'm down," he whispered over the comm link.

"Copy," McCarter sent back. "We're on the way."

Hawkins had started for the edge of the wall when he caught a glimpse of movement and dropped back down. A man in beret and boots with an assault rifle slung over his back was standing at the far side of the roof, apparently looking out into the night. Hawkins had searched for signs of guards on his way down, but he had missed this guy. All it would take was one more mistake like that to ruin his whole day.

Slipping the silenced .22 Ruger pistol from his shoulder holster, he started down the wall. He didn't know why this guy hadn't heard him coming in, but the wind had to have masked the sound of the rush of air past his chute.

When Hawkins got close enough to take his shot, he raised the Ruger and crossed his wrists to steady his aim. When he had acquired the target, he half pulled the trigger, activating the red-dot laser sight to double-check his aim. Seeing the dot appear on the back of the guard's head, he squeezed the trigger the rest of the way. The subsonic puff of the silenced pistol was almost too quiet for even him to hear.

The Teflon-coated .22 LR slug drove through the base of the guard's skull and mushroomed to the diameter of a dime in his brain. With his neural synapses cut at the core, the guard instantly went limp. Since his weapon was slung over his back, the body made little noise as it fell face-first.

Hawkins kept the pistol trained on the corpse as

he moved in to check his kill. He knew the man was dead; the laser dot had been right on the juncture of his spinal column and skull. But it was always the ones you didn't check who came alive at the wrong moment. A quick touch behind the point of the man's jaw, though, was all it took to rule this guy out of action.

The Phoenix Force commando paused to take a close look at his kill. The guard was wearing a desert-camouflage uniform, and he also had the expected AK-47 assault rife slung over his shoulder and a chest-pack magazine carrier. What wasn't expected was the set of night-vision goggles hanging on a strap around his neck. Whoever these guys were, they were well equipped. But as this guy had just found out, night goggles really didn't help much if you weren't using them properly.

"One down," Hawkins reported in a whisper. "And be advised that he was wearing night goggles."

"Copy."

Since he had missed this guy, Hawkins decided to make sure that he really did have the roof all to himself. When he was satisfied that the top of the fortress was clear, he took the roll of nylon rappeling rope from his butt pack and tied the end around one of the battlements. After making sure that the ground below him was clear, he dropped the other end of the rope over the side of the wall. After slinging his

MP-5, he clipped the rope onto the carabiner on his rappeling harness and got ready for the trip down.

Taking up the slack in the rope with his left hand, he stepped backward over the battlement. Stopping for one last look, he drew the .22 with his right hand and flicked it off safety. For this short rappel, he would risk making a one-handed drop for the security of being able to shoot if anyone showed up.

He checked his descent a foot off the ground and eased himself the rest of the way down. "I'm on the ground, and it's clear," he radioed.

"We'll be there in zero-five," McCarter radioed back.

Keeping his back to the wall, Hawkins waited in the dark. Breaking into a fortress was never easy, and ancient or not, this one wasn't going to be an exception to the rule. As soon as the rest of the team showed up, they would recon the walls for the best way in.

ENTRANCE TO the fortress proved to be as simple as finding a small door that was secured with an antique padlock. Taking the bolt cutters from his pack, Manning cut through the lock and had the door open in seconds. Behind the door, a tunnel through the thick stone wall opened up onto a courtyard. After checking to make sure that no sentries had been posted, they moved in.

Kurtzman hadn't been able to locate a plan of the castle for the team. But since it was traditional to house prisoners in the lower levels of stone fortresses, when Phoenix Force came to the stairs leading below ground level, they headed there first. If they didn't find Richard Lacy in the basement, then they would start searching the rock pile room by room. Doing that would put Lacy in great peril, however. As soon as the first shot was fired, the hostage would be as good as dead.

James slid along the right side of the curving stone stairs, his back pressed against the damp wall. If there was a guard posted at the bottom of the stairs, the chances were more than good that he would be stationed on the right side so his weapons hand would be free. Knowing human nature was a great part of being successful in this kind of combat.

When he'd traveled far enough down the stone steps, James's combat expectations were met. A man was standing on the right side of the archway with his back against the wall. His AK was slung over his shoulder, and he looked to be half-asleep.

Even though the guard had made himself an easy target, James didn't know if he had a buddy down there and decided to silently take him out with cold steel. Shooting him with the silenced MP-5 would have been his first choice, but he couldn't risk his making a noise when he fell, so a little knife work was called for. Slinging his subgun out of the way, he drew the Ka-bar knife from his boot-top sheath.

Moving slowly and silently, he closed the gap until he was within arm's reach of his target. Though the guard wasn't completely alert, something in the back of his mind warned of the commando's presence. When he started to turn, James was on him, his left hand clamping over the man's mouth and snapping his head back to expose his neck. The knife flashed, slicing through the veins and tendons of his neck.

James held the guard until his feet stopped kicking. Then, holding the corpse for cover and his silenced H & K at the ready, he looked to see if another guard was stationed at the other end of the dimly lit room. When he saw that the dungeon was empty, he double-clicked the radio to signal the rest of the team to join him.

Though there had been signs of renovations and modernization elsewhere in the fortress, the dungeon looked untouched. Cells flanked both sides of the corridor, but only two looked to have their antique iron locks slid shut.

Rafael Encizo went to the first locked cell and shone his flashlight through the crude iron bars over the opening in the thick wooden door. The man lying on the narrow bed along the wall was the right age and, though his clothes were dirty, they looked to be Western style.

When Encizo opened the door and walked in, the man opened his eyes. "I'm Richard Lacy," he announced. "Ex–U.S. State Department."

"We've been looking for you, Mr. Lacy," Encizo said. "Are you able to walk?"

Lacy nodded and tried to stand. "I'm okay."

When he faltered, Encizo offered his hand. "Let me help you up."

At the other end of the line of cells, Hawkins was checking each one to see who else might be imprisoned. Shining his flashlight through the cell opening, he spotted a man on a cot wearing a military flight suit.

"Over here, Striker," Hawkins whispered over the comm link. "I found a hot one. I think it's that pilot who went down."

"I'll be there in a minute. Check him out."

"Roger."

The man blinked when the flashlight beam hit his eyes and raised his hands to shield his face.

"Are you Air Force Major John Hammer?" Hawkins asked.

The pilot painfully raised himself from the cot. "Yeah, that's me. Who are you, the Marines?"

"Nope, the cavalry." Hawkins grinned. "Can you walk?"

"I can flap my arms and fly if it'll get me out of this place."

"Save that for when we get cut off. Then you can carry all of us out."

"Do you guys have a chopper waiting somewhere?"

"It's waiting in Italy," Hawkins replied. "We have to call for it."

"Oh, shit."

"What's the problem?"

"The Iranians have this place covered with radar and ground-to-air missiles."

"Iranians?" Hawkins frowned. "We were told that this was a Bosnian stronghold."

"It is," Hammer answered. "But there's a large Iranian contingent here, as well. It looks like they're some kind of commando unit working for the Bosnians. And I saw a couple of Strellas in one of their jeeps."

"Damn!" Hawkins clicked in his comm link, "Striker, we've got a problem."

"What's that?" Bolan asked.

"I've got the pilot, but he says that there's some kind of Iranian commando unit here and that they're armed with antiaircraft missiles."

Bolan cursed under his breath. "Okay, let's get out of here."

When Hammer reached the dead guard, he paused to pick up his AK-47 and strip the corpse's magazine carrier.

"Do you know how to use that thing?" Encizo asked when he saw the pilot go for the weapon and ammunition.

The pilot grinned. "Damned straight I do, mister. I have one of these at home, and I use it all the time to relieve stress."

"Just remember where the safety is," the Cuban cautioned.

"And the 'rock and roll' switch."

"You'll do," Encizo said. "Just follow us."

Lacy was in worse shape than he had thought, so James stayed with him, ready to throw him over his shoulder and run if it came to that. Hammer had been roughed up, too, but the pilot was a lot younger and kept himself in good shape.

Once they were outside the walls, Manning and James supported Lacy as they started off across the plain at a dogtrot. Since Kurtzman had picked up numerous tire tracks in the valley from his satellite photos, they knew that they wouldn't be in the clear until they reached safety in the rocks at the base of the cliffs. If someone made a late-night check on the prisoners and found them gone, they'd have vehicles chasing after them.

MANNING AND JAMES were carrying Lacy between them by the time they reached the base of the cliffs below the ridgeline. The diplomat had tried his best, but his ordeal in the castle had taken its toll.

As the team's mountaineer, Manning went up the cliff face freehand, then threw down two rappeling ropes for the others to climb. After clipping a safety rope to his harness, James took Lacy on his back and started up the rope hand over hand. At the top of the cliff, Manning belayed the safety rope in case the big man slipped with his load.

Hammer was able to make it on his own and was quickly followed by the rest of the team. Now that they were above the plain, Bolan took the time to talk to Lacy.

"We're safe from their vehicles now," Bolan told him, "but we need to keep on going. Do you think you can keep up with us?"

Lacy was beat and felt like he could sleep for a week, but he nodded. "I'll try."

"Good man."

MAJOR NASLIN ALWAYS WOKE well before dawn to praise God for having given him another day to bring death to the infidels. After his prayers, he headed downstairs in the dimly lit castle to check on the two Yankees who had fallen into his hands. Once more God had given him a gift exactly when he had needed it most.

The Bosnian crisis was reaching a climax. Years of planning were coming together. In a few short weeks, the Serbian and Croatian factions in Bosnia would find themselves in utter chaos and unable to stop the Muslims from taking control of the entire nation. But for the plan to succeed, he had to make sure that the United States wouldn't get involved, and the prisoners would do a lot to relieve the minds of the planners in Tehran.

He hated to admit, though, that he had been impressed with the courage of the Yankee pilot, and he didn't think that he could be made to talk anytime soon. As he well knew, any man would talk if he was worked on long enough. But there was no point in wasting valuable time on the pilot when he had Lacy, the so-called diplomat, in his hands. He was an old man and he was weak. Naslin was confident that he could break him today or tomorrow. Then they would find out what the Great Satan was plotting in Bosnia.

The major was surprised when he didn't see the guard at his post at the bottom of the stairs. Although the guard was one of Asdik's men, Naslin had expected better of him than to sleep on duty. He would have to talk to the Bosnian leader and insist that one of his Iranians stand guard over the Yankee prisoners from now on.

In the dim light at the bottom of the stairs, the Iranian officer failed to see the thickening pool of blood where the guard had been killed. Walking up to the cell that had held Richard Lacy, he immediately saw that the door wasn't closed and locked. The cell was empty.

Running back to the guard post by the stairs, he slammed the butt of his hand on the alarm button on the wall. As the wail of the siren sounded, he turned and ran back to see if the Yankee pilot had been taken, as well.

When he saw that cell was also empty, he turned again and raced for the stairs. When he met Dragan Asdik coming down the stairs, he shouted, "The prisoners have escaped!"

"What happened?"

"They've escaped! The Yankees came and took them away." Naslin shouted, his face distorted with rage. "After them!"

CHAPTER FIVE

Asdik was enraged to learn that the prisoners were gone, too, but he held it in check. He had learned long ago that rage should be used as a weapon and not squandered as a constant frame of mind.

"Show me."

When Naslin led him into the dungeon, it was obvious that the prisoners hadn't freed themselves. The locks to the doors hadn't been forced, and the guard had been killed at his post. Since no one had heard a shout or a shot, he'd been killed with a silenced weapon. Asdik knew that the Iranian was right when he said that commandos had raided the fortress and released them.

Exactly who the raiders were wasn't really important to the Bosnian, but his gut told him that they were Americans, not NATO troops. And they wouldn't be planning to walk out of the mountain that surrounded the fortress.

Since there had been no radar alarm during the night, more than likely the raiders had parachuted in. And now that they had what they had come for, they would call for a helicopter to come in and pick them up. But he had the perfect way to deal with that situation.

Calling two of his subordinates to his side, he gave orders. "Issue the missiles," he told the first man. "I want every search team to carry at least two Strellas with them. If they see an airplane, particularly a helicopter, they are to fire on it immediately."

"Yes, sir."

The second man stepped forward. "Tell the radar operators to be extra-alert for low-flying aircraft. They are to radio the search parties as soon as they make visual contact."

"As you command."

In minutes, three Toyota four-wheel-drive pickups packed with Iranian troops raced across the castle's drawbridge, their headlights stabbing into the breaking dawn. Each pickup had two Strella missiles on board.

As soon as the vehicles were away, Asdik went to his radio room to inform the Bosnian high command of the situation. Lacy and the pilot hadn't been central to the plans that were being set in motion, but the fact that someone had raided the remote fortress was of critical importance. It had been thought that NATO didn't know about Castle Asdik, and precautions would have to be taken now that it did.

THE STONEY MAN TEAM had gotten the two ex-captives to safety in the rugged mountains before dawn broke. After finding a good hiding place where they could watch the approaches, McCarter and Bolan huddled with Major Hammer to question him about what he had seen in the fortress.

"What's the story on those missiles you mentioned?" McCarter asked him. "We have a chopper scheduled to come in and get us."

"You'd better call it off," the pilot said as he chewed on an MRE ration bar. His captors hadn't been big on feeding him. "Strellas are death to choppers."

"How do you know that they were Strellas?" McCarter asked.

Hammer smiled. "I'm a pilot, and that means that I'm a little paranoid about things that can shoot down planes and I study them. I probably know more about those damned things than the bastard who designed them. They were Strellas, and I can clue you that they're bad news for low-flying aircraft. You're not going to get a chopper in here without having it blasted from the sky."

"You also mentioned something about radar," Bolan said.

"Right. My Night Owl was equipped with all kinds of threat-warning gear. I started picking up radar emissions fifty miles out, and it was pretty dense. I don't think you'll be able to sneak past it even on the deck."

McCarter looked across at Bolan. "Go to Plan B?"

"I think we have to." Bolan nodded and glanced over at the rescued diplomat, who had fallen into an exhausted sleep. "They won't let us risk Lacy under those circumstances."

"So I'm expendable?" Hammer asked.

"We didn't come for you, Major," McCarter said bluntly. "You were an unexpected bonus, so to speak. And if it comes down to it, since you're military, you get to take the same risks we do."

That set Hammer back. "By the way, who in the hell are you guys anyway, Project Delta?"

"We have a Delta graduate," McCarter said, "but we're a DLJ team."

Hammer frowned. He thought he was up on all the special-warfare units assigned to PROFOR, but he'd never heard those initials before. "I've never heard of DLJ."

"It stands for Dirty Little Jobs."

"Oh." Hammer looked surprised. "The Company."

"Not really, but you don't have a need to know."

"Okay." Hammer shrugged. "I can live with that. You mentioned a Plan B for the extraction. What's that?"

Now McCarter smiled. "We don't bloody well know yet."

"You're making this up as you go along?" Hammer's voice rose a couple of notches.

"You might say that."

The pilot slowly shook his head. "Now I know

you guys are from the Company. Those bastards never get it right the first time.''

McCarter grinned. ''Welcome to the world of clandestine operations.''

''You also mentioned something about Iranian troops in the fortress,'' Bolan prompted, getting back on track. ''What's the story on them?''

Hammer briefly went through his observations and conclusions about the man he called the Spider and the troops he'd seen.

When he was finished, Bolan locked eyes with McCarter. ''We'd better talk to Katz about this.''

''Also,'' Hammer said, ''when you're talking to whomever you guys work for, you might want to mention the fact that my airplane was down somewhere around here. Since it's the most classified thing in the air right now, they might not want it to fall into unfriendly hands.''

Stony Man Farm

''WE JUST GOT a change in plan,'' Barbara Price told Hal Brognola. ''The team got Lacy out of the castle, but the chopper extraction had to be called off.''

''What happened?''

''Well, Mack did more than spring your man Lacy out of there. He also rescued the pilot of that downed TR-3, and he explained the facts of life to them.''

Brognola didn't want to hear what was coming, but he knew that he had to. ''Which are?''

"Apparently they're not dealing with just a Bosnian warlord and a ragtag army this time. There's some kind of Islamic commando unit working out of that fortress, as well, and the pilot reported that they're armed with Russian shoulder-fired antiaircraft missiles."

Brognola didn't quite understand what law of nature it was that said that no military operation could ever go the way it was planned. But as long as he had been in this business, it never seemed to change. Just when it looked like you were in the clear, something went wrong.

"So, what are they doing now?"

"They managed to get away from the Bosnians," she answered. "For now at least. They're holed up in the mountains to the east to wait until Katz can come up with a Plan B for the extraction."

He sighed. "I need to talk to Katz."

"The video link is hot."

THE NEW VIDEO SATELLITE link equipment Able Team had set up in the command post made Katzenelenbogen's reports back to Stony Man Farm almost as good as if he were there in person. A big-screen monitor in the War Room displayed his face in living color and gave a glimpse of the command post and all of the communications gear behind him.

"The shoulder-fired Strella isn't as good as a Stinger missile, but it's a close second," Katz stated. "Its heat-seeking warhead can reach up to eight thousand feet or so and deliver a knockout punch. And since they're designed to kill armored ground-attack aircraft, they'd have no trouble taking out a helicopter with one shot.''

"Lovely.''

"Can we get NATO aircraft in there to suppress those missiles and radars?'' Katz asked.

"Nope,'' Brognola replied, shaking his head. "NATO involvement isn't on right now. The political situation won't allow it.''

"How about a carrier air strike, then?''

"That won't fly, either,'' Brognola said. "The situation is too explosive. Any official unilateral U.S. or NATO involvement will blow the peace accord and put us back to square one. That's why the Man tapped us for this operation in the first place.''

"What does the Man think they're going to do, then?''

"I'll have to talk to him. But I know that he'll be looking at a ground extraction. Anything that involves troops and equipment will be out.''

Katz shook his head. "I don't mean to be disrespectful and all that, but you might want to ask the President if he has a map anywhere in the Oval Office. If he does, I suggest that he take a good long look at it and figure out how many miles those guys are going to have to walk to reach anything that might be called safe ground. And to keep out of sight, they're going to have to move at night. It's going to take them weeks to get to the closest PRO-FOR unit.

"And," Katz added, "I'm talking about what the situation would be if they were completely on their own. Remember, they've got two recent hostages of uncertain physical condition with them. We don't know if those two guys are going to be up to a month-long walk in the woods."

"You got a better idea?" Brognola asked.

"Striker wants to try a balloon extraction for Lacy at least. But he's afraid that it'll only work one time, so we'll only be able to get the one man out."

"How about our guys?"

"They'll try to find the wreckage of the downed plane so it can't be salvaged and examined. If it wasn't completely destroyed in the crash, they want to help it along."

"That's not a bad idea."

"That's what Striker thought, and he wants to work something up to take care of it."

"If he thinks that he can get Lacy out of there safely, let's do that first and then we'll see what it looks like after that."

"That's what I told him."

"So," Brognola asked, "what about the balloon extraction?"

"I talked to some of the guys at the Special Forces unit stationed here at Aviano, and they've got one they said we could borrow."

"Go ahead with that," Brognola ordered. "I'll brief the President."

"I'll get back to you when we have it en route."

"Do that."

Brognola wasn't so sure about sending a man of Lacy's age into the air on the end of a balloon cable, but his importance to the Bosnian peace process made it imperative that he be returned as soon as possible. He wasn't going to tell the President how risky it was going to be, though. Sometimes the Man didn't need to know all the details of what was being done in his name.

Bosnia

WHEN KATZ RADIOED that Brognola had okayed the balloon extraction, McCarter went to break the news to Lacy. "Mr. Lacy," McCarter said, squatting on the rock next to the older man, "we've come up with a way to get you out of here."

"Please," Lacy said, "call me Rich."

"Okay, Rich. I'm David. Anyway, you don't happen to have an overwhelming fear of heights, do you?"

Lacy shrugged. "Not any more than the next man, why?"

"Well, as I said earlier, we had planned to call in a chopper to take us out, but we had to call it off because of the missiles Major Hammer reported that the opposition is carrying."

Being an old hand at the diplomatic game, Lacy knew when a compromise was being suggested. "What's the alternative to the helicopter?"

"It's called a STABO balloon extraction system. We fit you with a harness, tie it to a balloon that carries a cable up into the air where a plane catches onto it and reels you up."

Lacy blinked hard. He wasn't afraid of heights, but this was ridiculous. He was a diplomat, not a daredevil. "Like the proverbial skyhook, right?"

McCarter nodded.

"Are you sure it works?"

McCarter nodded. "I've used it several times to get out of a tight spot, and I know that it works. Have you ever seen the James Bond movies? They used it in a couple of them if I remember."

"Did you bring one of these things with you?"

"No. We'll have to hide out here until we can get a STABO rig flown in."

"But if a plane is coming in to deliver this equipment, why can't we fly out on it?"

"Good question, sir. But the plane will be dropping it from above missile range so it won't get shot down."

"Dropping it?"

"Like a laser-guided smart bomb, it will zero in on this location using a laser. But a parachute will slow it for a soft landing."

"If you can get that thing delivered," Lacy said, "I guess I'll try to ride it out of here."

"Good man." McCarter grinned and clapped him on the shoulder. "It will be something to tell your grandchildren about."

"That's going to be a bit of a shock for my wife." Lacy kept a straight face. "We don't have any children."

"You'll be okay, Rich."

CHAPTER SIX

Aviano Air Base, Italy

Yakov Katzenelenbogen soon learned that not only did the Special Forces unit at Aviano have a STABO rig available, but the Air Force also had one of the specially equipped AC-130E Hercules turboprops on hand. Equipped with the gear to hook on to the STABO balloon cable and reel it onboard, the plane also had a Pave Low laser-target-designator system mounted in the nose so the STABO rig could be accurately delivered to the Stony Man team's location.

Armed with faxed permission to use the plane, Jack Grimaldi went to the flight line to oversee the loading of the STABO canister. The STABO's aerial-delivery canister resembled a fat bomb. The laser-guidance unit that had been scavenged from a GBU-27 two-thousand-pound smart bomb bolted to the nose only added to the lethal look. Only the bulky parachute pack nestled in the canister's tail fins detracted from its deadly appearance.

Since the AC-130E did not have bomb racks fitted to it, Jack Grimaldi had the STABO canister hooked up to one of the plane's two external-fuel-tank pylons. Since the flight would be relatively short, he wouldn't need the extra fuel, and the fuel-tank pylons were fitted with quick-release hangers that could drop the canister as well as a conventional bomb rack could.

For this mission, both Gadgets Schwarz and Carl Lyons were going along with him. Schwarz would ride the right-hand seat in the cockpit and act as the bombardier to drop the canister. And when the balloon was launched, both of the Able Team commandos would operate the equipment in the cargo hold to capture the balloon cable and reel in the man on the other end of the line.

Within an hour of receiving the okay from the Farm, the camouflaged AC-130E was winging its way across the Adriatic for the coast of Bosnia.

Bosnia

"THOSE GUYS MIGHT BE okay in the desert," T. J. Hawkins said as he watched the Iranian officer lead his patrol up the rocky draw on the side of the mountain, "but they don't look worth diddly squat in this kind of terrain. They might as well be carrying signs saying Here We Are! Shoot At Us!"

Hawkins and Gary Manning were guarding the approach to the mountaintop clearing where the rest of the team waited for Grimaldi to deliver the STABO container. For the plan to extract Richard Lacy to be successful, they had to keep the opposition at bay long enough for the pickup to be made. Then they would find a place to hide out in the hills until the Farm could work up an extraction plan for them, as well.

All that, however, was contingent upon their keeping the enemy at bay, and that had now become a problem.

"The bastards don't have to be good if they get lucky," Manning reminded him. "Which they just did. If they keep going up that draw, they'll end up behind us."

"Well, then, I guess we'd better just up and see if we can change their luck a tad."

Like everyone else at Stony Man, Manning had gotten used to Hawkins's particular version of the English language and knew that he wasn't suggesting that they jump up and run down there. The problem could be taken care of where they were. The Stony Man warriors had found a perfect sniper's nest in the rocks four hundred yards from the draw, and they could hold off an army from that position.

"That's what we're here for," Manning said as he snuggled the butt of his Remington Model 700 sniper's rifle into his shoulder. "Spot for me."

"Start with their pointman," Hawkins suggested. "Four fingers to the right of that biggest boulder."

"Got him."

The field of vision of Manning's twenty-power ranging scope brought the Iranians into sharp focus as he took aim at the lead man. From the pistol in his hand, he identified him as their officer. And while it was great for morale when an officer actually led his troops from the front, it was also a good way to die.

Centering the crosshairs of his scope on the man, the Canadian focused it in to get the range. When he had the target and the range, he took a deep breath. Letting the air out slowly, he stroked the rifle's trigger. Since the 7.62 mm NATO round was supersonic, it made a small crack as the bullet left the muzzle, but the sound suppressor on the end of the barrel muffled most of the report.

Four hundred yards away, the round took the Iranian officer square in the middle of the chest. He was spun by the force of the blow and toppled from the rock he had just stepped up onto.

The troops below him scattered for cover, looking around to see where the silenced shot had come from.

"How about another one?" Hawkins asked. "I suggest you work on that guy in the middle who's carrying that RPG launcher."

"Good idea," Manning said as he shifted his sights. Again he ranged in and fired.

Watching through his field glasses, Hawkins saw the Iranian rocket gunner take the hit and go down. The RPG launcher fell from his lifeless hands and skidded downhill on the rocks.

Another man wearing a pistol belt stood up from the middle of the patrol and urged the troops forward with a wave of his arm. He took only two more steps before Manning's next round put him down.

With their last leader dead, the remaining Iranians started to slip back down the hill. Manning let them get away. The name of the game right now wasn't to kill them all, but to keep them from interfering until Lacy could be picked up. Once he was clear, then they would see about finishing up this mysterious bunch of Iranians.

Hawkins kept his field glasses trained on the retreating troops. "I remember reading somewhere that three out of ten is about all the casualties a unit can take without breaking. That certainly seems to be the case this time."

"I think it's because I took out their officers," Manning replied. "Most troops will fold when you pop their leaders."

"Whatever it was, it seemed to have worked."

"This time," Manning said as he glanced at his watch. "But Jack had better get his butt in here before too much longer. Now that they know where we are, they'll be back in force."

"Well—" Hawkins patted the stock of his H & K SMG "—if there's too many of them, we can always take turns. My dance card isn't full yet."

WHEN THEY GOT THE CALL that Jack Grimaldi was on his way in, the two snipers pulled back to the assembly area where the STABO equipment would be delivered. The trick to making the delivery, though, was to make sure that the mailbox was properly lit up.

Hawkins warmed up the laser target designator while Manning unfolded the portable reflector that would bounce the beam up into the sky so the STABO canister's guidance system could lock on to it. After planting the reflector in the middle of the small clearing, Hawkins took aim at it from several yards away and activated the laser.

"We're hot," he radioed up to the orbiting plane.

"Roger," Grimaldi radioed back.

In the Hercules, Schwarz was on the plane's laser target designator. After getting a GPS reading from the ground, he plugged in the numbers, and the detector picked up the laser almost instantly.

"I've got the laser," he told Grimaldi. "Go into an orbit while I wake up the canister's guidance unit."

As Grimaldi banked the aircraft, Schwarz locked the ground designator's signal into the canister's guidance head. "Locked and loaded," he said.

"Launch it."

Schwarz hit the pylon release, and the canister fell away. "Bomb's away."

"It's coming at you," Grimaldi informed the Stony Man team. With the canister gone, he put the Hercules into a high orbit to wait until they were ready for the pickup.

CALVIN JAMES WAS the first to spot the falling STABO canister. Since it was shaped like a bomb, it was falling bomb fast. "There it is," he called out, pointing at the black spot in the sky.

"I've got it," McCarter replied.

"Come on, come on," James muttered as the spot grew larger. "Pop the damned chute."

If the parachute pack failed to open, the canister would drill a hole in the rocky ground like a dud bomb, and they'd have to fall back on Plan C. The problem was that there wasn't a Plan C. They'd have to run for it while Katz tried to put something else together.

As if it had heard James's plea, the parachute pack's altimeter tripped and the parachute blossomed open. The falling canister suddenly slowed and started oscillating under the canopy. In seconds it hit the ground, smashing the guidance unit, but it had done its job perfectly.

"That's not half-bad," Manning said as the canister's parachute collapsed. "It almost hit the reflector dead center."

The team quickly opened the canister and got to work. Packed inside was the folded balloon, the STABO harness, the cable box and the helium tanks needed to inflate the balloon. While McCarter helped Lacy into the jumpsuit and harness, James and Encizo made sure that the cable reel was ready to feed out the several thousand feet of steel-and-nylon cable. A kink in the cable could cause it to break when the retrieval hook caught it, and that could send Lacy plummeting back to earth. McCarter clipped the loop on the end of the cable into the ring on the back of Lacy's harness and inserted the lock pin.

After sitting Lacy down in the correct position for the pickup, Bolan handed him the helmet and goggles that completed his STABO outfit. "You're going to need this up there. It gets a little windy."

"I still don't know who in the hell you guys are," the State Department man said. "And when I get back to D.C., I'm not going to try to find out. But I can't even begin to tell you how much I appreciate everything you've done for me. If it was up to me, I'd see that you all got a Medal of Honor for this."

"Don't worry about that," Bolan said with a chuckle. "We all draw a regular paycheck."

Lacy shook his head. "Whatever they're paying you people, it isn't enough."

"Can I get that in writing?" McCarter asked.

"Any time."

JACK GRIMALDI WAS cruising at eight thousand feet in the AC-130E when he got Bolan's call that they were ready to launch the balloon as soon as he could get in position to retrieve it.

"I'm inbound on a heading of zero-eight-six," the pilot replied. "If you launch now, I should be able to pick it up on the first run and get the hell out of here. I'm above Strella range, but there's too much radar operating down there for my taste."

"Roger," Bolan sent back.

When they got the nod, James and Manning held the balloon's restraining ropes while Hawkins turned the valve to the helium canister. As the bomb-shaped balloon filled with the lighter-than-air gas, the two men faced it into the wind. When the balloon's stubby fins inflated, they caught the wind and stabilized it. By the time the canister was empty, the twelve-foot-long balloon was straining against the ropes.

"We're go," James said as he pulled the disconnect on the canister.

"Launch it," Bolan ordered.

When James and Manning released the balloon, it swiftly rose into the air. McCarter and Encizo fed out the cable, making sure that it didn't kink as it came off of the roll. When the last of the cable was played out, Bolan keyed his throat mike.

"Come and get it," he radioed to the waiting Grimaldi.

"On the way."

GRIMALDI SPOTTED the blinking strobe light on the bottom of the balloon as soon as it broke through the clouds. The winds had caught it, however, and it wasn't on-line with his flight path.

"I'm going to have to go around again," he radioed to the ground team. "I've got a nasty crosswind up here, and I don't want to snag the cable. I have to come in straight at it to make a good snatch."

"Get a move on it if you can," Bolan sent back. "The opposition's starting to get nasty about wanting this mountaintop back."

A minute later, Grimaldi's voice sounded in Bolan's earphone. "I'm coming up on it now and will give you a long count."

"Get ready," Bolan told Lacy as he listened to Grimaldi's approach count down. "Four…three… two…one," he counted down on his fingers. "Now!"

When Bolan's last finger snapped out, Lacy felt like someone had ignited a rocket strapped to his behind. One instant he was sitting on the ground with his legs out in front of him, and the next he was being jerked upward faster than a space shuttle launching. Even with the helmet covering his ears, he could hear the air screaming past his head. It was in harmony to his own unvoiced screams. He gulped hard to keep his stomach down where it belonged.

He had no way of knowing how long he had been flying through the air before he felt a jerk on the cable. Suddenly he was being pulled backward even faster than before. An instant later, he saw the tail of the camouflaged Hercules appear above him and he slammed to a halt. The cable was caught in a steel claw that was pulling him into the open rear ramp of the plane. Hands reached out to grab his harness and pull him inside the plane.

"You okay, sir?" one of the two men shouted

over the roar of the engines and the rush of air from the open ramp.

"Jesus!" Lacy muttered as he swayed on his shaking legs.

"Are you okay?" the man repeated.

"Yes, I'm in one piece."

As one of the men helped him to a seat, the other hit a lever that closed the rear ramp.

"Welcome to Air Bosnia, Mr. Lacy," Schwarz said with a straight face. "May I see your boarding pass, please?"

"How about that," Lacy replied, playing the straight man and patting his empty pockets. "I seem to have misplaced it."

Stony Man Farm

"THEY PICKED UP Richard Lacy," Barbara Price reported to Hal Brognola on the Farm's intercom. "And he's safely on his way back to Italy."

"Outstanding! The President will be very glad to hear that. Lacy's needed at the upcoming round of election negotiations scheduled for next week, and we were going to have to postpone them if we couldn't get him back."

"Do you want the report on the team, too?" Price broke in on his reverie.

"Of course."

"While they were waiting for Grimaldi to deliver the balloon, they ambushed a patrol looking for them and sent them packing. Now that Lacy's gone, they're going to shift gears and try to see if they can find that crashed plane. When they find it, they'll assess if it needs to be destroyed. And if it has to be blown up to keep it from being salvaged, since the team doesn't have demo packs with them this time, Katz wants permission to use a stealth fighter to drop a two-thousand-pound smart bomb on it.''

"I'll try to clear that with the White House."

"Please try to clear it fast," she said. "We have to be ready to keep that thing out of enemy hands."

"I'm going, I'm going."

She smiled. "The chopper's waiting for you."

Brognola knew that Stony Man had been located in the Shenandoah Valley to keep it away from the political insanity of the Beltway. Secrecy aside, he sincerely wished that he didn't have to fly ninety minutes anytime he wanted to talk to his boss. But then, collecting frequent-flier miles was part of his job description.

CHAPTER SEVEN

Bosnia

Dragan Asdik smiled to himself when Major Naslin's men reported their defeat in the mountains. They claimed that they had been ambushed by a company-sized unit and had inflicted heavy casualties on the Yankees before they had been forced to withdraw. As an experienced mountain fighter, the Bosnian doubted that their story was anywhere close to being accurate. More than likely, they had stumbled into a small force that had a better position and had been able to bring accurate fire down on them.

Although the Yankees were his enemies, too, he wasn't unhappy to see the arrogant Iranian major humbled. Even though they were supposed to be Islamic brothers, Naslin looked down on the Bosnians, including Asdik, as not being pure. It was true that Asdik's Turkish ancestors had conquered the region in the 1600s and had married the local women over the centuries. But the Prophet's warriors had always done that, even when they had swept into Naslin's homeland.

It was only in this century that a Persian-Arab half-breed like Naslin could have ever tried to lord it over a Turk. Though he called himself a Bosnian now, Asdik could trace his ancestry back to a Turkish warrior, a leader of a thousand, in the Ottoman army of Süleyman the Magnificent, which had brought this part of the world under the domination of Islam. The Ottoman Turks had been the mightiest warriors in all of Islamic history, and they had also conquered the land that was now known as Iran when they had carried the green banners of Islam into the Middle East. For all he knew, Naslin himself carried Turkish blood in his veins.

To make it even worse, the Iranian was a Shiite fanatic, not a Sunni like the Bosnians were. It was true that the Shiites were Muslims, too, but as far as a Sunni Muslim like Asdik was concerned, the difference showed. Asdik had noticed early on that Major Naslin's leadership style seemed to be based on rage. The louder he screamed, the faster his men hustled. This time, though, it hadn't seemed to have worked.

It was more than apparent now that the Iranians weren't good in the mountains. Asdik's own men had been born and raised in these hills, and they knew how to move through the rugged terrain without being obvious about it. The Iranians, however, tried to fight the rocks rather than treat them as their friends and allies. Now that Asdik knew where the Yankees had gone, he decided that it was time to let his troops handle them. Asdik's mountain men were too valuable for him to waste, but this was a good opportunity to show the arrogant Naslin how to use troops in the mountains.

"I will send my men into the mountains after those raiders," Asdik announced when the major was finished ranting and raving. "They know the area well and are used to hunting in it."

Since his men had been turned back, there was nothing that Naslin could say to the Bosnian's proposal.

Half an hour later, several groups of experienced mountaineers were driven up to the base of the cliffs. After checking their gear, including mountain-climbing ropes, they started for the area where the Iranians had been ambushed. They would pick the trail up there and find these elusive Yankees.

Italy

WHILE THE IRANIAN government didn't have official representation in the UN contingent that oversaw the operations of the Bosnian protection force, they weren't ignorant about what went on at the Aviano air base. The stakes were high in the struggle for the future of Muslim Bosnia. The imams of Tehran had more than a passing interest in the outcome of what they saw as a religious battle against the West. If

Bosnia could be turned into a revolutionary Islamic state, it would be a dagger in the soft underbelly of their decadent enemies—a dagger that could be used to bring about the triumph of the Islamic revolution that much faster.

But without an official presence, Tehran kept itself informed through a network of agents as was the case in the rest of Europe. Few of Tehran's agents in this part of Italy were Iranian. The imams had long ago learned that the power of money could be as useful to their struggle as religious fervor. It was particularly useful in the decadent West, where men had no real loyalties except to money. Their money had bought a dozen agents who had infiltrated the air base at Aviano to report on Tehran's enemies.

As a result, Tehran had learned about the arrival of the commando team almost before the wheels of their plane had stopped rolling. The agents hadn't been able to learn any more about them than the fact that they were working out of a small building surrounded by a chain-link fence. But it was apparent that some kind of classified operation aimed at Bosnia was being run out of the small building. And any clandestine American interest in Bosnia was of interest to Tehran.

When Richard Lacy was flown in and immediately hustled away to this new group's headquarters, the Iranian agent controller could wait no longer. He had to learn more about what was happening in that small building, and there was only one way to find out.

Making a phone call, he ordered one of his teams into action.

GADGETS SCHWARZ WALKED out of the base exchange in the U.S. section of the air base with his bagged purchases under his arm. Since it looked like they were going to be there for a while, they might as well try to live like humans. He had bought some fixings for their coffee, paper plates, plastic eating utensils and napkins, as well as a good stock of snacks. A man had to do something while standing radio watch, and dry roasted peanuts were a favorite of his.

He was walking up to his jeep in the parking lot when three men stepped out from behind the van parked beside his vehicle. Two of them were dressed in the baggy OD uniforms he had seen worn by the Italian troops on the base, but the third wore civilian clothing. The particular combination of clothes he had on and his dark features tripped an alarm bell in Schwarz's mind.

The third man was no more a native Italian than Schwarz was. And when the man's hand dived inside his unzipped jacket, all doubt ended.

Dropping his shopping bag, Schwarz went for the Beretta holstered under his own jacket. The 9 mm pistol cleared leather, and he was diving for cover before the paper bag could hit the pavement.

His first shot was a little off target as he was moving when he fired. Nonetheless, he saw the dark-complected man jerk, so he knew he had scored. The two Italians in uniform were a little slow getting to their concealed weapons, so Schwarz had more than enough time to make sure of his kills before he proceeded to take them out.

The first 9 mm round drilled into the head of the nearer Italian, and he dropped his pistol abruptly before following it to the ground.

The surviving gunner had gotten his pistol into target acquisition by the time Schwarz could get to him. But his first shot missed, and the Able Team commando didn't give him a chance to take another. A double tap over the heart sent his second shot wild, and he joined his buddy on the pavement.

Schwarz was swinging back to put an insurance round in the guy in civvies when he saw the jeep full of Italian air police racing toward him with their M-16s at the ready. Carefully laying his pistol on the ground, he raised both of his hands and stood stock-still.

It was one thing to have taken out the three thugs. But he didn't want to exchange rounds with their NATO allies; it wasn't good form. As he was cuffed and led away, he saw one of them bend down and pick up his bag of PX goodies. At least he wouldn't have to go back and buy new supplies.

"WE'VE GOT A PROBLEM HERE." Katz's face on the video screen in the Farm's computer room was grim.

"What now?" Aaron Kurtzman asked.

"We had hostiles make a move on us here."

"How bad was it?"

"We're okay, but they have two dead and another one wounded. The base is in an uproar, and Schwarz isn't in good odor around here. In fact the NATO security people are grilling him right now."

"Just a second," Kurtzman said. "Let me get Hal in on this."

Brognola had just returned from Washington, but he hurried to the computer room after Kurtzman buzzed him in his office, followed by Price.

"What's this about Gadgets being held by NATO?" Brognola snapped. "What happened?"

Katz filled Brognola and Price in quickly. "The gun battle attracted base security and they're holding him for questioning right now," he concluded.

"Dammit," Brognola exploded. "That wasn't supposed to have happened. You guys were supposed to be keeping a low profile."

The success of Stony Man's operations depended upon the tight ring of security that surrounded the teams and their operations. The Farm's security made breaking into Fort Knox look easy, but any time they moved away from home, they had to be extracareful. Even so, the initiative was always with the attacker and incidents happened.

"He didn't initiate the contact," Katz reminded him. "And Schwarz had little choice but to take action. The last thing we need is to have one of the team kidnapped."

"You're right," Brognola conceded. "But we can't have him in NATO hands."

"That's why I called. I need you to have the Man spring him."

"I'll get on the horn to him right away."

"The U.S. commander here is an Air Force Colonel Ralph Waters."

"I'll get right on it."

"What about the wounded attacker?" Price asked as soon as Brognola left to make his call to the President. "Have you been able to get anything out of him?"

"Surprisingly enough," Katz said, "they have gotten a little information. It appears that he's an Iranian."

"You're joking."

"I wish," Katz said. "He claims that he's a member of some kind of revolutionary Islamic commando group. If this is the case, it gives the operation a new wrinkle."

"Striker did say that Major Hammer mentioned running into a Middle Eastern contingent at the castle."

"I know," Katz said with his characteristic understatement. "And if they're Iranian commandos, too, we have a big problem. If they have connected the two operations, we may have to tell the team to bunker down and wait until we can make the extraction later."

Price hadn't liked this mission from the beginning.

It had been put together far too quickly and contingencies like this hadn't been planned for. But it was typical of a politically driven assignment. The Stony Man team was on the ground in hostile territory without a ready means of extraction, and now they could be facing a large group of Islamic fanatics.

"Start working on a way to get them out of there," she told Katz. "And plan to use anything you have at your disposal. I'll start hammering on Hal to get the Man on board so we can do whatever we have to do to make it work."

"Short of sending in a Marine landing force," Katz said, "they're stuck there."

"You take care of the plan, and I'll work on the political clearance. If we have to use Marines, I'll do what I can to get them cleared for it."

Knowing how slim a chance she had of accomplishing that, he wished her luck.

"Thanks, I'll need it."

WHEN KATZENELENBOGEN killed the video connection to the Farm, his eyes drifted to the map on the wall. He knew that Barbara Price was sincere when she said that she'd tweak the Oval Office, but he also knew the realities of Bosnia. The UN and NATO weren't likely to go along with any unilateral American plans to move forces into the region even for a rescue. And even if they did, it would only be after months of bickering and biting about who would get the credit if the plan worked and who would take the blame if it failed. Plus, if there were Islamic agents working inside Aviano, there was no chance that the plan wouldn't be leaked by the time it had been hashed out.

The only chance the Stony Man team had was for him to come up with something that could be done quickly and with the resources he had at hand. He might have to borrow an airplane or two, but with Grimaldi available to take care of the flying chores, he wouldn't have to get the Air Force involved beyond supplying the hardware. That way they could always plead ignorance about what happened after it took off.

First, though, he had to get Schwarz back from base security. Even though Brognola said that he would get the President working on that ASAP, again Katz knew the realities and he wanted him back right now.

Reaching into his kit bag, he took out the identity papers the Farm had prepared for this mission. According to his ID, he was Bob Brown, a GS-14 in the CIA. The name was so fake that it might as well have been John Doe, but it would work. Schwarz was Joe Green this time, Lyons was Bill White and Blancanales was Jim Black.

He was going to have to talk to Price about these names when he got back. Until then, he would have to use what he had been given. Grabbing his leather jacket from the back of his chair, he headed out the door.

"Do you need an escort?" Lyons asked.

"Not this time," Katz said. "You and Rosario hold the fort until I get back. I'll call you if I need you."

"We'll be waiting."

Bosnia

DRAGAN ASDIK FROWNED as he listened to the reports of the search teams he had sent into the mountains. They had found the sniper's nest where the raiders had turned Naslin's men back, and recovered the three bodies they had left behind. As he had thought, it had been a small force who had ambushed them, not the company-sized unit the Iranians had reported to their leader. But though the one team had found the site, it hadn't been able to track the men from there. It was always difficult to find tracks in rocky terrain, and the enemy was good—the intruder had left no trail.

Another search team reported that it had found what looked like an empty bomb casing with a parachute attached. They said that it looked like some kind of aerial-delivery device and had found a couple of gas canisters along with other debris in the same place. But once again, there were few tracks leading away from the area.

Asdik ordered his men to keep searching and went to find the Iranian major. Like it or not, he would also have to report failure.

CHAPTER EIGHT

Aviano Air Base, Italy

The fake CIA ID immediately got Katzenelenbogen shown into the office of Colonel Ralph Waters, the commander of the U.S. contingent at the air base. But when he demanded that Schwarz be released ASAP, he ran into resistance.

"You have to understand," Waters said soothingly. "This incident occurred at an Italian base, and our host country has its own way of—"

"I don't want to hear any of this 'host country' crap, Colonel," Katz cut him off. "The Italians have one of my men, and I want him back ASAP. The 'incident,' as you call it, took place in the U.S. sector of the base, and you should be the one investigating it, not a foreign officer."

"I don't think you understand, Mr. Brown," Waters said with the same tone that he would use to speak to a child. "We have a delicate situation here. Two men, local nationals, were killed, and a third was wounded. We have to get to the bottom of this.

The Italian base commander, Colonel Alazono, and I have—''

Katz leaned over the man's desk. If there was anything he disliked, it was a man who didn't know where his primary loyalties lay. ''Is this 'situation' as delicate as your pension status, Colonel?''

''What do you mean?''

''I mean that I can pick up that phone, call the Oval Office and have your butt on the next flight back to the States. Mr. Green is an American under my command, and you have allowed him to be taken into custody by a foreign power. That may not exactly be treason according to the UCMJ, but I don't think that you're going to like having to explain what you have done to a closed-door congressional committee. There are some congressmen who may not appreciate the subtle difference. If you wanted to be a diplomat, you should have joined the State Department not the United States Air Force.

''But,'' Katz went on, smiling for the first time, ''if you want, I can see that you're made a civilian damned quick. Maybe even before you leave here.''

That brought Waters to his feet. ''You can't come into my office and threaten me like that.''

''I just did, Colonel,'' Katz replied calmly. ''What are you going to do about it?''

''I'm going to talk to your superiors about this.''

''If you don't have the President's red-phone number, Colonel, I'll be glad to give it to you,'' he offered. ''I'm sure he would love to talk to you about this matter. Maybe you can explain to him what an American government agent is doing in the hands of a foreign power.''

Something about Katz's demeanor warned the colonel that he was in way over his head. He was on the generals list, and the last thing in the world he needed was to have his career shot down in flames over something like this. He liked Alazono, but he knew when to cut his losses. He didn't know who this guy thought he was, but he didn't want to have to find out the hard way.

"I'll see what I can do.''

"You'll do better than that, Colonel,'' Katz warned. "If he's not standing in front of me in fifteen minutes, I suggest that you start packing your bags. Your replacement will send a car to take you to your plane.''

"Yes, sir,'' Colonel Waters responded, surrendering completely.

"Good. I'm glad that we understand each other. Also I want a copy of everything you have on the attackers on my desk by the time Green gets back.''

"Yes, sir,'' Waters repeated.

The colonel sat and stared out the window for a minute or two once he was alone again. Words couldn't express the disgust he felt about his having been tapped to command this particular installation. Of all of the assignments he could have gotten, he had to have been given something that had so much political input. Damn all politicians and double damn all spooks.

Reaching out, he picked up the phone to call his friend, Colonel Alazono.

WATERS WAS AS GOOD as his word, and Schwarz was delivered to the Stony Man compound right after Katz returned himself.

"Thanks, guys." Schwarz waved to the two American APs who had driven him back well over the speed limit.

"You did a great job of springing me, Katz," Schwarz said with a grin when Katzenelenbogen met him at the door. "They hadn't even gotten around to using the rubber hoses on me yet, so I want to thank you."

"It was nothing," the former Israeli commando said, grinning. "It felt good to kick ass again. Hal had the President working on getting you out, but I didn't want to have to wait that long."

The courtesies over, Schwarz got down to business. "What do you have on the guys who tried to make the snatch?"

"Not much. Two of them were Italian locals who had security clearance for the base workforce. The third one, though, the one you left alive, is a ringer. He's an Iranian commando of some kind."

"It looks like I left the right one alive for a change."

"That's one way of looking at it."

"So, what do we do about this?"

"Nothing." Katz shook his head. "We still need to keep a low profile, so we just hang tight and hope it was a one-shot thing. But the next time you guys step outside the fence, go in pairs."

"You got that right."

CARL LYONS DIDN'T LIKE having idle time on his hands, and it was driving him crazy. He didn't mind helping Katzenelenbogen around the command post, but sitting around waiting for something to happen just wasn't his style. He hadn't earned his "Ironman" moniker because of his inertia. He liked to be out there charging hard all the time. On this gig, though, the only ones who were having fun were Bolan and Phoenix Force. But this was a foreign operation, and McCarter's people were the specialists in that arena.

Able Team had been set up to handle domestic situations for Stony Man and usually operated in the States or, at the most, in Latin America. But even with Phoenix Force taking care of the Farm's foreign missions, that didn't mean that Lyons and his teammates weren't up to a little foreign adventure. They were more than able to do it. All they needed was a chance to show their stuff. And as far as Lyons was concerned, the time had come for them to do it. The attempt on Schwarz couldn't be allowed to go unanswered.

When the ex–LAPD cop walked into the CP,

Schwarz didn't look any the worse for wear after his short stay in the base slammer. In fact he and Katz were back doing what they had been doing most of the time since they had arrived in Italy—nothing.

It was true that Schwarz was fiddling around with the communications gear making sure that the satellite link was operating, but give him anything with more than three parts and he was content to spend hours messing with it. Katz was doing his thing as the operations wizard, but this far from the action, there was only so much he could do. He could only read through the Farm's latest faxes and look at the satellite photos so many times.

In short, everyone was waiting for something to happen, and Lyons was tired of waiting. He wanted to get out there and kick some ass.

"Have we gotten anything more on those guys who jumped Gadgets?" he asked Katz.

The Israeli shook his head. "The Italians haven't been able to get much more out of the survivor. He keeps giving them the Islamic revolutionary party line. 'Death to the infidels' and all that crap."

"Give me five minutes with the bastard," Lyons growled, "and I'll get him to talk to me."

"I really wish I could," Katz admitted. "Because I don't have any idea of the size of the opposition we're dealing with here. Obviously someone's on to us, and one decent-sized car bomb getting past the Italian air police would be all it would take to put us out of business."

"Well," Lyons said, trying to sound casual, "since there's not a hell of a lot going on around this place right now, why don't Pol and I hit the bricks and see what shakes out? We might be able to develop something and save us from another nasty surprise."

"Blancanales does speak Italian, doesn't he?" Katz warmed to the suggestion. Like Lyons, he had spent so long in the trenches that he didn't like sitting around, either. But even if his job now kept him in a chair much of the time, that didn't mean that he couldn't get something going. He could use the big ex-cop as his surrogate.

"I think he can get by," Lyons replied. "I'm told that it's a lot like Spanish."

Katz knew that he was falling into what was called "mission creep" in Washington, and that he should clear it with Brognola first. But, what the hell. The big Fed hadn't specifically said that they couldn't defend themselves. "Wake him up and get him in here."

Rosario Blancanales, the third man of Able Team, had been taking the night shift at the CP, so he was sleeping during the day. "What's happening?" he asked when Lyons jostled him awake.

"Katz is cutting us loose."

"Good," Blancanales said as he sat up and reached for his shoes. "This has been a drag so far, and I can catch up on my sleep later."

When Lyons came back with Blancanales in tow,

Katz was ready for a mission briefing. "We don't have a lot to work with," he began. "But I do have the home addresses of those two Italians Schwarz waxed. Maybe you can canvass their neighborhoods and see if you can come up with their watering holes, their drinking buddies or something like that. For a couple of locals to have been involved with something like this, they would have had to have been in personal contact with Iranian agents somewhere along the line. And this is not the kind of place that you would expect to find too many Muslim immigrants."

"Won't the local police have done that already?" Blancanales asked. Like all of Able Team, he hated trying to work a case after the cops had already gone through and screwed it up.

"Probably," Katz replied. "But if they have, they haven't come up with anything or I would have heard of it. I put the fear of God into the American base commander, and if he hears something, he'll tell me."

"Even if the Italians have muddied the water," Lyons said, getting to his feet, "it beats the hell out of sitting on our butts around here trying not to be a target."

Blancanales smiled to see the Ironman come alive again. It was time that they got back to work.

AT FIRST, IT WAS slow going. As Lyons had said, Blancanales could get by in Italian, but only slowly and the local dialect was difficult to understand. By the early afternoon, however, they had managed to glean a little information, including the name of the garage the two men had used. Most of the information was useless neighborhood gossip, but the tip about the garage interested Lyons.

As with everything else they did, the Europeans handled automobile maintenance differently than how it was done in southern California. Rather than having a string of gas stations, dealerships and specialty garages along major streets, the Italians sent their cars to the small neighborhood garages for gas, maintenance, repair and parking. The garages also served as hangouts for the local wastrels, low-grade hoods and other social riffraff. It might be a good place to check out.

Lyons liked the garage a lot more when Blancanales drove their rented Lancia past it and saw that it was closed during business hours. Everything else on the block, including the smaller garage on the next corner, was open, so that place should be, too. The fact that it wasn't could be significant if it was being used as a safehouse.

"Pull over," he said. "We need to find someone to talk to about who owns that place."

The small grocery store two doors down looked like a good start. With much hand waving and using several English words, Blancanales got the story on the garage. According to the grocer, the garage had been sold to foreigners a year or so ago, and the new owners didn't seem to want much business. He said that they were only in there at night, and they didn't open up when someone honked for service.

The grocer's take on the garage's new owners was enough for Lyons. As soon as they were back in their car, he reached for the cellular phone. "Find a place to stash this thing where we can keep an eye on that place," he said. "I'll call Katz and let him know where we are."

"How about that corner two blocks down?"

Lyons glanced to the left and saw the alley. "Yeah, pull in there."

PULLING A STAKEOUT in Aviano, Italy, wasn't like keeping an eye on a gang hangout in East L.A. Two guys, particularly two foreigners, sitting in a car were bound to attract unwanted attention. But since nothing was going on, even the local kids had lost interest in them by nightfall.

The two men waited for an hour after dark before making their move. When they did, getting into the building was as simple as picking a lock. When their night goggles showed them that the place was empty, they flicked on their flashlights and started to look around.

"We need Gadgets here," Blancanales said when he saw the computer equipment on the table against the back wall.

Lyons handed him the cellular phone. "Call him while I look the place over."

Schwarz answered on the first ring. "What's up?"

"I thought you'd like to know that we found a computer and fax in here," Blancanales told him.

"Great. Fire it up and see what's in it."

Blancanales booted the system, but when the screen came on, it showed that a password was needed to get in. "It wants a password," he told Schwarz.

"You said there's a fax machine and modem?"

"Yes."

"No sweat," Schwarz replied. "That means they're on-line. Give me the make and model number of the equipment."

Using his flashlight, Blancanales read off the names and model numbers of the computer, fax and modem.

"Okay, I got them," Schwarz said. "Now, what's the street address there?"

"It's 109 Via del la Rosa."

"Hang on while I get into the web. I'm going to try to find their E-mail address."

A moment later, Schwarz was back on the phone. "Okay, I got their address. Now let me see if I can break their password."

The screen message suddenly changed to a DOS prompt. "I did it," Schwarz said, cackling. "Now we can get to work transferring whatever they have stored in there. Are you ready?"

With Schwarz talking him through it, Blancanales

sent the entire electronic contents of the computer via modem to Schwarz at the Stony CP.

"Okay," Schwarz said triumphantly. "They have a fast modem, so it came through quickly. I'll be able to read everything they have stored in that thing. Now I need to figure out a way to block their access to the machine without destroying it."

"Why don't we just take it with us?"

"You don't want them to know that we're onto them, do you?"

"Can't you change the security password?"

"I can, but that's too easy to bypass," Schwarz replied, sounding thoughtful. "I've got another idea. Hang on for a couple of seconds."

Suddenly the screen in front of Blancanales filled with numbers that flashed almost too fast for the human eye to see. "This screen's gone crazy," Blancanales said. "What did you do to it?"

"I just told the computer to compute pi to a million places. That will keep it busy for several days and we'll be back in the States by the time it gets done, if it ever does. But until it does, it can't work on anything else. Even turning it off won't work because I programmed it to boot to the new program."

"So you've cut off their communications to Iran?"

"At least on that machine." Schwarz laughed. "They'll have to buy a new computer and modem and go through the setup, and that should buy us enough time to track them down."

"The miracle of modern electronics."

CHAPTER NINE

Rosario Blancanales was shutting down the computer when Carl Lyons suddenly killed his flashlight. "Someone just drove up," he whispered over the comm link.

Slipping silently out of his chair, Blancanales snapped down his night-vision goggles and reached for his SPAS assault shotgun. He had hoped to get out of there clean, but he was ready if it came to a firefight.

Lyons could hear the sound of voices approaching the garage, speaking a foreign language. He couldn't tell how many men were out there, but there were too many of them to simply overpower. If these guys were connected to the Iranian commandos as he suspected, a firefight was in the offing.

He quickly took up a position against the front wall away from the door while Blancanales crouched behind a drum against the back wall in a classic L-shaped ambush.

No sooner were they in place than the door opened and five men walked in. They closed and locked the door behind them before turning on the overhead lights. Seeing the move, the Able Team commandos slipped their night-vision goggles up so the sudden glare wouldn't blind them.

"Freeze!" Lyons shouted in English. Thanks to Hollywood and television, almost everyone in the world knew that one distinctly American word.

This time, though, it didn't work. All five of the men were armed, and they responded by pulling their pieces. One gunman had his Beretta minisubmachine gun on a sling at his side, and it snapped up, spraying lead.

The long burst went wild, and Lyons's .357 Colt Python barked in response. The Magnum round took out the submachine gunner by blowing the back of his head off. Blancanales's 12-gauge SPAS roared at the same time, the buckshot slamming another thug against the wall.

Scrambling for cover, one of the three remaining gunmen started to dive behind a gray Fiat sedan parked near the far wall. One of his partners screamed something and waved his hands urgently.

Almost in midjump, the gunman skidded to a halt and reversed direction. His change in plan, however, was fatal. Lyons caught him halfway to cover with two rounds from his Python. The .357 Magnum slugs slammed him sideways as they tore through his rib cage and smashed his heart.

Pivoting to the left, Lyons spun to face the gunman whose spray of 9 mm lead had driven Blancanales to the ground. He tripped the Colt's hammer two times in rapid fire and saw the rounds punch two close-spaced holes in the upper left quadrant of the target's jacket.

Finding himself suddenly alone, the last gunman tried to make a break for it. Ripping off a long burst from his little Beretta subgun as he ran, he sprinted for the closed door. Had the gunners left the door unlocked, he might have escaped the carnage in the garage. But when he was forced to stop to open it, Blancanales's SPAS belched buckshot.

At that range, the lead balls didn't have time to spread out much, and they hit him in an eight-inch pattern. Any one of the balls would have been enough to kill him, and the entire load tore him open like he'd run into a buzz saw.

"Check them out," Lyons said as he turned to the cars parked against the wall.

He couldn't get the image out of his mind of the one gunman diving for cover behind the Fiat and then running away from it. The car would have provided him a hell of a lot better cover than where he had tried to go, so there had to be a compelling reason why he had turned back from it. Walking over to the car, Lyons shone his flashlight inside.

The bottom cushion of the back seat had been removed, and a plywood box had been installed in its place. A cluster of electrical wires ran out from under the floor carpet into a hole in the front side of the wooden compartment, and the ends of the wires had detonating caps attached to them.

The car had been rigged to be a bomb, and only the blocks of RDX explosive were missing. With the timers and firing wires in place, all the terrorists needed to do was put the explosive charges in the compartment, fit the wires and lay a blanket over it. Then it would be ready.

"I got their wallets and papers," Blancanales said after frisking the last of the bodies.

Lyons holstered his Python. "This damned thing is rigged as a car bomb, but I'm going to leave it for the Italians to mess with. Let's go."

Warbling police sirens were sounding in the distance when Lyons started the Lancia and drove away from the garage. It had been a good evening's work, and he was ready for a cup of coffee.

Stony Man Farm

BARBARA PRICE NOTICED that Hal Brognola looked a little more ragged than usual when he stepped out of the chopper at the Farm's landing pad. He usually showed the signs of a mission more than the rest of the Farm team, but this time, he seemed a lot worse for wear.

As always, Brognola kept silent on the short walk from the landing pad. After keying the security code into the main door, Price opened it for him and stepped aside to let him enter first. No sooner had his foot crossed the threshold than he started to talk. "We have a problem."

"We sure as hell do," she agreed. "But I'm not sure that we're talking about the same problem."

"The President is concerned about the Iranian Schwarz encountered in Italy. He thinks that the mission has been compromised."

"That's the same topic as the problem we came up with, but a different location."

"What do you mean?"

"Well, Aaron came up with what looks like hard evidence that the Islamic freedom fighters mentioned in the Dayton Accord didn't leave Bosnia as they were supposed to."

That stopped the big Fed in midstride. "But we saw them leave Sarajevo. They got on the planes," he said. "And the UN international observers signed off on it."

She smiled slowly. "We saw somebody leave town, true. But Aaron says he has proof that the guys who marched onto those planes weren't the guys they were supposed to be. Plus he did a little snooping in the files and came up with what the Islamic commandos have been doing since they didn't leave."

"And that is?"

She shrugged. "The same thing they were doing before the cease-fire—killing Serbs and Croats."

"I need to see this ASAP."

"It's waiting in the War Room."

The key players were waiting around the conference table when Brognola and Price walked into the War Room. No one looked as bad as he did, but it was obvious that they had been working long hours and drinking too much coffee.

"What's this about those Islamic freedom fighters?" Brognola growled as he popped two antacid tabs from the fresh roll in his jacket pocket.

"The bottom line is that they didn't leave as per the Dayton Accord," Aaron Kurtzman stated.

"Who the hell did leave, then?"

"My best bet is that they were students who were headed for graduate work at the University of Tehran's school of murder and mayhem. I think that we can expect them back on the scene after they've learned the finer points of terroristic slaughter."

Brognola closed his eyes as if he were trying to make the world go away.

Kurtzman anticipated the next question. "I know that the UN weenies certified that all of the so-called Islamic freedom fighters had been shipped out, but it simply didn't happen and I can prove it."

"The President will need to see that proof."

"It's ready for him."

"And what is this about their still being active in Bosnia?"

"I'll let Hunt give you the background. He's the one who tracked it."

Dr. Huntington Wethers was usually the best-dressed man at Stony Man Farm. He always looked like the distinguished academic he had been before

Kurtzman lured him away from the ivory towers of academia. Today, though, he looked as scruffy as any of the overworked cybernetics team. The long hours and Kurtzman's brew were beginning to take their toll on him, too.

"When this came up," Wethers said, "something started nagging at the back of my mind. During the war, we kept getting field intelligence that the so-called freedom fighters were operating as mobile search-and-destroy teams targeted against leaders and functionaries of the other two factions."

"They were assassinating them," Brognola said, cutting through the jargon.

"In short, yes. And apparently they were rather successful at it. They were hitting the infrastructure and high level—"

"And you think that they're back at it?" Brognola asked.

"I'm convinced they are," Wethers replied, nodding. "About a month after the so-called return of the Iranians, mysterious deaths started to occur again in Bosnia. We could attribute this to happenstance, except that none of the victims have been Muslims. All of them have been Serbs and Croatians."

"Do we have any hard evidence of this or do you expect me to take statistics to the Man?"

Wethers looked offended. Even though he was well aware of their limitations, statistics were holy to him. As far as he was concerned, if the world paid more attention to statistics, it would be a better place to live. "We have the men who attacked Schwarz in Italy and the Islamic troops Phoenix Force and Striker ran into as hard evidence."

"That doesn't mean that there are Islamic hit teams operating in Bosnia."

"This does, though." Wethers hit the button that flashed a newspaper up on the screen.

"Can you give that to me in English?" Brognola asked dryly. "My Serbo-Croation is a bit rusty."

"This came out of a Serb paper last week, and it says that the mayor of one of the contested towns was ambushed by gunmen on his way home and killed. This time, though, there were witnesses who claimed that they heard the attackers shouting to each other in what sounded like the Arabic language."

"Who were these witnesses?"

"A British observation team seconded to the UN mission. And they went on to say that the attackers were wearing desert-camouflage uniforms and green berets."

"Okay, okay," Brognola said. "I'll take it up with the President."

"I told Striker about the attack on the guys in Italy," Price told him. "And the guys are taking extra precautions."

"How's the search going for the Night Owl crash site?" Brognola asked.

"Not well," Kurtzman said flatly. "I worked out the most likely area that the plane came down in, but they haven't been able to get there yet. The last call from Katz, however, said that they thought they were closing in on it.''

''Make sure he keeps us informed.''

Bosnia

As KURTZMAN HAD SAID, the search for Hammer's crashed Night Owl wasn't going well. For one thing, the pilot had only the vaguest idea where he had been when he had been forced to eject from the stricken plane. Nor did he know where he had landed and been captured. All he had to go on was an estimate of the length of time it had taken his captors to drive him to the fortress. Even with so little information, however, it wasn't as hopeless as it sounded.

Hammer knew that he had been taken in a westward direction to reach the castle. That meant that he had been captured to the east of it. Since he had been on an outward-bound leg of his search for Lacy's SAR beacon, the TR-3 had been heading east at the time of the collision. Wherever the plane had come to earth, the wreckage would have to be to the east of the fortress.

The other problem that the Stony Man Team was dealing with was the string of Bosnian teams who were searching the mountains for them. They had to make sure to keep out of sight and not to leave a trail. Nonetheless, they were covering a lot of ground, but had little to show for it so far.

Bolan had asked Katz to have the Farm check the

satellite runs over the area to see if they could spot the crash site, but to no avail. The problem was that the radar-defeating structure of the plane that kept it from being spotted in the air worked as well when it was on the ground. Even broken up, the carbon-fiber-composite wings and fuselage didn't give good radar returns. The optical scanning also failed to spot it because of the dense forest cover. This was one time that a high-tech approach had to take a back seat to old-fashioned footwork.

"That's the damned problem with terrain-following radar," the pilot grumbled during a break. "When you don't see the ground, you can't remember anything."

"You were flying at night," Hawkins reminded him. "So you wouldn't have seen diddly anyway."

"You'd be surprised what you can see at night up there," Hammer said. "And I wish the hell I was up there now."

"This infantry stuff starting to get to you, fly-boy?"

"I don't see how in the hell you guys do this day in and day out."

"You'll get used to it."

"Not in this lifetime."

With the enemy search parties in the hills, the Stony Man team was even being careful to keep out of sight at night. Since the guard at the fortress Hawkins had killed had been wearing night goggles, that meant that the others could be using them, too. They couldn't make fires to heat rations and had to sleep in the rocks to block their bodies' heat signatures from night-vision devices.

"We'll give this another day or so," Bolan told the pilot when they halted for the evening. "And then we're going to have to start thinking seriously about getting out of here. As you know, we didn't come equipped for this kind of mission. With the numbers of men looking for us, we can't afford the exposure. Sooner or later, someone's bound to spot us and we'll be forced into a fight we can't win."

Hammer saw the truth in Bolan's words. The commandos had gone the extra mile and then some to try to find the crash site. But the fate of his downed aircraft still loomed large in his thinking. He wouldn't be comfortable until he was satisfied that it was useless to anyone.

Aviano Air Base, Italy

"KATZ," SCHWARZ CALLED out from inside the CP, "the Bear's on the line. I think he got the files decoded."

The majority of the information they had pirated from the garage computer had been security coded. Since Schwarz didn't have the programs to try to break the codes, he had forwarded them to Stony Man for the computer-room crew to work on. Breaking cyber-codes was one of Kurtzman's favorite pastimes. In his off moments, he worked on them like other people did crossword puzzles.

Sliding in front of the video pickup, Katz saw that Kurtzman was grinning. "I take it you broke it. What's in there?"

"Mostly it's political garbage," Kurtzman said. "The usual ranting and raving of Islamic extremists. But there's also information about weapons shipments and terrorist cells. This group has been in place for some time now, and they've had a pipeline directly to Tripoli."

"The Libyans again?"

"I'm afraid so."

"Did you find anything about whoever is in charge of this mob?"

"Not his real name," Kurtzman answered. "But he goes by the nom de guerre of 'the Lebanese' so we can assume that he's from Lebanon, probably from Beirut."

The long civil war in Lebanon had produced hundreds of young Arabs who blamed the self-inflicted misfortunes of their homeland on the West. The terrorist states of Syria, Iran and Libya had welcomed many of these men and had provided them with new homes, as well as employment. The problem was they were employed as terrorists.

"I'll get right on this stuff," Katz said, "and get back to you as soon as I've gone through it."

"Better make it quick," Kurtzman urged. "Barbara and I haven't told Hal about Lyons's raid yet."

CHAPTER TEN

Stony Man Farm

As soon as Hal Brognola woke up the next morning, along with his coffee Barbara Price served him a briefing on Able Team's venture into counterterrorism in Italy.

"What in the hell does Lyons think he's doing?" Brognola snapped. "He knows that Able Team isn't supposed to be taking action. We didn't work up a legend for them, and they're only supposed to be helping Katz run the CP for the Bosnian operation."

A "legend" was the cover story for an agent operating in a foreign country and was an essential part of the Farm's operations. Without carefully prepared legends, the operatives were vulnerable if they were picked up by local police or intelligence services. The last thing Stony Man needed was for one of its men to go through a chemical interrogation and reveal information on the Farm. The shock wave could bring down the presidency.

"But Katz thinks they're onto something," Price

argued. "And since he's the man on the ground, he authorized their mission. If what they suspect is true, the PROFOR operation at Aviano is in real danger."

Brognola shook his head. This was supposed to have been a simple snatch job to get one of the President's advisers out of a jam. Piece of cake—a good troop of Girl Scouts should have been able to take care of it. Twelve hours in and out, no sweat. But no, that would be too simple. Instead, the mission had turned into some kind of Armageddon scenario with Islamic commandos, crashed stealth planes, terrorists and car bombs.

The world was going to hell in a handbag and he had Ironman Lyons and his merry band of tricksters bulling their way around northern Italy like characters in a made-for-TV action-adventure flick. The President was going to have his head if he didn't get this under control ASAP.

"Okay," he said. "Let's go back to the beginning. What prompted this exercise anyway?"

Price quickly ran through the facts about the two dead Italian gunmen who had tried to kidnap Schwarz and Katz's desire to learn more about them.

"So," he summed up from memory, "as a result of their little foray off the reservation, we have a half a dozen Iranian terrorists KIA and a car bomb in custody, right?"

"So far," Price said. "But I don't think that's the end of it. Aaron is working on the data Schwarz stole from their computer, and he thinks that there is still a threat to the air base. From what he and Katz have been able to figure out so far, the plan is to infiltrate a dozen or more vehicles laden with enough explosives to take out the entire air base. The first bomb is to go off next to the building housing their fire-fighting equipment and emergency vehicles.''

''Cute touch,'' Brognola murmured. ''Someone's been working overtime on this one.''

''Then,'' Price continued, ''they're going to take out the flight line, the pilots' ready room, the fuel storage area and the ammo dump.''

''What, no bomb in the officers' club? They might as well unleash a nuke on the place and have done with it.''

''I think they would if they could get their hands on one.''

''If this assessment is correct,'' Brognola said, ''and for the sake of argument, I'll accept that it is, this is a major escalation of terrorist activity in an area that's been quiet for a long time. Why does Katz think that they're going to do this?''

''So the PROFOR air assets won't be able to interfere with their activities in Bosnia.''

Brognola had worked with Katzenelenbogen for a long time and knew that the Farm's tactical adviser wasn't prone to flights of fancy. If he thought that he had proof of this, it had to be taken seriously. The question was how to deal with it without creating another UN/NATO mess. Simply putting the cards on the table would create a storm of unimaginable proportions.

More than likely, everyone would be so up in arms about the clandestine American operation that had uncovered this plot that they would ignore the threat itself. In the councils of the UN, placing blame always took precedence over doing anything useful. Not for the first time, he wished that the U.S. would cut itself loose from the UN and let the bastards screw up the rest of the world by themselves.

"What's Katz's input on how we should handle this?"

"Well," Price replied, "he thinks that we probably don't have enough lead time to run it through the PROFOR chain of command in time for anything to be done. He's suggesting that we send an anonymous tip to NATO warning of the attack while Able Team tries to short-stop it."

"There'll be hell to pay if anything goes wrong."

"There'll be hell to pay if we don't get this shut down ASAP," she said, pointing out the obvious. "The Italians don't have a good track record at counterterrorist operations, and the UN is completely useless. If the NATO forces tighten security at the base, it may limit the damage in case we can't get it stopped."

"If this gets screwed up, it's going to cost all of us our jobs, you know that, don't you?"

She smiled. "Probably. But at least I'll know that I went down fighting terrorists, not UN bureaucrats."

He sighed. "Tell them to do it."

"I already did."

Brognola took a deep breath. "You know, Barbara, someday you're going to jump the gun on me one too many times and I'm going to fire you myself."

She shrugged. "I've always wanted to start an Avon dealership."

"Dammit, I mean it."

"When I screw up—" she locked eyes with him "—I expect to be fired. But until then, I have a job to do and I'm going to do it the best way I know how. And sometimes that means getting a jump on the opposition by acting sooner rather than later."

Brognola hated it when she was right. And that was almost all of the time. "Okay, okay," he said in surrender. "But if you keep me informed, I'll be able to cover your ass if something doesn't work out."

Price smiled. "I'll keep that in mind next time, Hal."

Brognola shook his head.

Aviano Air Base, Italy

"OKAY," Yakov Katzenelenbogen said, turning to Carl Lyons, "we're sanctioned to operate here, and the Farm has posted your cover stories. Now when you get busted by the Italian police, I'll be able to get your butt out of jail sometime before the next millennium.''

''What's our cover this time?'' Schwarz asked.

''You're Justice Department, DEA, and you're tracking a gang of Middle Eastern heroin smugglers.''

''I'll bet we'll find that, too, before we're done with this,'' Schwarz predicted. ''These guys have to get the funds to pay for this somehow.''

''Just stick to busting car bombs,'' Katz said, ''and leave the rest of it to the locals. They're going to be angry at us enough as it is.''

''Only if they find out what we're doing.''

''It's going to be hard to cover up a dozen more bodies and as many car bombs.''

Schwarz shrugged. ''Maybe they'll think that it's just the Mafia or the Red Brigades acting up again.''

''Right.''

''Okay,'' Lyons said, ''let's figure out what we're going to do and where we're going to do it. What do you have for us?''

''I have a couple of likely targets,'' Katz answered. ''After running the E-mail addresses on as many of the messages as we could recover, we located two places nearby that may be worth checking out.''

''Do you know what they are?''

''One of them's another garage, and the other's a warehouse.''

''Let's get it, guys,'' Lyons said to his partners.

"It'll be dusk in a hour or two, and I want to get to work as soon as it's dark."

Bosnia

"I GOT SOME TREE DAMAGE up here," Gary Manning reported from the point position. "It looks like something heavy came down through here."

"Wait," David McCarter said. "We're coming up."

The Stony Man team and Major Hammer had been on the move again since first light and had covered a lot of ground. So far, they hadn't seen any sign of the enemy patrols and had been able to move fast. There were no guarantees, though, that they would be able to do this for long. The ball was in the enemy's court.

"I think I've found the crater," Manning called a few minutes later, "but it's empty. Someone beat us to it."

The trees surrounding the hole in the ground bore mute testimony to the fact that something had slammed into the earth in the not too distant past. The broken treetops and slashed-off branches showed the path the stricken spy plane had taken right before it had impacted. Since it hadn't rained since the Stony Man commandos had jumped into the mountains, none of the evidence had been washed away. But beyond the damage to the trees and the impact crater in the ground, only scattered scraps remained.

Someone had hauled almost everything away. Considering what the TR-3 Night Owl represented, it wasn't surprising.

Now that the cold war was over and the Russians were no longer bankrupting their shaky economy trying to keep up with the American aerospace industry, the United States was the undisputed leader of the aviation world. But while there was no other nation that could afford to do the research that had gone into the design and development of an aircraft like the TR-3, some other country would be able to steal the spy plane's secrets if it could get its hands on the wreckage.

"There was a plane crash here, all right," Air Force Major John Hammer said as he picked a small scrap of metal off the ground and turned it over in his hand. "And I think that it was mine."

"How's that?" McCarter asked.

He held out the chunk of aluminum. "See the markings? They're in English, and that sickly green paint is good old USAF zinc chromate primer."

"I thought your plane was made of some kind of plastic."

"Only on the outside. Inside, where it counts, it has as much metal as a regular fighter."

"Now what?" McCarter asked him.

Hammer looked at the small metal scrap in his hand. "I'll be damned if I know. But I'd still like to find out what they've done with it so we can destroy it."

"I've got an idea." Hawkins pointed to tire tracks in the floor of the forest. "Let's follow the tracks and see if we can find out where they took it. Maybe we can recover it."

Based on the tracks that had been left, it looked like at least three or four small trucks had been used to haul the pieces of the wreckage away. On top of that, there were boot prints of well over a dozen men in the well-trampled area. A blind man should be able to find out what had happened to the wreckage.

"We might as well," Bolan said. "Hal is going to want to know what happened to it so he can tell the Air Force."

A LITTLE OVER two hours later, the Stony Man team and Hammer found themselves back at the ridgeline overlooking the castle. The vehicle tracks had taken them to a road that cut through a break in the cliffs. The dirt road led downhill to the plain around the fortress, the last place they wanted to go again.

"We'll never be able to distinguish the tracks on that road," Hawkins said as he scanned the road through his field glasses. "But I know that they took that damned thing down there."

"Did Aaron come up with any information about the geology of this area?" Manning asked.

McCarter looked at him like he had two heads. "What does geology have to do with a missing plane?"

"It's wreckage, not a plane," Manning reminded him. "And it's easier to hide."

"What do you mean?"

"Well, we're assuming that the Bosnians took the wreckage, and the question is where they put it, right?"

McCarter nodded.

"Unless it all ended up as confetti like that chunk Hammer found, I don't think they could have gotten it through the gate of that fortress."

Bolan turned to Hammer. "What about that?"

The pilot shrugged. "It's hard to tell. But from other crashes I've seen, there should have been some pretty big pieces of it left no matter how hard it hit the ground. At least the jet engines would have survived almost intact, and they're ten, twelve feet long. Also, as you saw, there was no fire at the site, so there should have been some pretty big pieces left."

"Do you think they could have taken the wreckage into the castle?"

Hammer looked at the fortified main gate with its massive but narrow gate and shook his head. "I really doubt it."

"That's what I said," Manning interjected. "And that's why I asked about the geology of the area."

When McCarter's face looked blank, the Canadian continued. "In this part of the world, most of the mountains are limestone." He reached down and picked up a rock chip. "Like this. And as our newest recruit knows, limestone formations usually contain large caves that have been carved by the ground-water, right, T.J.?''

"I don't know much about geology," Hawkins admitted, "but I can say that leastways they have pretty big limestone caves in Georgia."

"You're saying that they put the pieces of the plane in a cave?''

"If it's still here and hasn't been moved on," Manning stated. "There's no other place to hide it around here. I don't think that they'd just stack it up in a big pile somewhere for the satellites to spot."

McCarter sighed. "Okay, I'll ask Katz to see if the Farm has any reports of caves in this area."

"And this cave would be guarded, right?'' James had been following the conversation over the comm link from his security position to the left of the group.

"More than likely," Bolan said. "What do you have?''

"I just spotted a couple of the opposition in a guard post at the base of the cliff about five hundred yards to the left of us. There's nothing I can see for them to be guarding down there, but I can't see if there's a cave from here. We'll have to go down to get in position to take a look."

"Think it's worth trying, Striker?'' McCarter asked Bolan.

"I think we should," Bolan replied. "We still may be able to get to it."

"Heads up, guys," Encizo broke in over the

comm link. "We've got a patrol coming down the road."

"Okay," McCarter said. "Let's get out of here. Fade to the left."

CHAPTER ELEVEN

Aviano Air Base, Italy

Since they were operating in a foreign country, Able Team didn't suit up in combat blacksuits and assault harnesses. That would be a little too obvious and would automatically draw unwanted attention from anyone who spotted them. Instead, dark pants, black turtlenecks over their Kevlar bulletproof vests and dark jackets worked almost as well. In that garb, they could pass for local working men once they ditched their hardware.

Their Beretta weapons were not out of place in Italy, either, nor was Blancanales's SPAS-12 assault shotgun. The two things that the Italians made best were fast cars and reliable firearms. Authorities checking cartridge cases and recovered bullets would not be surprised to see that they came from Italian weapons.

After a quick meal of freeze-dried rations with seconds on coffee, the trio made a final check of communications gear.

"I'll be monitoring your comm links," Katz said, "so I want you to keep talking so I'll know what you're doing. Also, that way if you get grabbed by the cops, I'll know about it and can start working on springing you."

"We're not going to get caught, Katz."

"I've heard that one before."

LYONS DECIDED that the first stop on their evening's itinerary would be the warehouse location Katz had uncovered rather than the new garage. Since it was probably the larger of the two buildings, it was the most likely place for them to find what they were looking for. Exactly what that was, he didn't really know. But more car bombs or other instruments of destruction were high on his list of expectations.

The warehouse was an hour's drive away in a small coastal town on the Adriatic. Lyons was glad to see that the business district was away from the residential area, which meant if something went wrong, they should be able to make their getaway before the local police showed up.

At first glance, the warehouse looked good. It sat far enough away from the other industrial buildings in the area that terrorists could conduct their clandestine business out of sight of prying eyes. Its isolation also made it perfect for what Lyons had in mind. The outside security lights were on, but that was a drawback that could be quickly overcome. The single-story building's windows had been painted over, though, so they couldn't see if the interior lights were on or if anyone was inside. But once they killed the power, it wouldn't matter. Anyone who was working in there would make his or her presence known then.

After studying the warehouse for half an hour and making mental notes on its layout, the three men were ready to make their move. On the way in, Lyons stopped the Lancia by a power pole and killed the headlights.

Since Italy was famous for its urban power outages, cutting the power wouldn't cause the same crisis that it would in the States. If people were working late in the surrounding buildings, they would simply go home and wait for the line to be repaired. All it took was two 9 mm rounds from Schwarz's silenced Beretta in the pole's transformer and the lights went out throughout the area.

"That should be good for all night," he said when he got back in the car. "I doubt anyone's going to come out and fix it until tomorrow."

After parking the Lancia in a lot behind one of the other buildings, Able Team walked the short distance to the warehouse. The parking lot in front of the building was empty, and no one had come out to see why the lights had gone out, so it wasn't likely that anyone was working inside.

Bypassing the front door because it was too obvious, they went around the corner of the building to a side entrance they had spotted earlier. If they tripped an alarm going in, they didn't want to leave signs that they had gone in the front way. With Lyons and Blancanales standing guard, it took less than a minute for Schwarz to pick the security lock in the door.

Another modern touch the Italians could use were electronic security locks. European key locks were just too easy to pick. But, even though they'd had a basic lock, Schwarz didn't fail to check for the presence of a security system. He knew he couldn't count on the opposition to be as stupid as he wanted them to be.

"Damn," Schwarz muttered when his suspicions were confirmed by a small red diode inside a panel by the side of the door. "They've got this place wired and the alarm's running on backup batteries."

"Can you bypass it, Gadgets?" Lyons asked.

"No sweat." Schwarz reached into his pants pocket for his electronic lock pick set. A few snips and a couple of bypass wires later, he stepped back. "That should do it."

With their night-vision goggles over their eyes, the trio slipped through the door. Inside, most of the broad expanse of floor was empty except for some large wooden crates stacked against one wall. Examination of an opened crate showed that it contained stuffed leather furniture, and the crate bore markings indicating that it had originated in Algeria. The shipments could be legitimate. But since Libya and Algeria were next-door neighbors, the crates could contain more than just cheap furniture. It was too easy to hide explosives or drugs in the seat cushions.

More important than the crates, however, were the four small Fiat sedans lined up against the other wall. Judging from what they had discovered on their raid of the garage, it was a good guess that they had found another car-bomb factory.

Lyons was headed to check out the cars when Blancanales called from his security position at the front windows of the warehouse. "We've got company coming. Two cars and they're coming on fast."

"Damn!" Schwarz whispered. "That alarm must have sent a signal when we killed the power and it switched over to the backup batteries."

The trio had been through this drill so many times that their response was automatic.

Checking the magazine load in his SPAS, Blancanales slipped back out the side door and took up a position around the corner from the front of the building. "I'm in place," he whispered over the comm link.

Inside, both Lyons and Schwarz had taken cover behind the wooden furniture crates. The stuffed furniture would soak up bullets almost as well as a thick mattress. "We're set," Lyons answered.

The two cars, both BMW sport sedans, skidded to a halt, and almost a dozen men poured out with weapons in their hands. The raid on the garage had taught these guys to be prepared. But exactly how prepared they were for what they were walking into remained to be seen.

"You have nine of them on the way in," Blancanales whispered over his comm link. "And they're packing."

"Copy," Lyons answered. "You take care of any of them that get away."

Lyons didn't plan to give their visitors a chance to prove their good intentions. The fact that they were packing was proof enough that they were who he thought they were. Legitimate businessmen didn't come calling with heat in their hands. He waited until they were all inside the warehouse, but he didn't yell out for them to freeze this time. The last time he had tried that, it hadn't worked and he saw no reason to waste his breath.

Lining up his Python's glowing night sights on the last man through the door, he thumbed the hammer back for a smoother first-round, single-action shot. The roar of the Colt .357 would be the signal for the action to begin.

Tripping the Python's hammer, Lyons didn't wait to see if his first round had connected. Before the shot had even echoed away, he fired again.

Schwarz didn't lag more than a microsecond behind his teammate. His Beretta Model 12 submachine gun swept the area in front of him, dumping a full magazine of 9 mm slugs in one burst. When he ducked to change magazines, Lyons snapped off two more quick shots.

Though they had been caught flat-footed, the terrorists responded well. Ignoring the cries of their wounded and dying comrades, they dropped for cover and returned fire.

Lyons and Schwarz were on the floor offering as small a target as possible as they picked their shots. With Schwarz's subgun spitting flame to cover him, Lyons snapped open the cylinder of his Python, fed it six rounds from a speed loader and snapped it shut as he thumbed the hammer back to get back in action.

His first round scored on a man trying to edge around to the right.

When the bolt on Schwarz's Beretta locked back on an empty magazine, he felt a tug at his sleeve and wood splinters from the crate stung his cheek. Damn! One of them had worked his way along the side wall.

"Flash-bang!" he warned as he pulled the grenade from his pocket. Pulling the pin, he closed his eyes and rolled the bomb across the floor.

Three seconds later, he had a fresh magazine in his subgun when the inside of the warehouse lit up like a football stadium at a night game. The detonation that accompanied the flash charge was deafening, stunning the attackers.

In the brief glare of the grenade, Schwarz spotted his flanker and stitched him with a 6-round burst. The man screamed as he was slammed back against the wall.

According to the muzzle-flashes, only four men

remained in the fight and they were trying to pull back.

Lyons and Schwarz each scored one more. But in the brief flurry of gunfire, the other two made it out the door.

"Two of them coming your way," Lyons shouted to Blancanales.

"I'm on them."

When the front door slammed open, the two men who raced out of the warehouse moved right into Blancanales's line of fire.

"Halt!" he called out loudly in Italian as he sighted in on them.

He shouldn't have wasted his breath. The two gunmen spun at the sound of his voice and started firing into the dark. He had no choice but to respond in kind.

The SPAS roared on semiauto, spitting out a barrage of double-aught buck that swept the space between the car and the front of the building. Nothing made of flesh and blood could stand up to that kind of firepower, and the last two terrorists went down.

After six 12-gauge rounds had spoken, all was quiet. The two gunmen lay sprawled on the gravel, bleeding from multiple wounds.

"You okay, Pol?" Lyons called over the comm link.

"Clear out here," Blancanales answered.

"The bastards ruined my jacket," Schwarz stated. "Someone shot a hole in it."

"Let's check them out," Lyons said as he got to his feet, the Colt still ready in his hand. The air was thick with the reek of blood and burned cordite, but it was like perfume to him. Smelling it meant that once more, he was alive and his opponents weren't.

"Are we going to hit that other garage tonight?" Blancanales asked as he loaded fresh buckshot rounds into the magazine of his SPAS.

"No," Lyons replied. "I think we've done enough damage for one night. We'll save the garage for another time in case we need to send the cops another message."

"If they don't get this message," Schwarz said, "they need hearing aids."

"Gadgets, check those cars while Pol and I go through the bodies and the office files."

AS THEY HAD EXPECTED, Schwarz discovered that the small sedans had been rigged as car bombs. But unlike the one they had found at the garage, the first one he looked at had the blocks of explosive in place and the detonators attached. All anyone needed to do was set the timer and it would go off.

"This first one is fully rigged," Schwarz called out over the comm link. "Do you want me to activate the timer and let it go off after we leave?"

Lyons shook his head. "No. I don't want to risk damaging the surrounding buildings. When the cops get here, they'll get the message without our having to rub it in."

"I can disable it and leave a 'bang, you're dead' charge behind to make sure that they notice it."

Now Lyons grinned. Using booby-trapped, non-lethal charges to send a message worked wonders to wake people up. There was something about almost being blown to bits that was more effective than actually killing someone.

"Go ahead, but make sure that you kill that bomb."

"No sweat. I'll cut off the detonators and put the flash charge on a trembler."

After finding that the other three Fiats were also loaded with explosives and ready to go, he disabled them, too, before rigging the first car with the flash charge.

Leaving the terrorists' weapons with their bodies, the trio went out by the side door and locked it behind them and reactivated the alarm.

THE NEXT MORNING at the Aviano air base, the aftermath of Able Team's raid on the terrorists' warehouse resulted in increased security measures. Once Able Team was safely away from the scene, Katz had informed the Italian police about the gun battle and they had responded to find the bodies and the car bombs that had been left for them. Apparently, as Schwarz had planned, someone tripped his little booby trap and, while no real damage was done, except to a couple of officers' shorts, they got the message.

The result was frantic activity at Aviano. Warbling European police sirens sounded every few minutes as more and more trucks and vans full of troops and police poured into the air base. Italian and NATO units of every description were stampeding into any cleared area they could find, trying to set up their command posts. The air police were working overtime trying to keep the runways cleared so operational flights could continue.

Katzenelenbogen joined Lyons in the open door of the Stony Man CP building. "You boys certainly seem to have started people thinking about base security around here," he commented as he watched the chaos outside the chain-link fence.

"We sure as hell got someone's attention," Lyons said, grinning. "I haven't seen such a rat screw since the Democrats invented the free lunch."

"That was the purpose of the exercise, wasn't it?" Katz said. "To wake these people up and point them in the direction of the coffeepot?"

Lyons shook his head. "Now we need to give them all downers before they hurt themselves."

Katz laughed.

CHAPTER TWELVE

Ali Nadal wasn't the kind of man who was going to let the setbacks at the warehouse and the garage get in the way of accomplishing his mission. An Israeli air force attack on an apartment building in Beirut twelve years earlier had made sure of that. Ever since the day when he had been dug out of the rubble of the collapsed apartment more dead than alive, the only survivor of his family, his life had been a gift from God, who had saved him from death at the hands of the Yankee imperialists and their Israeli dogs so that he could do his bidding.

After Nadal recovered from his injuries, he considered his future and how he could repay God for his life. It was apparent to anyone with half a brain that Lebanon was doomed to drown in its own blood. Egged on by foreign interests, the embittered sectarian infighting had shattered his country and showed no signs of ending in his lifetime. If he stayed in Beirut, he would be drawn into the fighting. But there would be little chance that he would ever have the opportunity to strike a blow to avenge his family.

To fight against the Great Satan, he needed to find powerful allies, and the only two Islamic nations that were strong enough to stand up to the Americans were Iran and Libya. As a Shiite, Nadal favored the imams of Tehran, but he knew that the Libyans were more active in the war against the Yankees and decided to throw in with them. Getting to Libya wasn't a problem, and when he arrived, he presented himself to the authorities and was accepted as a freedom fighter.

He had done well at the Libyan desert training camps he was sent to. Many of the other freedom fighters in training had been Palestinians, but there had been several Lebanese like himself. There had also been men from a dozen other freedom-loving nations, and not all of them had been Islamic. Libya welcomed all men who were willing to put their lives on the line in the never ending battle against the evil of Western imperialism. Irishmen, Germans, a few Americans and several Latin Americans trained beside him as he learned the skills of a holy warrior.

Nadal had a gift for learning languages. In the camp, he had helped teach Arabic to the foreigners and helped translate instructions. His language skills had been noted, and after the training camp, the Libyans picked him to go to Italy to set up a network of agents and to stockpile weapons for future operations.

The longtime ties between Italy and Libya, her one-time colony, had made his entry into the West relatively easy. Regardless of the UN economic sanctions against his adopted homeland, trade between the two nations hadn't ended. Nor had the smuggling of contraband going both ways been in any way curtailed; the Sicilian Mafia made sure of that. Hightech equipment and manufactured goods were still going south to Libya in exchange for drugs and weapons.

Nadal had been in Italy for two years now, and his organization was one of the largest Libyan terrorist cells in all of Europe. His dealings with the Mafia had provided enough money for him to recruit dozens of Italians in all walks of life to augment his intelligence base. As a result, there was little that went on in southern Europe that he wasn't made aware of. Since the beginning of the Bosnian truce, he had been the major conduit for intelligence information about the UN PROFOR operations to the Islamic world.

This unexpected attack on his organization and the destruction of the car bombs had set back his plan to attack the Aviano air base, but it hadn't ended it. Among the stockpiles of weapons he had built up over the months were mortars and RPG rocket launchers, and they would serve in place of the lost car bombs. He would have to use more of his men than he had planned, but the attack could still take place on time.

His agents on the Aviano workforce had given him up-to-the-minute reports of the increased security measures that the NATO and Italian forces had taken at the base. But those measures would only protect them against a car-bomb attack. In a standoff attack using RPGs and mortars, the increased manpower would provide only more targets, not security. And the more targets he had, the greater the body count would be. Even without the car bombs, when he was done, the NATO air base at Aviano would be out of action for some time.

This was the first chance he'd had to strike at his enemies and he would let nothing stand in the way of his long-awaited vengeance. A few quick phone calls sent his orders to the leaders of the units that would carry out the attack. More calls alerted the units that would provide the covering fire for the assault group while it made its getaway.

Though he usually kept himself far from the actions of his agents, Nadal decided that he would watch when his men made this attack. When the history of the Islamic triumph over the decadent Western world was written, this attack would be a major event and he wanted to witness it himself. He also wanted to see the infidels die as so many of his countrymen had.

"YOU KNOW," Carl Lyons said as he and Yakov Katzenelenbogen continued to sift through the material Aaron Kurtzman had forwarded, "from what I'm reading here, car bombs should be the least of our worries."

"I couldn't agree more. These people seem to have enough small arms and crew-served weapons stockpiled to equip a light-infantry battalion, and they didn't go to all of the trouble of smuggling them in-country for nothing. They're planning to do something spectacular with those weapons sooner or later."

Lyons looked thoughtful. "If those car-bomb attacks were planned to coincide with something in Bosnia, do you think that they'll call them off or go to Plan B and use the infantry weapons?"

Katz got a faraway look in his eyes. He had fought Arabs almost all of his life, losing an arm in the service of Israel during the Six Day War. He spoke the language like a native and was as familiar with their thinking processes as any non-Arab could be. But, as he had told Lyons, the mercurial minds of Islamic fanatics were impossible to second-guess. Rational thought was always the first casualty whenever a man thought that God was on his side.

"I know you guys think that I can get into an enemy's mind," Katz said, "but all I do is lay out as many of the possibilities as I can think of and hope that I choose the right one. If we were facing Westerners here, I'd be inclined to say that your raid would have set their timetable back if not canceled it altogether.

"But—" he raised a cautionary finger "—we're dealing with Islamic fanatics this time. We have Bosnians, Iranians and now Libyans that we're dealing with. That's quite a stew of Islamic fanaticism to try to get through to find the scraps of rational meat in the bottom of the pot.''

He shrugged. ''I haven't got the slightest idea what they're going to do, and I couldn't even begin to guess. All I'm willing to bet is that whatever it is, it will be nasty and will indiscriminately kill a lot of people. That has always been their trademark, and I don't see it changing anytime soon.''

''That's a sucker's bet,'' Lyons replied. ''But I think you're right. The question is, is there anything we can do about it? Will it do any good to warn the authorities?''

''If we were in the States, I would say yes. But we're not. We have to go through too many layers of bureaucrats, and I'm not confident that our warnings will do any good. Our best bet is to hunker down, take every precaution we can to survive any attack and do everything we can to help the Stony Man team short-stop this thing. Whatever it is.

''We have the RPG screen,'' Katz continued, referring to the chain-link fence surrounding their small building. ''Maybe we can get some sandbags from the military and build a mortar bunker inside the CP. That way, we should be able to survive an attack with anything short of artillery.''

That wasn't what Lyons wanted to hear. He wanted Katz to pull another rabbit out of the hat as he had so many times in the past and come up with a plan to turn this situation around. Being a target wasn't one of his favorite things to be. And sitting around waiting for something to happen was what had gotten them into this in the first place.

"Whatever they're planning," Lyons said, "rather than just sit around here waiting for it to happen, I think that we should try to shut it down before it happens. At the very least, Rosario and I can go out there and provide some early warning if they do decide on making a ground attack on the base."

"That might not be a bad idea," Katz agreed. "With all of the NATO forces guarding against car bombs coming into the base, I'd bet no one is watching the approaches."

"I'll see if I can get us a van and find a place to park it."

Bosnia

MORNING FOUND the Stony Man warriors in the rocks where they had spent the night. After spotting the enemy patrol in the area of the cliffs, they had been forced to keep moving until they found a safe hiding place to spend the night.

"Are we going back to the cliffs?" Major Hammer asked McCarter and Bolan as they shared a cold breakfast of MREs.

Bolan nodded. "I think it's worth taking a good look at. We'd have done it last night if that patrol hadn't shown up."

Hammer put the discarded wrappers of his rations

into the pockets of his flight suit. "I'm ready when you are."

It took almost two hours for the team to get back to its observation point at the top of the cliffs. And when it arrived, the plain below wasn't empty. Several small pickup trucks and two dozen troops had gathered as if they were waiting for something to happen.

"We've got a plane coming in from the south," Manning warned, "and it looks like it's going to land."

Hammer's trained eyes instantly identified it. "What the hell is that doing here?" he said. "That's one of ours, a C-130 Hercules!"

"Everybody and their brother are flying those now," McCarter accurately stated, "including a lot of people who aren't too friendly to us."

"I knew that was a landing strip," Encizo said as the turboprop transport dropped its flaps and landing gear and lined up with the long cleared area in front of the caves.

"It's Iranian air force," Manning reported as he read the red, white and green insignia rondels on the plane's fuselage with his field glasses.

"That answers the question as to why one of America's finest airplanes is landing here," the Cuban said when he saw several more pickups drive out of the fortress. "I'll bet it's a resupply bird, and the locals are waiting to off-load its cargo."

It was no news that the Iranians had been supplying the Bosnian Muslims with weapons and equipment. But this was the first time that anyone had actually seen a resupply flight come in.

When the desert-camouflage C-130 reached the end of the grass landing strip, it turned before coming to a halt with its tail facing the caves. When the rear ramp descended, more than a dozen troops poured out the back. They were wearing desert-camouflage battle dress that looked out of place in the greenness of Bosnia, but they looked to be well armed as they fanned out to secure the plane.

With a word of command from a man who looked to be an officer, the Iranian troops headed to the base of the cliffs at a dead run. The troops that had been waiting for the plane busied themselves off-loading the cargo and putting it in the trucks.

FROM THE TOWER of his fortress, Dragan Asdik watched Naslin's Iranians off-load the transport and carry the supplies to the trucks. Usually the supply missions were flown at night to keep the Iranian involvement in Bosnia as secret as possible. The lure of the wrecked Yankee spy plane, though, had made the Tehran imams overanxious. Asdik didn't like the change from the routine that had worked so well for so long. But this was only one more indication that the Bosnians were the junior partners in this venture.

Though the aid and supplies were welcome in the fight against the Serbs and Croatians, Asdik would be glad when Bosnia was strong enough to go it on her own. Tehran's arrogance was wearing thin. As the man who was in charge of the secret airstrip and the stockpiling of the supplies that were being flown in, he had more day-to-day contact with the Iranians than anyone else in the Bosnian government. He hoped, though, that as soon as the Iranian master plan was put into action, he could go back to being a simple fighting man and leader of other fighting men, instead of a clerk.

As soon as the cargo-laden trucks were on their way back to the castle, the Iranians started bringing material out of the caves to reload the plane.

"I'LL BE DAMNED!" Hammer was indignant when he saw what the Iranians were doing. "They're loading up the wreckage of my plane."

During the transfer of cargo, the Iranian pilot kept the inboard port-side turbine running to provide internal power while the troops labored to load the jagged pieces of the crashed Night Owl into the cargo hold. There was no hope of ever returning the Night Own to the air, so the Iranians weren't being careful about how they handled their valuable cargo.

Hammer winced when he saw one of them take an ax to one wing panel to shorten it so it would fit inside the transport plane. "Morons," he muttered. "All they needed to do was to fold the wing panel. It's designed to fit inside a C-5A."

Hawkins shook his head as he surveyed the scene below. "Man, there's no way the seven of us can go down there and kill all of those guys and get that plane of yours back. There's just too many of them.''

"We've got to do something.'' Hammer looked like he was about to explode. ''That's the most advanced spy plane in the world they're stealing. Even in pieces, it's worth millions and I'm the guy who signed that sucker out. I'll have to stay in the Air Force for five hundred years just to make the interest payments if I don't take it back where I got it.''

"Striker,'' McCarter said thoughtfully, ''I think that Hammer and I might be able to sneak down there if the rest of you give us a little diversion.''

"And do what, blow it up?''

"No,'' the former British SAS commando replied. ''I was thinking of hijacking it. I can fly a bloody Herky Bird in my sleep. And if I have our resident flyboy here riding along with me, he can talk us through the NATO fighter cover over Italy so we don't get shot down by some trigger-happy fighter jock.''

Bolan turned to Hammer. ''What do you think, Jack?''

The pilot didn't blink. ''Like I said, I'm signed out with that aircraft, and no one said anything about my having to bring it back under its own power or even in one piece. The only thing that counts is keeping it out of the hands of the enemy. I'm game to try it.''

"How good are you on a rappeling rope?'' McCarter asked Hammer.

"It's been a while," he admitted, "but I do know the difference between a Swiss chair and a 'beaner.' We did a little of that when I was at the academy."

"You'll do. It's like riding a bicycle."

"Except that you fall a lot harder."

"There is that."

McCarter was already stripping off most of his combat gear. The only thing he'd need down there were his weapons, ammunition and radio. If the attempt failed and they had to pull back, he could always retrieve the rest of his gear later. Taking his combat cosmetics from his assault pack, he renewed his face paint and recoated his hands. It wasn't going to do him much good out in the open, but he always liked to dress before the ball.

"Come here," he told the Air Force pilot. "We need to rig your Swiss chair."

While Hammer was being fitted with his rappeling harness, James and Manning got out two dark nylon ropes and secured them at the top of the cliff.

"Whatever you guys do," McCarter cautioned the rest of the team, "don't get excited and hit the bloody plane. We're going to need it."

"Got you covered," Manning replied as he unlimbered his scoped Remington 700. "If I have to shoot at the plane, I promise not to hit anything vital."

CHAPTER THIRTEEN

David McCarter hugged the rocks as he slowly worked his way down the face of the cliff on the rappeling rope. With the enemy so close to them, he couldn't kick free of the cliff and make a standard rappeling free fall; that would be sure to catch someone's eye. Six feet from his left side, Hammer tried his best to keep up with the Phoenix Force warrior, but wasn't quite making it. The inexperienced pilot was having trouble with the outcroppings he kept running into.

When McCarter reached the jumble of rocks and boulders at the base of the cliff, he moved over to secure Hammer's line for the final few feet. The pilot landed with a heavy thump, but got right to his feet.

After unclipping the rappeling rope from his assault harness, McCarter grinned at his involuntary teammate. "For a flyboy, you're not half-bad at this grunt drill."

Hammer smiled as he puffed to catch his breath. It had been a long time since he had trusted his body to a quarter-inch-thick nylon rope. But as the Briton had told him, rappeling was something that you never forgot. If you did, you would die on the rope.

"God knows I'm trying, but this isn't like working out on the golf course."

"This is the original workout."

"I hear that."

"We're in the rocks at the bottom," McCarter radioed to the commandos on the top of the cliff.

"You'd better get a move on it," Bolan answered. "It looks like they're about finished loading the wreckage."

"We're on the way."

As McCarter watched the Iranians carry the last few parts of the Night Owl into the C-130, he saw that Bolan was right. They had to make their move now. With the wreckage on board, the Iranian pilots wouldn't want to stay on the ground any longer than was absolutely necessary. Not during daylight hours. They were taking a risk as it was and would want to trim their exposure time.

After checking his H & K assault rifle one last time, McCarter clicked in his throat mike. "Let's do it, Striker," he radioed.

On command, the ridgeline erupted in a storm of automatic fire. Caught out in the open with their weapons slung, the Iranians were stunned. Dropping for what little cover they could find on the plain, they responded quickly, though. All eyes were on the ridge as AK fire arched up at the Stony Man team.

With the enemy's attention focused elsewhere,

McCarter made his move. "We're going for it!" he shouted to Hammer, and took off across the open ground for the Hercules without looking back to see if the pilot was keeping up with him. At the sound of the first shot, the C-130's pilots had fired up a second turbine and were cranking the other two. Since turboprop engines have a short run-up time, the plane would be rolling in another few seconds.

A ground crewman cut across McCarter's charge, racing for the plane's open rear ramp. The Briton snapped a short burst at him, cutting his legs out from under him. Behind him, he heard Hammer put a couple more rounds in the man for insurance.

Two men suddenly appeared in the plane's open ramp door with their AKs in their hands. Seeing the two Americans running toward them, they started to fire. McCarter skidded to a halt to take careful aim. The last thing he needed was for a stray round to clip something important in that machine. The C-130 was a tough old bird and could soak up a lot of damage, but he had to fly that aircraft all the way to Italy and he wanted it intact.

Firing on single shot, McCarter spun one of the Iranians with his first round, causing him to stumble and fall off the ramp. The second shot hit the other gunner dead center in the chest. His arms flew wide and he collapsed, falling back inside the plane.

By now, all four of the aircraft's turboprops were churning and the plane started to roll when the pilots came off the brakes. McCarter was pelted by a blizzard of dust and debris thrown back by the prop wash as he leaped for the ramp door. As soon as he had his footing, he turned back to give Hammer a hand up.

The pilot grasped his arm and, catching the edge of the ramp with the toe of his boot, pulled himself up.

"Stay here," McCarter shouted to him over the roar of the engines. "And make damned sure that no one tries to join us."

Hammer nodded and instinctively ducked for cover around the ramp opening. He knew that the thin aluminum skin of the aircraft wouldn't stop an AK round, but he liked having it between him and the people who were shooting at him. Even though the plane was rolling too fast now for anyone to catch up on foot, he stepped out just far enough to send several quick bursts at the gunmen closest to him.

In the cockpit, the Iranian pilots were busy concentrating on getting the C-130 off the ground and out of the line of fire. They didn't spot McCarter until he had made his way up to the flight deck and was drawing a bead on them with his 9 mm Beretta. The copilot shouted a warning and clawed at his shoulder holster for his own pistol.

McCarter's quick shot took him in the throat. Clawing at his neck, the copilot toppled from his seat.

Catching the pilot's move from the corner of his eye, McCarter dropped into a half crouch and pivoted to the left to swing his Beretta into play. The pilot's frantic shot sizzled past his head and harmlessly punched through the aircraft's fuselage skin. McCarter's double-tap, 9 mm response was dead on target.

The dying pilot's hand dragged the throttles back, and with no one at the wheel, the plane abruptly slowed and slewed to the left. The gunmen on the ground scattered as the whirling props turned in their direction. The confusion below them gave the Stony Man team several good shots, and they took advantage of the targets.

In the Hercules, McCarter pushed through the narrow confines of the cockpit to drag the pilot's body from behind the seat before sliding into his place. Not even pausing to belt himself in, he kicked down on the rudder pedal to check the plane's swing and bring it back on the runway. He slammed the throttle levers forward, the four turboprops roared anew and the plane leaped forward again.

That little excursion through the pucker brush had brought them dangerously close to the end of the already too short runway, but since they couldn't abort and try it again, he was committed. With both hands on the control wheel, he watched the airspeed indicator slowly unwind as the four bladed props clawed at the air.

As the plane accelerated, Hammer slipped into the copilot's seat and reached across for the flap lever. "I'm going to give you another five degrees of flap," he yelled over the roar of eighteen-thousand turbo-prop horsepower. "We're loaded down."

"Do it," McCarter snapped as an AK round punched a star-shaped hole through the canopy right over his head.

The instant the flaps came down, McCarter felt the wings lighten up. Another few miles per hour, and he'd try to take off. With the trees at the end of the clearing coming on fast, he took a firm grip on the control wheel. "I'm going for it!" he shouted over to his copilot.

"Do it!" Hammer yelled back.

With the props thundering and the turbines screaming, McCarter pulled back on the control column and the heavily laden Hercules responded. In the right-hand seat, Hammer watched the trees rushing at them as he slammed the gear-retraction lever forward to bring the wheels up and clean up the airframe.

It was going to be close, too close, and he didn't want to snag a wheel on the treetops.

At the end of the runway, the belly of the C-130 cleared the treetops by less than a foot. But rather than climb for altitude, McCarter kept the plane on the deck to try to use the trees to shield him from the storm of missiles that were sure to follow them.

Suddenly the radio crackled with a frantic voice shouting in Arabic. McCarter didn't have to know the language to know what the guy was asking. He wanted to know what in the hell was going on. Keying the mike, Hammer spoke a short Arabic phrase in return and the radio fell silent.

"What did you tell that guy?" McCarter asked.

Hammer smiled. "One of the more useful Arabic phrases I picked up when I was stationed in Riyadh. I told him that his mother enjoyed having public sexual intercourse with diseased men. I wasn't sure if he was aware of it and thought that he'd want to know."

McCarter tried not to laugh out loud. He liked Hammer, but having the pilot around was going to get all of them killed. Rubbing salt in the wound wasn't going to make this any easier for them.

"Is that load tied down back there?" McCarter shouted as he jinked the aircraft to throw off the missile gunners' aim. "I don't know if they had time to secure it and I'd hate to lose it now."

"I'll check it," Hammer yelled back.

BOLAN WATCHED the C-130 as McCarter kept the plane's belly on the treetops rather than try to climb out to gain altitude. It was dangerous to fly that low, but it was less risky than it would be to climb up into missile range. If McCarter could keep from going into the trees for a few more miles, he'd be out of the range of the heat-seeking warheads of the Strellas.

Even though the Hercules's hot exhausts were being shielded by the trees and prevented the heat-seeking warheads from acquiring the target, the Iranians triggered off two of their missiles anyway. Since the gunners couldn't get a guidance lock-on, they just aimed the Strellas in the direction of the fleeing plane and fired.

The first missile went straight into the trees at the edge of the clearing and exploded harmlessly. The heat-seeking warhead of the second Strella got a lock on the setting sun and streaked after it. Reaching the end of its trajectory, the time fuse triggered the warhead, but it didn't explode anywhere near the C-130.

Now that the C-130 was safely away, Manning had switched back to using his H&K assault rifle. Zeroing in on the guy who looked to be in charge down there—at least he was the one standing up, waving his arms and shouting—he gave him a short burst in his chest for his efforts. These guys were going to have to learn to keep down when they were giving orders.

No one else stood up to take the dead man's place, but the Iranians weren't giving it up. Now that the C-130 was out of missile range, all of their attention was focused on the ridgeline above them. A renewed storm of fire kept the Stony Man warriors' heads down.

Seeing that the Iranians were getting their act together, Bolan keyed his throat mike. "Let's get out of here, guys. Gary, you and T.J. pull rear guard."

With James leading, the team headed back for the safety of the mountain to wait out the next phase of the mission, their extraction. Hopefully Katzenelenbogen wouldn't take too long putting it together, because they had really angered the locals now.

Stony Man Farm

BARBARA PRICE and Hal Brognola were crowded into the computer room again as they waited to hear the results of the Night Owl snatch. When Yakov Katzenelenbogen's face flashed onto the video monitor, they didn't need to hear his words to know that McCarter had been successful. It was written all over his face.

"They did it," he crowed. "They hijacked the Iranian plane with the Night Owl's wreckage on board and they're on the way back now."

"You'd better make sure that the NATO pilots know that they're coming in an Iranian-marked aircraft," Brognola suggested. "We don't need for them to get shot down now."

"The word has been put out," Katz reassured them. "And the fighters on this interception are all USAF, so there won't be any itchy fingers on the triggers looking for a cheap kill to put on their scoreboard."

"Let me know as soon as they land," Brognola ordered. "The President's waiting for the news."

"Will do."

"Tell Striker that we're working up an extraction plan right now," Price informed him. "The guys may have to walk a ways to get to the LZ, but we'll try to make it as close to them as we can. But until then, tell them to keep out of trouble if they can. We've had enough excitement around here for a while."

"I'll pass that on, too."

When Katz killed the connection, he sat back. So far, so good. They had gotten Lacy out, and Hammer was coming back with what was left of his plane. Now all they had to do was to get the rest of the team out of Bosnia, and they could rack up another win for the good guys.

Someone else could worry about the Iranians. Maybe PROFOR could get their hands dirty for a change. He knew that there was little chance of that, but a man could still hope.

Bosnia

MAJOR NASLIN COULDN'T believe that the Yankees had been able to hijack the Hercules transport with the prized stealth fighter on board. The imams of Tehran would have his blood for the loss of the two planes and it wouldn't be an easy death. There was no way of getting them back now, and his only hope of redeeming himself was to kill the raiders who had done this to him. Plus, for him to be able to carry out the primary mission he had been sent to Bosnia for, he couldn't afford to have these American commandos running loose.

He had to admit that for infidels, the Yankees were

good, especially the devil with the silenced rifle. This sniper had taken several of his most experienced group leaders, and he had been forced to promote some of the younger, less experienced men to take their places. The dead men were basking in God's Paradise now, but carrying out the plan would be more difficult without them.

"I am going to put the plan on hold," he told the Bosnian. "Until we can run down those Yankee devils, it is too dangerous to continue with it until we know that they are dead."

Dragan Asdik wasn't sorry to hear the Iranian's decision to delay Tehran's plan and would have preferred to see it canceled outright. He didn't mind killing his Serb and Croatian enemies; he had done that all of his life, it seemed. But killing them with poison gas offended his sense of righteousness.

Enemies were for killing, but for killing man-to-man and face-to-face. Even though he knew that the Iranian plan would advance the cause of his people, he had never liked it. He wanted a Bosnia free of the Serb and Croat infidels as much as any son of the Prophet, but he didn't think that a merciful God wanted them to be killed like sheep the way the Iranians planned to do.

"And," the Iranian continued, "I will need to use your men, as well as mine, to make sure that we can kill them as soon as we can."

"As I told you," Asdik said, "my men are my men and they fight for me. A handful of Yankees can do me no harm here. Plus, they have taken back everything they came for, both the men and that damned airplane. Now they will leave and go home. They will be gone from here in a day or two.''

"But they made us both look like fools."

"Not us," Asdik said. "It was your idea to keep the Americans prisoner, and it was your plan to try to fly that wreckage back to Tehran."

"The commandos have acted against the will of God," the Iranian insisted. "They have cast dung in the faces of the faithful, and God demands that they be punished for their crimes."

Asdik thought of himself as a good Muslim, but he wasn't as sure that he knew what God wanted as the Iranian seemed to be. To Naslin, everything that happened was either God's will or the hand of Satan working against the Almighty. Asdik knew that nothing was ever that simple and that luck played a large part of any military action. The Yankees had proved that. Only blind luck could have placed them on the ridgeline when the plane had flown in. Their skills as warriors, though, had let them successfully exploit that luck.

Asdik was man enough to admit that he had seriously miscalculated the danger the Yankees had presented. This was one time that Naslin's paranoia had been accurate. Whoever those men were, they were good. Nonetheless, he was convinced that they no longer represented a danger, at least not to him.

"If that is true," he told the major. "I am content to let God punish them. They will be leaving now, and things will get back to normal."

"We will see," the Iranian almost hissed.

CHAPTER FOURTEEN

Aviano Air Base, Italy

The flight of the Iranian C-130 carrying the wreckage of the Night Owl back to the Aviano air base went off without a hitch. With Hammer talking them in, they had been met halfway across the Adriatic by a flight of four American F-16 Falcons from the base. The fighters were fully armed, but Hammer knew all of the right code words, and one of the pilots was a drinking buddy of his. With the fighters flying off both wings, no one bothered them.

They were cleared to land immediately, and once he was on the ground, McCarter taxied the Hercules to the big hangar at the far end of the flight line as Hammer directed. When the waiting ground crewman signaled him to stop, he killed the fuel feed to the turboprops.

"Home, sweet home," Hammer said as the American Air Police rushed to throw a cordon around the Iranian plane. "You know the drill, get out of the plane with your hands up and assume the position."

"Been there," McCarter said, grinning, "done that."

Katz had made the necessary arrangements for McCarter and Hammer to be driven directly to the Stony Man CP for a debriefing before anyone else talked to them. The only thing the Air Force needed to know right then was they had their secret spy plane back and they would have to be satisfied with that. They didn't need to know the details of how they had gotten it back.

Hammer stood back and looked at the makeshift CP. He had never seen so much electronic gear thrown together in one place outside of a repair facility. Some of it was easily recognizable, but much of it was as foreign to him as a microwave oven would be to a bushman. He still didn't know who the hell he had gotten mixed up with, but they certainly didn't lack resources. A maid, however, wouldn't be out of order.

Without waiting for an invitation, he walked over to the coffeepot, pawed through the debris piled around it to find a semiclean cup and poured himself a hot one. If he was violating some kind of protocol by serving himself, they could shoot him later. Right now he needed a cup of coffee.

"This is Major John Hammer," McCarter introduced him, "the Night Owl pilot we came across in the castle."

"I'm Yakov Katzenelenbogen," said the older

man with a stainless steel prothesis in place of his right arm. "But everyone just calls me Katz."

"They call me Jack," Hammer stated, taking his hand. "I'm pleased to be here, wherever here is."

Katz smiled. "This is just a little CP operation we threw together for this mission."

Hammer also didn't know what "this mission" was, but he now knew better than to ask. He was tired of being told that he didn't have a need to know.

"I'm Hermann Schwarz," the man behind the biggest bank of commo gear said, waving. "Everyone calls me Gadgets."

Hammer raised his coffee cup in salute.

"The other guys are busy right now, so you probably won't meet them for a while."

Hammer's rough count was coming up with a dozen guys associated with whatever this was. But again, he didn't have a need to know.

"You want me to tell the Farm that they're here?" Schwarz asked Katz.

"Go ahead."

Hammer tried not to be too obvious as he sipped his coffee to cover his listening in to Schwarz's short conversation. The woman's voice on the other end intrigued him. He couldn't quite see women working with this gang of commandos and spooks.

"You present a bit of a problem to us, Jack," Katz told Hammer after showing him to a chair beside the single desk in the room. "Usually we don't let outsiders get this close to one of our operations. But since you got yourself dragooned, as it were, I guess that we'll just have to accommodate you for a little while more. In fact you'll be seconded to us for the duration.''

''If you don't mind,'' Hammer replied, ''I'd like to check that out with my chain of command first. They're going to want to get a—''

''That's already been taken care of,'' Katz interrupted him. ''As of the time we pulled you out of that fortress, you've been on detached duty with us. I have a hard copy if you'd like to see it. It's signed off by the Air Force chief of staff.

''That's so we can keep you quiet,'' Katz explained when he saw the look on the pilot's face. ''This thing isn't over yet, and we have to maintain absolute security until it is. As the pilot of a classified aircraft, I'm sure you understand things like that.''

Hammer took a deep breath. If he didn't understand it, he sure as hell was going to pretend that he did. He was just a down-home fighter jock, and spook games were a little out of his league, but it looked like he was locked in and had to ride it out. ''Okay,'' he said. ''I'll play.''

''Good. Gadgets will show you where you can bunk down and get cleaned up. Let me know if there's anything you need, and I'll have it sent over ASAP.''

Hammer leaned back in his chair. ''Well, there is this waitress at the officers' club.''

Schwarz laughed and Katz grinned. "You're going to fit in well around here."

Stony Man Farm

AARON KURTZMAN WAS happy to hear that McCarter and the Air Force major had made it safely back to Italy with their hijacked Hercules and its classified cargo. The loss of the Night Owl would have been devastating to the security of the United States. Now, all they had to do was to get the Stony Man team to someplace where they could be extracted by chopper without the threat of a gauntlet of deadly Strella missiles.

There was something about those Strellas that had been nagging at the back of his mind. It was true that since the breakup of the old Evil Empire, ex-Soviet weapons were showing up more and more on the arms black markets of the world. But even the Russians weren't so money hungry that they wanted to see weapons like that get into the hands of Islamic fanatics.

With the trouble the new Russian state was having with their own Muslims, they were very leery of who got hold of weapons that could so easily be turned against them. They hadn't forgotten what the American Stinger missiles in the hands of the mujahideen had done to them in Afghanistan. One of the old Soviet generals had even said that they were the single thing that had tipped the balance against the Russian army and had forced its withdrawal.

Regardless of Russian concern, it was true that a few Strellas had slipped out, particularly a batch or two from an unguarded armory in what had once been East Germany. But for Iran to have enough of the valuable weapons on hand to be willing to issue them to the freedom fighters in Bosnia didn't make sense to Kurtzman. The missiles were there for a reason, and it bothered him that he didn't know what it was. There was a big piece to this puzzle that was missing, and he hated missing pieces.

After discovering that the mysterious Islamic commandos at the fortress were Iranians, he had been able to match them to the political assassinations that had taken place in Bosnia since the signing of the so-called peace accord. The assumption was that this was the Iranian contingent's primary mission. That by killing enough Serb and Croat leaders, the Bosnian Muslims would have an easier time of gaining control of the fragmented state and could impose their will on the non-Muslim population.

He still thought that was a valid assumption, but it didn't explain the antiaircraft missiles. The problem was that the assassination of leaders in that region was a game as old as time. Even the War to End All Wars had been started by the assassination of a political figure in Sarajevo in 1914, the Archduke Ferdinand of Austria. But he wasn't sure that assassination alone would swing the balance far enough to the side of the Muslims to make an appreciable difference this time.

It wouldn't hurt the Muslim cause to have fewer capable men opposing them—that was true. But he knew that for every man who was killed, another one would stand up in his place and vow to carry on the fight. The only way to dramatically shift the balance of power in the region was genocide pure and simple. The Serbs had gotten a good start on that with the concentration camps and mass killings that had taken place during the war. As evil as it had been, a few thousand men, women and children more or less simply didn't make any difference in the real world.

For these Iranian commandos to make a radical difference in the politics of the region, they would have to kill tens of thousands of Serbs and Croats, and there simply weren't enough of them to do that. Unless, of course, they planned to use weapons of mass destruction, as they had come to be known. Calling up a menu, he clicked on a file to take a look at the latest information he had on weapons of mass destruction in the Middle East.

It was only by the grace of God and the courage of mortal men that the only member of the nuclear club in the region was the state of Israel. The Israelis had nuclear weapons, and they had made sure that all of their bellicose neighbors knew about them. This was the primary reason that the Jews and Arabs had quit going to war every couple of years as they had done in the fifties, sixties and seventies. If the state of Israel felt threatened enough, it was well-known they would use their nuclear weapons to defend themselves.

But while the Arab states didn't have nuclear weapons, it didn't mean that they didn't have weapons of mass destruction. There were other ways to kill large numbers of people without using nuclear bombs. Chemical and biological weapons worked just as well if they were employed properly. Iraq's biological- and chemical-weapons programs were a proved factor. Only the threat of nuclear retaliation had kept them from using them during the Gulf War.

What was less well-known was that the Iranians also had a sizable chemical arsenal. Back when the Russians had been supporting them, they had sent scientists to Tehran to set up a chemical-weapons-development program. In particular, an East German team from a chemical firm in Dresden had spent more than a year there setting up a state-of-the-art facility for the manufacture of nerve gas and blister agents like mustard gas.

Scrolling through the latest intel updates, he looked for reports of unusual activity at the known Iranian chemical-weapons storage sites. These were all hidden facilities camouflaged to look like anything but weapons-storage areas.

When Kurtzman found what he had suspected, he ran the tapes of the past few months' worth of recon-satellite passes over the facility. Like nearly everyone else in the world, the Iranians knew when America's spy birds were overhead and made sure that they didn't do anything that would look suspicious while their cameras were watching. But often what they didn't do when they could be seen was as informative as what they did when they couldn't.

For instance, for the past several months at the Jeziel storage facility, the Iranians hadn't done anything that would look bad on tape. In fact they had gone to great lengths to ensure that everything would look normal to the space spies. But since the place was being passed off as an agricultural machinery factory, it didn't make sense that no one was working during daylight hours. It also didn't make sense that the same half-completed tractors were in the same place for run after run.

But if this was a chemical-weapons facility, it would make sense that it would have a growing pile of junk in back that on the highest magnification turned out to be the original packing crates for Russian high-explosive rockets. And tire tracks of heavy trucks leading to the airfield nearby were always fresh. An enhanced oblique camera shot showed him the distinctive tall tail of a C-130 parked in the big hangar at the airfield, and there was no need to fly tractors anywhere in Iran.

When Kurtzman was completely satisfied that he had his answer, he picked up his phone and hit the speed dial. "Hal," he said when it was picked up on the second ring, "I think you need to come down here and look at something. And bring Barbara with you.''

WHEN BROGNOLA AND PRICE arrived ten minutes later, it was apparent that Kurtzman had rousted the rest of the cybernetics team, as well. They were all at their workstations, and the high-speed printers were spitting out paper as fast as it could be loaded into them.

''What do you have, Aaron?'' Price asked.

''I think I've found out why those Islamic commandos are hiding out in Bosnia.''

''Couldn't this have waited until the morning briefing?'' Brognola growled. ''Unlike you, I have to get some sleep every now and then.''

''It could have waited, yes,'' he admitted. ''But I thought that you'd want to get this to the President as soon as you could.''

''Get what to him?''

''The information about the Iranian chemical weapons that have been transferred to Bosnia.''

That woke up Brognola in a hurry. ''How about starting from the beginning, Aaron? Some of us haven't been awake all night doing whatever you've been doing.''

As Price headed for the coffeepot, Kurtzman started relating how he had spent the night. When he was done, Brognola looked considerably more haggard than he had when he first walked in. ''How soon can you have hard copy on all of that ready for me?''

Kurtzman glanced at the printers. ''It should be ready any moment now.''

''I'll get the chopper ready,'' Price said.

''I already notified the pilot,'' Kurtzman stated, ''and he's standing by.''

''The Man is going to love this,'' Brognola muttered as he was handed the heavily laden briefcase with the security-handcuff lock.

CHAPTER FIFTEEN

Bosnia

The Stony Man team had found a secure hiding place in the rocks while they waited for extraction. Their mountain refuge gave them good all-around vision of the approaches and had a natural "back door" if they were discovered. It was a good place to hunker down until Katzenelenbogen could put together their return flight.

"That's about the last of the MREs," James said as he crumpled the brown plastic wrapping of his meal and stuffed it in his assault pack.

"If we get too hungry," Hawkins suggested, "I've got a pretty good recipe for bootlace soup. My daddy always said that it came down from his great-granddaddy, and that the Army of Northern Virginia really liked it. He even said that Bobby Lee himself stopped by one day and had some."

"I'll put my gym-sock stew up against it any old time," James said. "It was the hit of the Chicago neighborhood where I grew up."

"The problem with using old sweat socks as a soup base," Hawkins said seriously, "is that you get that residual rubbery taste from the shoes and have to use too much pepper to cover it up."

"Everyone knows that stone soup's best," Encizo said, putting an end to the argument. "But you need to have a village nearby to get the condiments it really needs. I can remember one time when I was—"

"Can it, guys," Manning radioed from his lookout. "We have another patrol moving toward us, and it looks like it's the mountain men this time."

They had gotten away clean from the hijacking of the C-130, but the opposition hadn't been content to let it rest there. Ever since they had gotten back to their hiding place, both vehicle and foot patrols had been working the forest day and night. The Iranians had been joined by men in dark olive battle dress and carrying ropes on their rucksacks. The new force had the look of locals and, from the ropes, they had to be trained mountain troops.

The Stony Man warriors knew that it was unlikely that the Iranians would try to climb the rocks to get to them. But the locals were a different story. They would have no fears of rocks and sheer cliffs.

Picking up their weapons, the commandos moved to their prepared positions to see what developed this time. Their ammunition situation wasn't critical yet, but they were down to only a third of their basic load and couldn't afford to get into a long firefight.

Aviano Air Base, Italy

CARL LYONS and Rosario Blancanales were on the afternoon of their second day of watching the western approach to the air base from their hilltop observation point. After making a map study of the area surrounding the air base, Katzenelenbogen had decided that any attacker would come from that direction because of the easy access to the road networks. They would want to get in and out of their attack positions quickly, and the roads were best to the west.

Figuring that the terrorists would want to strike at night, Lyons and Blancanales had stayed awake the night before and now were taking turns sleeping during the day. On an assignment like this, it was essential that they get their rest whenever they could. Blancanales was sacked out in the back of the van this shift while Lyons kept watch. His eyes were on autopilot, scanning every vehicle that passed in traffic, when he saw a large van in the right-hand lane slow and pull off the road.

"Heads up, guys," he called the CP over the comm link. "I've got what looks like a moving van, or something like that, pulling over to the side of the road. It's not a normal parking area, and there doesn't seem to be anything wrong with the truck."

"Maybe the driver's just got to take a leak," Schwarz called back. "They have to do that in Italy, too, you know."

"Four men have gotten out," Lyons continued his report. "No, make that six, and they're opening up the doors in the back of the truck."

"This is it!" Lyons shouted when he recognized what the men were pulling out of the van. The shape of a mortar base plate couldn't be mistaken for anything else. Not when the tube and bipod were brought out a second later and fitted to it. "They're setting up a heavy mortar."

Blancanales had woken in the back of the van and was scrambling to get into the passenger's seat as Lyons fired up the engine and shifted the transmission into first gear.

It took but a few seconds for the gunners to lay their weapon and drop the first round down the tube. The mortar fired with the characteristic coughing thump, and the first 120 mm mortar round was on its way, arcing through the sky. It hit at the end of the flight line, and the gunners cranked the traverse wheel to bring the weapon to bear on the hangars.

By the time the second mortar round was in the air, a dozen more men stood up along the base perimeter fence at the end of the runway with RPG-7 antitank rocket launchers on their shoulders. Since the chain-link fences would detonate the rocket warheads if they tried to fire directly through at the fence, they angled the launchers up to fire over the fence like artillery.

The 85 mm RPG warheads didn't carry the explosive charge of the larger 120 mm mortar rounds. But since they were shaped-charge warheads designed to penetrate tank armor, they made good bunker busters. Also they had a good antipersonnel effect when they detonated against concrete and sprayed the fragments like shrapnel.

On the flight line, the Italian pilots of the pair of F-16 Fighting Falcons on ramp alert raced for their planes at the sound of the first explosion. The ground crews had already started the jet engines, and as soon as the pilots were strapped in, they pulled their throttles past the stops into afterburner, released the brakes and took off screaming down the runway.

The RPG gunners heard the whining scream of the turbines and shifted their aim to the fighters trying to take off. Trailing dirty white smoke, a volley of half a dozen rockets arched over the fence for the runway. The gunners' aim wasn't precise, but enough of the rockets hit the tarmac to do the job.

One of the shaped-charge warheads detonated right in front of the lead F-16. Jagged chunks of concrete were sucked into the fighter's intake, and the engine exploded.

"Seven Niner, punch out! Punch out!" the control tower screamed at the pilot.

The pilot needed no prompting and had already pulled the bang-seat handle. The zero-length ejection seat rocketed him high enough into the air that his chute could open and return him to earth.

The pilot of the first fighter was still in the air when his wingman took a direct hit on the left wing.

The antitank warhead cut through the aircraft's main spar like a hot knife. When the wing folded, it knocked out the landing gear on that side, and the F-16 slammed sideways onto the runway at well over a hundred miles per hour. This time, the pilot had presence of mind enough not to eject and risk getting killed from the seat rocketing him into the ground.

All of this happened in the first 120 seconds of the attack. It took another 120 seconds before any of the base security forces responded. By that time, the fuel tank farm was blazing, one of the ammunition bunkers had exploded and more than a dozen planes on the flight line had been destroyed or damaged by shell fragments.

Now, though, sirens were wailing all over the base, and men were running for their alert stations. Helicopter gunships were cranking up, and fire trucks were racing to try to put out the fires before the flames spread. One of the trucks drove into a falling mortar round and was blown off its wheels.

The stunned security forces tried to return fire at the RPG gunners outside the fence, but they were met with a hail of AK fire from the second group of terrorists who had been lying in wait for them. The advantage lay with the attackers, who had taken cover in the drainage ditches.

ON THE HILL overlooking the carnage, Lyons and Blancanales were racing for the terrorists with the 120 mm mortar. If they could put the tube out of action, they could limit the damage that was being done.

As Lyons drove, Blancanales loaded a 40 mm grenade into the breach of the M-203 grenade launcher he had borrowed from Schwarz. For this kind of work, his 12-gauge SPAS just didn't have the range or the firepower.

IN THE STONY MAN CP, Katz and Schwarz had their hands full. When Lyons sent the warning about the mortars, Katz immediately called the base security office, but had been put on hold. In frustration, he tried to get through to the UN PROFOR headquarters, but hadn't been able to talk to anyone in charge. The man on radio watch didn't speak enough English to understand what the problem was and kept shouting that they were under attack.

Major Hammer had been catching up on his sleep when the first mortar explosion brought him out of his bunk. Racing into the main room, he saw Schwarz diving for cover inside the sandbag bunker that had been built against the far wall. When Katz yelled at him to do the same, the pilot didn't argue.

"We're coming up on that mortar," Lyons called into the CP. "Can you get someone up here to back us up?"

"I'm afraid that you're going to have to handle that one yourselves," Katz answered.

"We're in the process of doing that right now," Lyons said, "but we could use a little help."

"I think you're going to be on your own for a while. The base security people are a little busy right now. They're trying to get their fingers out."

"Good luck."

Stony Man Farm

AARON KURTZMAN'S voice broke in over Barbara Price's intercom. "Barb, Katz just called, and the air base in Aviano is being attacked."

"I'm coming."

On her quick trip down the hall, Price used her comm link to talk to the blacksuit on duty in the radio room. "Put a priority call through to Hal Brognola," she ordered. "Tell him that Aviano is under attack and I need him back here ASAP."

"Will do, ma'am."

Brognola was probably on the way to the airfield for the flight back to the Farm with the President's decision about the nerve-gas rockets as it was. But with this new escalation of the situation, they needed to talk immediately, and even encrypted radio didn't cut it.

The computer room looked a little busier than usual. Hunt Wethers had a monitor screen showing a satellite view of the air base. Akira Tokaido looked like he was running radio intercepts of the traffic of the Aviano security forces, and Kurtzman had Katz's face on his screen.

"...and so far," Katz spoke loudly to be heard

over the scream of sirens and rumble of explosions in the background, "we haven't taken any hits. I've got everyone else under cover and—"

Just then there was a thunderous explosion that sounded close in the background.

Katz looked as unflappable as ever as he turned away from the video pickup to see what the noise was. "We just took an RPG round in the chain-link fence," he said, "but it didn't penetrate. RPG screen works every time."

Price leaned down so she could be seen by the video camera. "Katz," she said, "you'd better get your butt under cover, as well. I don't want to lose you and have to put the Ironman in charge over there. I'd never hear the end of it from Hal."

Katz grinned. "He and Rosario are a little busy right now anyway. They're outside the perimeter trying to knock out a mortar."

"Just get your butt under cover until it's over," Price snapped. "That's an order."

"Yes, ma'am."

Price's comm link beeped and she answered it. "Price."

"Mr. Brognola's inbound," the blacksuit in the radio room stated.

"Good. Tell him to come directly to the computer room."

Aviano Air Base, Italy

CARL LYONS DROVE to within fifty yards of the mortar before the terrorists caught sight of the van. One of the men handing ammo to the loader shouted a warning as he grabbed for the Beretta subgun slung over his shoulder. A long burst of 9 mm rounds cut across the front of the vehicle, smashing the headlights, radiator and bodywork.

"Hang on!" Lyons shouted as he hunched lower in the cab. Cranking the wheel hard over, he trod on the brakes to spin the van, sliding it broadside to the enemy fire. Killing the engine, he was out of his door before the vehicle stopped rolling, his man-killing Python filling his fist. His first two shots took out the thug with the subgun, and another two slugs scattered the rest of the crew.

Blancanales was out of the driver's door of the cab right on Lyons's heels. Crouching behind the hood, he used the engine block for armor as he aimed the M-16/M-203 over-and-under combo and triggered the grenade launcher. The 40 mm round arched out and dropped long, well behind the mortar. The black puff of smoke that marked the detonation didn't seem to affect the enemy.

Ejecting the empty, he shoved another round into the launcher to try it again.

The entire gun crew was firing at them now, their 120 mm mortar forgotten. That was a good start, Lyons observed as he snapped off the last two rounds in the Colt's cylinder.

Blancanales dropped his second grenade right next

to the mortar's base plate. The little warhead didn't have much of a burst radius, only five yards, but the crew was bunched up, well within that range. Two of them went down from the blast, and, flipping over to the M-16, he dumped a full magazine into the rest.

By the time he dropped down to eject his empty magazine, Lyons had his Python back in action, and four .357 Magnum rounds later, it was all over.

Stony Man Farm

"HOW BAD IS IT?" Brognola looked a little out of breath from his sprint from the chopper landing pad.

"We don't know yet," Price answered. "But none of the team has been hit."

"It's a major attack, though," Kurtzman said. "Mortars, RPGs and the whole nine yards."

"I'd say that something we've been doing has stirred them up." Brognola sounded satisfied.

"I'm not so sure about that," Kurtzman replied. "Since they aren't directly targeting the CP, there must be something else behind this. Damned if I know what, though."

That wasn't exactly what Brognola wanted to hear right then. He was having a difficult enough time explaining the situation to the President as it was without this new twist.

Aviano Air Base, Italy

SOMEONE IN ONE of the NATO security units finally called up armored cars and sent them in against the terrorists in the ditch outside of the perimeter. The vehicles weren't well enough armored to withstand RPG rounds and would be taken out of action if they took a hit. But once they could get close enough to the chain-link fence, they would be protected because the warheads would detonate when they hit the wire.

One of the vehicles took a hit on the way in, but the crew was able to bail out before the fuel tanks went up in a roiling ball of flame. With their turret machine guns hammering, the other cars raced for the fence. When the vehicles' charge brought them to the wire, the battle was effectively over.

With no way to knock out the vehicles, the terrorists couldn't stand up to the blazing turret guns. They turned and fled only to be cut down.

"CAN YOU SEND someone out to pick us up?" Lyons called the CP. "Our van is kind of shot up."

"Wait there," Katz replied. "I'll send Gadgets and Hammer to pick you up."

"Also, tell the UN guys that there's six bodies and a mortar up here for their trophy room."

CHAPTER SIXTEEN

The next morning, the damage to the air base looked worse than it really was. Unfortunately, though, almost a dozen casualties had resulted from the attack, and many more men had been wounded. But the damaged aircraft and vehicles could be replaced and the facilities quickly repaired. Aviano would be back in full operation in a couple of days at the most. Already, the runways were clear enough for the fighters of the PROFOR Bosnian patrol to take off on schedule.

The only good thing that came out of the attack was that both the Italians and NATO were taking the terrorist threat seriously now. Along with the infantry reinforcements inside the perimeter, armored vehicles and foot patrols were working all the areas around the base within mortar range. Security checkpoints had been set up along all of the roads leading in and were screening all traffic.

None of this, however, affected the small building that housed the Stony Man CP. Although the chain-link fence had soaked up one stray RPG rocket, the

CP had gone untouched; none of the mortar rounds had fallen near them. So, while the workmen were putting the base back to good working order, Katzenelenbogen went over the information he had just received from the Farm before calling Striker with the bad news that the mission had been extended.

The new mission didn't sit well with Katz. For one thing, the team wasn't equipped to stay in the field that long. The ammunition and ration loads they had been dropped in with were the standard three-day load appropriate for their original snatch mission. With the fighting they had done so far, they would be running low on ammunition, far too low for them to get into a sustained firefight. And while the rations weren't as critical as firepower, a fighting man had to eat, as well as shoot.

Plus he didn't like the odds the team would be facing, particularly when the opposition knew that they were there. This would be the third time that they had gone up against the same target, and the element of surprise had long since evaporated. They'd been very lucky to have pulled off the C-130 hijacking, but counting on luck alone was a good way to get killed.

At the bottom of it, though, was the fact that he didn't like anything that was associated with chemical weapons of any kind. As far as he was concerned, anyone who was found with them should be stood against a wall and shot dead.

Something as serious as the presence of chemical

weapons in the area should be handed over to the UN PROFOR, and they should send in troops who were equipped to deal with a chemical environment. The Stony Man warriors didn't even have gas masks with them. Not that they would do any good against what Kurtzman thought was involved.

If Kurtzman was right, the Iranians had shipped nerve-gas weapons to Bosnia. The gas involved was most likely sarin, the original German nerve gas of World War II vintage rather than the more modern VX nerve agent. But sarin was deadly. In fact home-made sarin had been used in the terrorist attacks on the Tokyo subways, and a gas mask was no defense against it. A single drop of it on the skin could kill, to say nothing of a lungful of droplets.

With the next round of Bosnian elections scheduled to take place in the near future, finding the targets for the rockets would be no problem. When the Serbs and Croats gathered to vote, a single round would kill hundreds if not thousands or tens of thousands of people. And since Kurtzman's information indicated that the Iranian chemical warheads had been mounted on Katusha rocket rounds, they could be fired from a distance great enough to allow the attackers to escape the effects of the gas.

The results would be complete disruption of the peace process and a chance for the Muslim Bosnians to eradicate their enemies like so many flies. And by the time the UN PROFOR could react to the threat, the Bosnian problem would have been solved by the destruction of the non-Muslim population in another ethnic cleansing.

The Western world would view such an attack with sheer horror, but Katz knew that the Iranians couldn't care less about Western public opinion. As long as they had their oil reserves, they were immune to that kind of pressure. It was one of God's cruelest jokes to have given those people a monopoly on a commodity that the world needed as much as it did. But until someone figured out a way for the modern technological world to get along without oil, the Islamic oil-producing nations would continue to call the tunes to the detriment of the rest of the world.

Once he had thoroughly backgrounded himself, Katz reached for the radio to give Bolan the bad news.

Bosnia

DRAGAN ASDIK WAS man enough to admit that he had seriously miscalculated the danger that the Yankees presented. This was one time that Major Naslin's paranoia had been accurate. Whoever those men were, they were good and they still represented a danger. Both the vehicle and foot patrols had failed to find them, and according to the radar, no helicopters had flown into the area to take them out.

There was a faint chance that they had simply walked far enough away that a chopper could come in to pick them up and not be spotted, but he didn't think that had happened. His gut instinct told him that they were hiding in the mountains and waiting. The problem was that he didn't know what they were waiting for.

Naslin had been in almost hourly contact with his superiors in Tehran, and they were concerned about the Yankees, too. The Iranians were convinced that the actions against their agents in Italy were definitely connected with the activities of the commandos in Bosnia. Asdik didn't see the connection, but the Iranians were certain that it was there. In fact Naslin was on the radio to them again, and Asdik was waiting to see what further measures they wanted to take.

When the major came out of the radio room, he wasn't smiling. "Tehran is concerned about your security, and I have been ordered to move the chemical rockets out of here before the Yankees find them."

"Where will you take them?"

"I am to take them to the forest camp where the rocket launchers are."

Asdik didn't take offense at the implication that his security was lax. He knew that it wasn't, and he was well aware that a small group of well-trained men could stay hidden for as long as they wanted. In fact he was glad to see the deadly rockets leave his area. He had never been comfortable having them stored so close to his fortress. His men had gas masks, but he knew that they would be no defense if one of the rockets malfunctioned.

"So your plan is to go ahead, then?"

"Yes, it is." Naslin smiled. "There was never a doubt about it."

Unfortunately, Asdik thought.

Now that he had permission from Tehran to act, Naslin was in a hurry to get the nerve-gas rocket rounds joined up with the modified Katusha rocket launchers waiting at his other base camp. The launchers were an old Russian weapon dating back to WW II, but they hadn't outlived their usefulness. If nothing else, their rugged simplicity made them the perfect launchers for the chemical rockets.

The bulk of Naslin's freedom fighters weren't at Asdik's fortress. Another camp a hundred miles to the north had been established to hide the Islamic commandos who had been secreted away. Unlike the Bosnian's ancient castle, it was a proper military camp with interlocking fortifications, heavy weapons and facilities to support the troops until the time was ready for them to go into action again.

After the rockets were joined up with the launchers, the select teams who would launch the rockets would leave from there to make their attacks on the Serb and Croatian towns. Backing them up would be other units ready to exploit the results of the gas attacks. If God allowed the plan to be carried out, the major Serb and Croatian cities and strong points would soon be in Bosnian Muslim hands. And once that was accomplished, the new Bosnian government would ask their Iranian brothers for help.

That would be the signal for a massive airlift of Iranian troops and equipment to start. Tehran had the supplies stockpiled at the airfields, and the aircraft and the troops were standing by for their orders. In a matter of days, the green flags of Islam would proudly fly over a completely Muslim Bosnia.

MACK BOLAN WAS GRIM FACED when he called the remaining Phoenix Force warriors together. "I just talked to Katz, and we have a situation."

Everyone on the team had been around the military long enough to recognize trouble coming when he heard it. The use of the word *situation* could only be bad news. And the look on Bolan's face only reinforced their misgivings.

"The Farm thinks that we might have stumbled into a real hornet's nest."

"Whatever gave them that idea?" Encizo quipped. "I thought we were on a vacation in the mountains hundreds of miles from friendly territory with no way to get back except booting it."

"It's just become a little more complicated than that," Bolan said grimly. "The Bear thinks that the Iranians and the Bosnians here are getting ready to launch a chemical attack on the Serb and Croatian strongholds in Bosnia."

"From here?" Hawkins asked.

"That's what they want us to find out," Bolan replied. "Hal's convinced that Kurtzman's theory is worth looking into, and that means the Man wants us to do it.''

"Does that mean making a raid on that rock pile again?'' James asked.

"Maybe not," Bolan answered.

"I sure as hell hope not," Hawkins said. "'Cause I kind of used up all my chips flying in there the first time. And since I don't have another parasail handy, I don't think that flapping my arms is going to cut it.''

"I don't think that'll be necessary," Bolan replied. "If these guys have been stockpiling chemical weapons, I don't think they'd want them stored that close to their headquarters. They may be fanatics, but we can't count on them being that stupid."

"Hammer said something about seeing some of them carrying gas masks in the castle," Encizo recalled. "And I remember thinking that was a little strange because tear gas isn't a usual terrorist weapon.''

"That is an indicator," Bolan agreed. "But I think it's more likely that if they actually do have those weapons on hand, they're keeping them in the caves where they stored the wreckage of that plane.''

"At least we know where they are, then," James said. "We shouldn't have too much trouble getting in there.''

"Depending on how many troops they have guarding them," Manning cautioned. "If you'll remember, they had a couple of dozen guys there when they moved the wreckage of the major's plane.''

"We'll find that out tonight," Bolan said. "But in the meantime, I want everyone to get as much sleep today as they can.''

Aviano Air Base, Italy

SINCE THERE WAS nothing he could do to help with Bolan's and Phoenix Force's situation, Carl Lyons went back to working on the problem of the local bad guys. This situation had escalated to the point that they needed to do more than just make raids on safehouses. It was time to go after the head of the beast and cut it off.

"How much of this intel have you given to the UN?" Lyons asked Katz about the computer files they had stolen from the garage.

"None of the raw information," the Israeli replied. "Hal didn't want us to let the cat out of the bag, as it were. There would have been too many questions asked about how we had obtained it.''

"Good." Lyons smiled grimly.

"What do you mean?"

"What I mean is, that means we still have a chance at taking out that Lebanese guy who seems to be in charge of the Italian operation.''

Katz closed his weary eyes and took a deep breath. Running interference for the Ironman and his sidekicks could be a full-time job, particularly when Able

Team had too much time on its hands. "I assume that you're thinking about hunting him down and making him pay for the damage his men did to the air base?"

"Something like that." Lyons shrugged. "But I was thinking more along the line of killing him and leaving his body in a ditch somewhere as an object lesson. As we have seen, he's a danger to himself and others. If someone doesn't take this guy out soon, he's likely to pop up somewhere else and cause even more trouble."

"I agree," Katz said. "But I was thinking of leaving that job to the local authorities. After all, they have a much bigger stake in that than we do."

"But," Lyons said, "we have the information about this guy, and they don't. Just call it doing our part for creating a safer tomorrow. It won't be the first time that we've helped another country take out its garbage."

Katz had to admit that there was truth to that. "Okay," he conceded, "but let's sit down and work out a plan of action first. Racing around northern Italy with a trunk full of weapons might not be a particularly good idea right now. The cops are likely to shoot you first and ask for your passports later."

"What do you have in mind?"

"I was thinking of doing something a little more subtle. Your usual 'bull 'em and bash 'em' routine has worked well so far, but the Lebanese will be on guard against it by now. If he's any good at all, he'll be ready and waiting to blow you guys away the next time you show up to bust one of his hideouts.''

Lyons had to admit that there was merit in Katz's assessment, there always was. He had been an anti-terrorist fighter as long as there had been terrorists. ''What's your recommendation, then?''

''Let's do a real thorough background on this guy and find out where he lives. Knocking out his satellite facilities is good clean fun, but if you want to nail him personally, you need to know where he lives.''

''That's fair enough.''

''And,'' Katz continued, ''I want to get the Farm to fall in line on it. I'll get them to go through the computer files we sent them with a fine-tooth comb and see if they can dig him out.''

''What if Hal gets excited and tries to tell us to mind our own business?''

''I'll take care of Hal,'' Katz vowed. ''I think this has gotten complicated enough that he'll be glad to have you put at least this part of it to bed.''

''He'd better approve it,'' Lyons growled. ''I don't like being shot at.''

''How do you think the NATO guys feel?''

''That's why I want to nail that bastard. I don't want to feel the same way they do.''

CHAPTER SEVENTEEN

Stony Man Farm

When Barbara Price went down to the computer room, the place looked like a disaster. Half-full coffee cups rested on desks and several other flat surfaces, and it looked as if someone had emptied a small garbage bin in the middle of the room, then rigged it for demolition. Crumpled paper lay everywhere. To add to the doomsday effect, bodies were slumped over their desks in complete exhaustion.

Kurtzman looked to be the only one alive and he was just sitting in his wheel chair staring at his new screen saver. On his big monitor, animated snarling dinosaurs scampered across the screen in what looked like the dance of the sugar-plum fairies.

Price started to chuckle, but held it in check. Someone had obviously suffered a small mental burnout down here and had turned to the graphics software to save his sanity.

"Aaron?"

Kurtzman turned slowly as if he were awakening

from a long hibernation. "Barbara," he said, glancing at one of the clocks on the wall. "It's three in the morning. What're you doing here?"

"That's California time," she replied. "It's six in the morning here."

"Oh."

"When was the last time you went to bed?"

"I don't remember."

He ran his hand through his hair, but only messed it even more. "That's the problem with a mission like this," he said. "We're supposed to run strike forces here, not military units. We're designed to do the quick in, quick out stuff, slash 'em, mash 'em and move out smartly. We don't have the legs for this kind of thing."

"I know," she said gently. "But we got sucked into this mission. You know Hal. When the Man says he has a problem, Sir Hal steps up and offers us as a solution. This time, though, the problem is a hell of a lot bigger than we are."

"It's a good thing that Katz is in Italy to back the guys up," Kurtzman said. "We couldn't even do what we're doing if he wasn't."

He paused, got a quizzical look on his face and switched topics. "What're you doing down here, anyway?"

Price reached out and laid her hand on his broad right shoulder. "I came down here to see how you were and to try to get you to take a break. You need to get cleaned up and rest for a couple of hours so you'll be fresh.''

"I'm okay," he said. "I've been grabbing catnaps in the chair when I get tired."

"You're a mess, Aaron. You look like the second runner-up in a head-on collision with a garbage truck competition and—" she sniffed dramatically "—you need a shower, badly."

"Okay," he submitted meekly. "Get Hunt down here to take over, and I'll take a break."

"He's already here. In fact he's sleeping under his desk right now."

Kurtzman looked surprised. "Why's he doing that?"

"He's exhausted, Aaron. All of you are, and I'm going to institute a rotation schedule down here. You guys can't think straight if you're dead on your feet. Striker is closing in to try to find those gas rockets of yours, and I need your crew on the top of their form to back them up.

"So—" she reached for the push bar on the back of his wheelchair to pull him away from his keyboard "—it's time for a shower and bed for you. Then I'm going to send a crew down here to cart off the debris and sweep this dump out so you guys can trash it up all over again."

When Kurtzman didn't protest, she looked down and saw that he was dead asleep. Taking care not to jostle him, she pulled his chair out and pushed it through the narrow walkway to the hall outside. The shower would have to wait. Right now, he needed to sleep in a real bed.

Wethers stirred as she pushed Kurtzman's wheelchair past him, but she let him sleep, too. He'd wake up if anything important happened.

Bosnia

"STRIKER!" Encizo radioed, "I think you'd better get over here."

Bolan went to the edge of the wood line where Encizo and Manning were taking turns keeping an eye on the fortress and getting a little rest before the evening's activities. He didn't have to ask what the problem was when he saw the fleet of small pickup trucks crossing the plain.

"I think they're heading for that cave where they had the wreckage of Hammer's plane stashed," Encizo said.

"I'd have to agree."

"What are we going to do about it?" the Cuban asked. "If Aaron is right about the rockets being here, and if that's where they've been stored, we're going to lose them if we don't do something."

"Maybe not. If the Bear found out about them in the first place, he may be able to track them for us if they're taken away from here. He has a satellite parked in orbit over this part of the world, and he might be able to follow them."

"Even if he can, then what?" Encizo asked. "We're not exactly a mechanized force."

Bolan grinned. "We'll just borrow a truck. They won't miss just one."

"That may be easier said than done."

"Then we'll boot it. But first I need to talk to Katz again. I need him to get the Farm on-line trying to track those damned things and I want to check on our resupply."

"Please do," the Cuban said. "With T.J. and Calvin going on and on about their down-home recipes, a man gets a little hungry, even for MREs."

Bolan laughed.

Stony Man Farm

WHEN BARBARA PRICE returned to the computer room, she found that Hunt Wethers was awake and back on duty.

"Sorry about taking a nap like that," he said apologetically, "but Aaron said that he'd watch things for me."

"That's okay," she reassured him. "We've been hitting it pretty hard for a couple of days now, and the human body needs maintenance, too."

He nodded toward Akira Tokaido, who was lying on his desk. "I want to let Akira get some more sleep if I can. But if anything happens, I'll wake him."

"Let him sleep as long as possible."

"Is anyone awake over there?" Katz's voice said over the satellite link. "We need to talk."

"Good morning, Katz," Price replied as she clicked on to the video pickup. "What's happening?"

"It's midday over here for starters," he replied. "And Striker has spotted the opposition moving trucks to the cave where they stored the pieces of that crashed Night Owl. He thinks they're getting ready to move the gas rockets, and he wants to know if you can track their movement for him until he gets his resupply."

Wethers started punching in commands on his keyboard before Katz had even finished talking. Earlier, Kurtzman had been able to "borrow" one of the NRO's deep-space Keyhole spy birds and park it in a synchronous orbit that covered most of the Balkans. From that position hundred of miles above the earth, its cameras and sensors could easily cover all of Bosnia.

"I'm on it," he replied as his fingers flew over the keyboard. "Got to upload a program first."

The program Wethers was sending to the satellite would teach it what a Toyota pickup truck looked like from deep space. On an earlier mission, Kurtzman had worked up an identification program that would work just as well this time. With that information locked into its computer, it would be child's play for the satellite's electronic eyes to track the trucks as they were loaded and driven away.

"It's loaded," Wethers said as his fingers flew over the keyboard. "Now, let's see...."

The big-screen monitor changed to show an aerial view of a valley with a stone fortress in the middle and a wooded ridgeline to the east. Zooming in at a higher resolution, the half-dozen trucks showed up as big as Matchbox toy cars. One at a time, blinking red markers appeared over the trucks and each icon was numbered.

"There they are," Wethers said as he started typing a final command. "Now I'll instruct the onboard computer to ID them in multispectra and we'll be able to track them anywhere they go, rain or shine. As long as we can keep the satellite in position, that is."

He sat back and faced the video pickup. "That should be it, Katz," he said into the video pickup. "Tell Striker that he can relax and wait for his resupply to show up. When he's ready to go, I'll be able to tell him where they've gone."

"Thanks."

"That's what we're here for."

Aviano Air Base, Italy

"WE'RE LOADED UP and ready to go," Jack Grimaldi told Yakov Katzenelenbogen when he and John Hammer walked into the main room of the CP in Aviano. Both men were wearing Air Force-issue flight suits and carried pistols in the holsters of their survival vests.

"You think you can make it in there without getting shot down?" Katz asked.

Grimaldi nodded. "If I bend the throttle and keep it in the dirt all the way. Even a Strella needs a few seconds to achieve a lock-on, and a few seconds is all I need to clear the area."

The pilot had wanted to borrow a V-22 Osprey from the Marines to fly the resupply mission. The tilt-wing assault transport flew higher and faster than a chopper and could stay out of the line of fire of any missiles. But the nearest Osprey was tied down on the flight deck of the USS *Tarawa,* which was sailing in the Persian Gulf right now. Rather than wait to have one flown in, he was borrowing a UH-60 Black Hawk from the Air Force instead.

"Are David and Carl ready?" Grimaldi asked.

"We're go," McCarter said as he stepped out of the sleeping area in the rear of the building with Lyons at his side. After a personal refitting, McCarter was ready to rejoin his teammates when the supplies were delivered to them. Lyons was going along as the door gunner and supply kicker for the run. Both of them knew that the chances were good that they'd collect a Strella up the tailpipe for their efforts. But the effort had to be made.

"Here's your maps," Katz said as he handed over the packets. "I've included an updated terrain map for each one of you in case you have to walk back."

"Bite your tongue, Katz," Grimaldi said. "This flyboy doesn't walk any farther than from the flight line to the officers' club."

"You got that right," Hammer added. The Air Force pilot wasn't rotary-wing qualified, but he could ride the copilot's seat and take care of the radio and navigation chores for Grimaldi, and he had insisted that he be allowed to ride along. Grimaldi was glad to have the help. Nap-of-the-earth flying took all of his attention, and a second set of eyes would be useful.

"Keep in touch," Katz said in farewell.

As with the previous Stony Man flights from Aviano, the Black Hawk had been cordoned off by USAF Air Police. The crew's Justice ID passed them through the cordon, and they quickly took their places in the aircraft. The control tower gave them immediate takeoff clearance, and they were off the ground as soon as Grimaldi had the turbines burning.

Climbing for altitude, he turned the Black Hawk toward the east and Bosnia.

Bosnia

AFTER A NORMAL FLIGHT across the Adriatic, Jack Grimaldi dropped down as soon as he crossed the coast and was flying with the treetops tickling his belly.

Hammer was sweating in the copilot's seat. He had been known to fly too fast and too low on occasion himself, but this was incredible. The birds were flying higher than they were. Plus, like most fixed-wing pilots, Hammer had a secret distrust of helicopters. If God had intended men to fly with rotary wings, the Wright brothers would have built a chopper not a biplane.

"Look out for that tree coming up on the left," he said, trying to keep his voice calm.

"I got it," Grimaldi replied as he nudged the cyclic to pull the nose up a few inches as the tree flashed past underneath them.

"We're coming up on the LZ," the pilot called back to McCarter and Lyons on the intercom, "so get your fingers out back there."

"Roger," McCarter replied.

So far, Grimaldi had been able to keep them clear of the enemy, but coming in toward a landing zone always carried a risk. A smart enemy didn't attack the men waiting for the chopper—he waited for the chopper itself and then took it out along with the men.

Carl Lyons flicked his 7.62 mm Minigun off safe and got ready to fire suppressive fire as they approached the LZ. He knew that Bolan would have his guys out in position to secure the area, but it never hurt to be ready for a nasty surprise. And a nasty surprise it would be for anyone who took a potshot at them. The gun in his hands was capable of spitting out six thousand rounds per minute.

"GRIMALDI'S INBOUND," Calvin James called over the comm link.

"I've got him visual," Gary Manning also reported, "coming in from the west."

When Katz had sent word that the resupply aircraft was in the air, the Stony Man warriors had found a good LZ in the mountains. After putting out security around the clearing, they'd settled down to wait.

When T. J. Hawkins heard the sound of the rotors inbound, he ran out into the middle of the clearing and stood facing away from the wind with his assault rifle held stiff-armed over his head in both hands. That was the universal military signal to show an incoming chopper pilot the wind direction and landing spot.

Grimaldi spotted him and keyed his mike. "I've got visual on the Lima Zulu."

"Lima Zulu is clear," James called back.

Cutting low over the clearing, Grimaldi nosed the chopper into the wind and chopped the lift to the rotors. The Black Hawk flared out and came to a landing right in front of Hawkins.

"Go, go, go," the pilot yelled to Lyons and McCarter over the roar of the turbines. Even though the area was secured, he didn't want to be on the ground a minute longer that he absolutely had to. He had a phobia of Strellas.

In the back of the Black Hawk, Lyons and McCarter shoved the crates and boxes off a portable access ramp as quickly as they could. When the last crate was gone, McCarter grabbed his weapon, threw Lyons a thumbs-up sign and jumped to the ground.

"Get it out of here!" he called to Grimaldi as he ran to clear the rotor.

Twisting the throttle all the way up against the stop, Grimaldi pulled pitch on the collective and took the Black Hawk into a ground-effect hover. After flicking his eyes to the tachs to check his rpms, he nudged the cyclic stick forward to pick up a little forward momentum before hauling up all the way on the collective. The empty chopper shot out of the clearing like a rocket, but Grimaldi checked his climb before he had cleared the treetops by more than a few feet.

Until they reached the Adriatic, the return trip would be made on the deck, too.

"Tree coming up on the right," Hammer stated.

"I got it."

CHAPTER EIGHTEEN

"Damn," Rafael Encizo said, sniffing as he walked up to the freshly showered and shaved David McCarter, "if you don't smell good."

McCarter maneuvered to stand downwind from his old teammate. "I wish I could say the same about you. In fact all of you lads could use a little soap and a long hot shower."

"Lead me to it," Hawkins said. "I'm ready."

"Sorry. All I can offer you today is clean socks and more MREs."

"Hot damn." Hawkins grinned as he bent down to break open an MRE carton. "Just what I was craving, Meals Refused by Ethiopians. But since I haven't seen a Burger King anywhere around here, I guess they'll just have to do."

"They beat the hell out of your vaunted bootlace soup," James said. "After all that talking about it, it was a real disappointment."

Hawkins shrugged. "It just didn't get long enough to simmer."

"I've heard that excuse before."

It took almost half an hour for the team to break down the supplies and refit themselves to continue the mission. The radios, comm links, night-vision goggles and the GPS needed new batteries. Their empty magazines had to be reloaded, and the rations were broken down and packed away in their assault rucks.

Once they were refitted, the Stony Man team took the time to eat and make coffee. They had been re-filling their canteen from the mountain streams and purifying the water with chlorine tablets, so it was a welcome change to have pure water. Particularly when it came to making instant coffee; chlorine and caffeine didn't go together well.

When they were done with their meal, McCarter gave the order for them to clear the LZ.

"You want me to bury this stuff?" Hawkins asked as he pointed to the pile of debris left over from the ammunition and rations packing.

"Leave it. We'll be long gone from here by the time anyone finds it. And there isn't anything in there that can ID us anyway."

As with everything else that the commandos took with them into battle, the resupply load had been sterilized. Nothing was marked to indicate its country of origin, and all of the labeling was done in multiple languages to include Arabic and Chinese. Even the MREs had been multinationaled.

"Now we need to find a vehicle to borrow," Bolan told Encizo.

"If there was anyone within five miles of here when Grimaldi came in, they'll have noticed the chopper and will be coming to investigate. Maybe we can borrow their ride."

"That's what I'm counting on."

Aviano Air Base, Italy

NOW THAT THE Black Hawk was safely back at Aviano, Carl Lyons jumped right back into his Ironman mode. The Lebanese was still out there somewhere, and Lyons intended to find him. Seeing Hermann Schwarz sitting in front of the CP's computer, he walked over to him. "Do you have a lock on him yet?"

"The Lebanese guy?"

"Who else?"

"Not yet," Schwarz replied. "The Farm hasn't finished sorting through all the E-mail addresses."

"What's taking them so much time?"

"If you'll remember, they're a little busy tracking those nerve-gas rockets, too."

"And they can't do two things at once?" Lyons growled. "I want to know where that guy is so we can put him out of business before someone else gets hurt."

"We're working on it."

Stony Man Farm

LYONS'S PLAN TO GO after the Lebanese had been okayed by the Oval Office. As far as the President was concerned, anything that Able Team could come up with to put an end to the situation in Italy, as well as in Bosnia, was welcomed. And Stony Man wasn't the only agency looking for the terrorist. Hal Brognola had authorized Katzenelenbogen to share everything they had on the Italian situation with both NATO and the Italian authorities, and the race was on to find the man who was responsible for the attack at Aviano.

At the Farm, Aaron Kurtzman was putting his methodical mind and intimate knowledge of cyberspace to work on the problem of finding the terrorist leader. From the extensive computer files found at the garage, it was being assumed that the Lebanese was computer literate. And since computer freaks were the same the world over, it could be assumed that he had left electronic tracks somewhere in cyberspace. All Kurtzman had to do was to find them.

He was using a raider program on the E-mail addresses that had been retrieved from the garage computer. The raider called each address, broke into the computer with a password generator and, once it was in, dumped its contents into a file it could read later. Fortunately the terrorists hadn't been diligent about emptying their cybernetic trash cans and were probably unaware that they contained copies of past messages filed away on a microchip. Being able to use a computer wasn't the same as knowing how it worked.

When he started running the information he retrieved from the raider program through a homebrew macro program, Kurtzman came up with what he had been looking for. "Gotcha, you bastard," he muttered as he punched up the video to the Aviano command post.

"Rose's Cathouse and Pizzeria," Schwarz answered. "Will that be takeout, or will you eat it here?"

"Cut the crap, Gadgets, and put Katz on," Kurtzman snapped. His long sleep had restored his exhausted body, but had done nothing to affect his mood. Until this mission was terminated, he had no time for smart-ass from anyone, not even Schwarz.

"What do you have?" Katzenelenbogen broke in.

"I think I have what you guys have been looking for," he replied. "I keep coming up with one E-mail address that gets a lot of traffic both in and out. It also has the most hits to Libya and Iran, so I think it's the one you want."

"Send it."

Kurtzman flashed the physical address of the computer that had recorded so much traffic to Aviano. The nice thing about landline modems was that their access to the Internet and E-mail was provided by a phone-company line, and that meant there was a record of where the connection had been made. The only way to use E-mail and not let anyone know where you were sending it from was to have direct satellite links on both ends. But since that equipment was too expensive for nongovernment use, almost all civilian E-mail was sent by landline.

"Good work," Katz said when the address flashed up on his screen. "I'll get back to you if this turns out to be what we're looking for."

"Gadgets," he called out across the room, "Aaron came up with a lead on the Lebanese, and I need you to run the address."

"'Bout time." Schwarz's fingers flashed over his keyboard. His computer had a program loaded in that would give him a map of any location in Italy. Originally developed for Interpol counterterrorist operations, it was getting a real workout on this mission. And, so far, it had proved to be a hundred percent accurate.

"I've got it," Schwarz called out. "According to the software, the address is a remote villa on the outskirts of San Simone, a couple of hours to the north of here."

"Better let the Ironman know."

"Let me know what?" Lyons asked as he walked in.

"That the Bear finally got the Lebanese's address for us and we can go to work," Schwarz replied.

"I'll start loading the car," Lyons said as he turned to go into the makeshift arms room.

Bosnia

FINDING A VEHICLE took less time than Bolan had even hoped. By the time the Stony Man team reached the main road, they saw one of the tan Toyota pickups slowly cruising up the dirt road from the castle. This was one of the desert-vehicle conversions, in which the metal cab was removed and replaced with a canvas top so a machine gun could be mounted.

A full squad of Iranians was in the truck—the driver, a man on the machine gun and six men in the back.

With a whispered command over the comm link, the team spread out into an L-shaped ambush. Manning took the short leg of the L with his scoped Remington to take out the driver. The other five men put their assault rifles on single-shot fire. To save damaging the truck, they would take out its crew with well-aimed single shots.

Manning's silenced shot was the signal to pop the ambush, and his aim was true. The driver took the bullet and slumped over his wheel, his foot slipping off of the gas. James targeted the machine gunner and took him out with two rounds fired into his chest.

The six men in the back barely had time to bring their weapons up to fire before they, too, were cut down. Only one of them got off a burst, but it was cut short.

Hawkins ran out of the wood line and, sprinting to the slowly moving truck, swung himself up to reach out and kill the idling engine.

"Great," he said as he examined his catch.

"There's no embarrassing bullet holes in awkward places. It's almost as good as new."

The Stony Man team quickly dragged the bodies off the road and stashed them inside the tree line. Scooping up handfuls of dirt, they covered the blood before dropping their rucks in the back.

A quick call to Katz put them on the right road to chase their prey. After topping off the truck's fuel tank from the jerrican in the back, they moved out. James was behind the wheel with McCarter riding shotgun with the map, radio and GPS gear.

DRAGAN ASDIK HADN'T been sorry to see Major Naslin, his Iranian fanatics and his nerve-gas rockets leave his territory. Hopefully that would be the last he would ever see of the major. Now he could concentrate on doing what he had done before the Iranians arrived—run his own affairs and make sure that the men of his mountain battalion were ready when the call came for them to fight again.

Asdik was meeting with his subordinate commanders when the duty runner brought the news that Naslin's last truck had been ambushed and all of the men killed. "The truck?" he asked.

"They say it was missing, sir."

The Bosnian briefly considered radioing to the Iranian base camp to warn Naslin that the Yankee commandos had captured one of his trucks. He knew that it was his duty to warn his unwelcome ally, but he just couldn't bring himself to do it. In his heart, he knew that the Americans were no danger to him or his people. They were after the gas rockets. How they had learned of them, he had no idea. He was beginning to think that the Yankees had spies everywhere. Why they had waited this long to do something about the rockets, again he had no idea. But for once, he and the Americans were of one mind.

The rockets were no good and he put no stock in Naslin's claim that it was part of God's plan to bring all of Bosnia under the rule of Islam. The Iranian had talked endlessly about God's will, so Asdik decided to leave the Iranian's fate to God's hands.

If God wanted the rockets launched, he would act against the Yankees. If he didn't want to see thousands of civilians killed in his name, he would allow them to catch up with Naslin.

"Do you want the radio operator to tell the Iranians about this?" the runner asked.

"No," Asdik said. "It is in God's hands now."

"As you command."

Stony Man Farm

THE PLAN TO TRACK the Iranian trucks carrying the nerve-gas rockets was going very well. While Kurtzman was sleeping off his exhaustion, Hunt Wethers was keeping an eye on the information being sent from the spy satellite over Bosnia. With Akira Tokaido as his able assistant, they had watched the rockets being loaded into nine Toyota pickup trucks and then convoyed north.

Most of the route was open to the sky, but when the trucks disappeared under the trees, the Keyhole satellite switched from optical to its MAD sensors and continued tracking them anyway.

When Barbara Price stepped into the newly cleaned computer room to see how it was going, she was stunned to be able to see the floor of the entire room for once. It was such an improvement that she considered talking to the cleaning crew about making hourly visits from now on.

"How's it going?" Price asked Hunt Wethers.

"I sure wish we had one of these Keyhole satellites for our exclusive use," he said wistfully as he watched the computer-generated icons that represented the Iranian trucks slowly traverse the map of eastern Bosnia. "We should be able to do this all the time."

"It would break our budget for the next twenty years to have one put in orbit for us," Price replied. "And why buy a cow when the milk is free?"

"Someday, someone in the NRO is going to figure out what we're doing and slam the door on us and lock it so we can't get back in."

She smiled. "They already have, but Aaron keeps finding where they hide the keys."

"They've stopped moving," Tokaido announced.

"Let's see where they are." Wethers's fingers

clicked on his keyboard and brought up a larger-scale map.

The radar map showed a rocky bluff with a flat area in front of it and mountains on each side. The readouts indicated that the flat area was densely forested, but that was to be expected if this location was in fact a major base camp. "This may be it," he said. "This looks to me like a good place to hide."

"You'd better call Katz and have him pass that on to Striker."

"Will do."

Bosnia

McCARTER TOOK the radio call from Katzenelenbogen. "The trucks have probably reached their destination," he told Bolan as he held out his marked map. "At least they stopped in what looks like some kind of forest hideout this time."

Bolan wasn't surprised to hear that. If as many Iranians had remained behind in Bosnia as Kurtzman thought, the fortress they had left wasn't big enough to hold all of them.

"How far away is it?"

"About sixty miles. We should reach it in three or four hours."

"It'll still be dark then," Bolan said, "and that will let us get in close without being spotted."

CHAPTER NINETEEN

Northern Italy

After loading the tools of their trade into their rented Lancia sedan at Aviano, Able Team had gotten a good night's rest before hitting the road for San Simone on the scenic Adriatic coast and the Lebanese's remote villa to the north of the town.

Like most small towns in that part of Italy, San Simone's origins probably went back to Roman times if not earlier. As Able Team approached the town, many of the buildings had stone walls that didn't look like anything that had been built in recent memory. Interspaced with the older buildings were, of course, modern, slablike concrete-block structures with all of the charm of a large cardboard box. Nonetheless, the place was charming; too charming to be the home of a terrorist.

"We should stop for lunch," Rosario Blancanales suggested as they started into the town.

"I had a big breakfast," Lyons countered, "and I want to get on with this."

"Talking to the locals may save us a lot of hassle later," Blancanales reminded him. "In a little country place like this, they're bound to know what's going on at the villa."

"You have a point," Lyons admitted.

"Good," Schwarz announced as he awakened from his nap. "I'm starving."

Like in all older Italian towns, the twisting streets were narrow and a smart person parked his car halfway up on the sidewalk and hoped a bus didn't sideswipe it on the way past.

"The one on the right or the left?" Schwarz asked, eyeing the two sidewalk cafés, unable to make up his mind.

"The left-hand side. It's in the shade."

The trio didn't have to wait long after seating themselves at an outdoor table adorned with a checkered tablecloth and a small bouquet of mountain flowers in a glass vase.

"Can I help you?" the waiter asked in heavily accented English.

"What would you recommend for lunch?" Blancanales asked, glad not to have to use his clumsy Italian. He was getting better at it, but still had a ways to go.

After taking their orders for the daily special, the waiter departed.

"This is the life," Schwarz said as he tore off a chunk of bread from the loaf the waiter had left and slathered it with butter. "When this gig is over, maybe we can do a little R and R up here."

"In your dreams, Gadgets," Lyons told him, reaching for the bread himself. "Hal will want us back home ASAP to check in on the latest crisis that someone has invented. We're not authorized to take time off. It's not in our contract."

"Bummer."

"Excuse me," Blancanales called to the waiter after they had finished their meal.

"Yes, sir?"

"We came up here to take a look at the Villa del Norte. Do you know anything about the current owners?"

The waiter's face tightened. "I would not advise you to go up there, sir. The owner is a foreigner, and he does not welcome visitors."

"We would be willing to compensate him for his time."

"He has no need of money," the waiter said. "Though the Virgin knows that he spends little enough of it here in San Simone. He thinks that he is—how do you say it?—too good for simple people like us."

"Is he a German, then, or English?"

The waiter laughed. "No, but he is just as bad. He is an Arab."

Bingo. Lyons smiled to himself. It seemed the first mistake terrorists always made was to anger the locals. Whoever this Lebanese guy was, he should have read Mao's *Little Red Book* before embarking on a career of terrorism. Mao had written a manual for guerrilla fighters, but the same principles worked for terrorists, as well. If their prey had alienated the locals, they wouldn't be keen on watching the place for him or warning him if trouble was coming.

"We may try our luck anyway," Blancanales said as he paid the tab and included a respectable tip. "Thanks for the information."

"My pleasure."

AS THE NAME IMPLIED, the villa was situated on a low, barren hill to the north of town. After driving past it on the main highway for a closer look, Schwarz drove the Lancia up a cow path and parked under a grove of olive trees behind the crest of another low hill to the east. Taking their weapons and surveillance gear out of the trunk, they walked to the crest of the hill and set up to watch the villa.

"There's not a hell of a lot of cover and concealment around that place," Schwarz noted. "We'll have to crawl in on our bellies to keep from being seen."

"We'll hit it at night, then," Lyons said.

"Did you see the lights on the poles around the compound when we went by?" Blancanales commented. "He's got the place lit up like a Christmas tree."

"And," Schwarz added, "I just spotted the dog kennel in the back of the main house. They're penned up now, but you know that he's going to turn them loose at night.''

Lyons's instincts always pointed him toward using immediate, overwhelming force to solve a problem, any problem, which was why he was called the Ironman. This didn't mean, however, that he couldn't be patient or subtle when he had to be, but patience was always his second choice.

With the lights and dogs to deal with, a more subtle approach was clearly called for this time. ''What's your call, Pol?'' he asked.

''I say we keep an eye on this place and try to see if we can establish their routine. If it looks like it's going to be too much for us to handle, we may have to call in the Italians to take care of him.''

That would be Lyons's last choice, but Blancanales had a point. Regardless of their will to win, there was only so much the three of them could do by themselves.

''If we're going to be staying here for a while,'' Schwarz said cheerfully, ''I'm going back to the restaurant and get a little more of that bread and wine. Maybe they'll have a nice cheese to go with it.''

''If you're hungry,'' Lyons said dispassionately, ''we've got MREs in the trunk.''

''Give me a break, Ironman. We're in Italy. We can use the MREs to poison the dogs.''

''Just get back on your earphones and we'll eat later.''

THE SUN WAS GOING DOWN over the Villa del Norte and there had still been no activity that Able Team had been able to see. The same black BMW sedan was parked in the front of the main entrance, and the curtains were still drawn on all the windows.

"It's about time to shift to the night-vision goggles," Blancanales said.

"I wouldn't bother," Schwarz replied. "When those lights go on, you won't be able to see a damned thing. We'll be better off using our day glasses."

"You want me to go back and get our sleeping gear?" Blancanales asked Lyons. Now that the sun was going down, the wind was picking up, and as high as they were in the mountains, the air was taking on a chill.

"And bring down some MREs, too," Lyons said.

"Heads up," Schwarz called out. "I've got a car turning off for the villa."

The villa was well off the highway and had about a quarter-mile private road leading up to it. From their observation point, they could watch the road all the way from the turnoff up to the villa.

"I make it out to be another BMW sedan," Blancanales said. "A white one this time."

That was another mistake terrorists tended to make, to pick out a favorite kind of car and stick to it to the point that it became a signature. The car bombs they were making had all been planted in Fiats, but it seemed that the terrorists liked to drive BMWs. They would have blended in better with the local population had they driven the humble little Fiats, but they were putting style before common sense. They thought that they were important, and in Italy, big men simply didn't ride in Fiats.

Lyons had his field glasses focused on the front door when the white BMW came to a halt while Blancanales watched the car itself. Though the sun was quickly setting, it was still light enough to see that the man who opened the door wasn't Italian. Neither were the three men who got out of the vehicle. Their physical appearance and choice of clothing marked them as being from the Middle East. The difference was subtle, but it was there if you knew what to look for.

"I think we just found our man," Lyons said. "Definitely Middle Eastern, late twenties, early thirties, five-ten, dark over dark. It's got to be him."

"And he just turned the lights on around his house," Schwarz commented.

As Schwarz had predicted, the lights illuminated the entire area, making it too bright for them to watch the villa with their night-vision goggles.

FOR THE FIRST TIME in his career as an Islamic freedom fighter, Ali Nadal was concerned. He wouldn't allow himself to even think of the word *frightened*, but his actions were clearly those of a frightened man. After the attack on the air base had been broken up, he had fled to the safety of his villa. He was convinced that there was a spy in his organization and the only men who knew about it were men he knew he could trust.

It was true that he had struck a blow for the revolution at Aviano, but he had just received a report that the air base was back in operation already. And if the planes were taking off for their patrols over Bosnia again, that meant that he had failed. In the Libyan desert, he had been taught that failure wasn't an option. At least not a failure you lived to tell about. For the revolution to triumph, Islam's holy warriors were expected to win or to die fighting, surrounded by the broken bodies of their enemies.

He now realized that trying to attack the base on the ground had been a mistake. But with the car bombs being discovered, he'd had no choice. Taking the car bombs away from him had been the critical turning point in a plan that had been worked on for months. And with the timetable he had been given, he'd had no choice but to try to destroy the base any way he could. That he had at least tried, though, wouldn't be taken well. He had failed and he was still alive.

The only way he could see to regain his status in the organization, and maybe save his own life, was to find the man who had betrayed him and make him pay the price for his betrayal.

Looking back, he now realized that he should have acted sooner. The raid on the garage should have set him off. But he hadn't taken it seriously because he hadn't had any warnings from his web of informants in the Italian police and local governments. Usually he had more than enough warning of what were called antiterrorist raids. A police official would call him and tell him if one of his warehouses was to be raided or even inspected. He also got tips from his Mafia connections because they depended on him to be part of the smuggling pipeline.

The only conclusion he could come to was that there had to be a traitor within his organization, and that traitor was somehow connected to that small group of Americans who were operating out of the Aviano air base. Even though he was targeted against any and all enemies of Islam, the Yankees were the Great Satan that had to be destroyed at all costs. That was why he had sent the team in to try to capture one of them. Had the Yankee been captured, he would have told Nadal everything he knew before he died.

It could be that in his haste to learn more about this mysterious group of infidels, he had made a mistake. He had been told that all of the team he had sent in had been killed by that one man, but he doubted that now. And he should have doubted it much earlier. Had he done so, he could have taken better precautions. But that was all in the past now. He wouldn't make the same mistake twice.

Nadal broke from his self-recriminations when his bodyguard, Ahmed, told him that the car was entering the driveway to the villa. It was bringing his three most trusted lieutenants for a council of war. He might have failed to take out Aviano air base, but he hadn't been defeated. When he received his new orders, he wanted to be ready to move on them.

Nadal went to the front door to greet his visitors, the two Palestinians and the Syrian who commanded his subunits. A fourth man, another Lebanese, had died in the attack on Aviano, and Nadal had taken over his cell himself until a replacement could be sent out from Libya.

After Ahmed brought a tray of sweet tea and almond cakes, Nadal got right to business. As were all of their discussions, the meeting was conducted in Italian or English. To keep a mistake from happening in public, Arabic couldn't be spoken as long as they were in Italy.

"I know that there is a spy in our ranks," Nadal stated flatly. "I just don't know who he is. I want you to find him and kill him immediately. And at the same time, I want you to take a careful look at all of our Italian informants. If you find any reason, however slight, to suspect anyone's loyalty, I want them eliminated, as well. When I make my report to Tripoli, I want to be able to tell them that we have eliminated the weakness in the organization."

"Some of our informants are highly placed," one of the Palestinians protested. "It might bring attention to us if they disappear."

"People disappear all the time," Nadal countered. "If it is done right, there will be no connection to us."

"What are we going to do about Aviano?" the other Palestinian asked.

"We will do as we have always done, Nazir—obey our orders," Nadal said. "If we are ordered to make another attack, we will make it."

"Even though they are on guard against us now? It would be suicide to try it again."

"No matter what they do, we will obey our orders."

"But," Nazir began, attempting to continue the conversation, "we will be—"

Without changing the expression on his face, Nadal reached for the 9 mm Beretta holstered at the small of his back. Drawing and aiming the pistol with one swift movement, he fired a single shot into Nazir's chest.

Ignoring the blood leaking onto his Algerian beige leather couch, Nadal holstered the pistol. "Are there any more questions?"

The other two men didn't meet his eyes, and there were no further questions.

Ahmed had come running at the sound of the shot, his Beretta subgun ready. "Take him out and feed him to the dogs," Nadal ordered, nodding at the corpse. "And you help him," he ordered the remaining Palestinian.

Being eaten by dogs was the worst fate that could befall a man. But the Palestinian dared not protest. He knew how fast Nadal was with that pistol.

CHAPTER TWENTY

Bosnia

The trip to the Iranian camp had taken the Stony Man team considerably longer than Bolan had thought it would, but it couldn't be helped. For one thing, they had driven the entire route with their night-vision goggles rather than risk someone seeing their headlights, and that had slowed them. For another, even with the Keyhole satellite and the GPS to guide them, the roads had turned out to be little more than dirt tracks through the mountains and had been difficult to follow.

With all the delays, it was daylight before they closed in on the target, but the Farm passed the word on that the trucks hadn't left yet, so there was still time. Stopping a little more than a mile short of the objective, David McCarter took a final GPS reading of their location and checked it against the reading from the satellite.

"They're about eight hundred meters on the other side of that point up ahead," he told Bolan.

"We'll take it the rest of the way on foot."

Getting back into their rucksacks, the commandos moved out in a tactical formation. This close to their camp, the Iranians were sure to have put out some kind of security. Strangely enough, though, they didn't encounter any sentries or guard posts along the rocky route. That kind of overconfidence was welcome, because it usually had fatal consequences.

Once they reached the mountain peak, the Iranian camp lay directly in front of them, secreted under the trees. From the air, there would be little or no sign of it. But from a vantage point to the side and a little above, such as the one the Stony Man team now occupied, it could be seen.

"It looks like they've got at least a battalion down there, Striker," McCarter said as he handed his field glasses to Bolan. "Heavy weapons and all."

Bolan focused the glasses, and the scene jumped out at him. Whoever was in charge of those troops was good. The camp had a proper perimeter with machine-gun bunkers, guard posts and what looked like mortar pits all hidden under the trees. He couldn't see any barracks or mess halls and figured that they had been built inside the cave so their heat signatures wouldn't register on the sensors of recon planes or satellites.

It was a thoroughly professional job, and at least a full battalion of infantry with armor and artillery support would be required to knock it out. Either that or a massive air raid. But even if he could get strike aircraft in, the Iranians could retreat to their cave and be safe. Unless, of course, the aircraft could deliver something big enough to drop the roof of the cave on their heads.

"We need to talk to Katz about this," Bolan said. "We need his help on this one."

"What's he going to do for us?"

"Find us a couple of one-ton smart bombs to bring that cave down on top of them."

The Briton grinned. "That's a good idea. I rather didn't fancy climbing down there myself."

While Bolan placed the call, the rest of the team got comfortable in the rocks and watched the activities below.

Aviano Air Base, Italy

NOW THAT Able Team had gone after the Lebanese, Jack Grimaldi and Major Hammer were working in the Stony Man CP taking turns with the communications gear. When Bolan's call came in, Katzenelenbogen already had the satellite photos of the Iranian camp on his desk and was able to confirm Bolan's assessment of the situation. The question was how to best deal with it. Since Brognola had "borrowed" Hammer from the Air Force to be their air adviser until the situation was over, this was the time for him to start earning his pay.

Calling him over, Katz pointed to the photos.

"What's the best way to take out a place like that? A pinpoint attack or mass bombing?"

Hammer looked at the satellite recon photos and the topographical map of the Iranian camp. "That cave makes it a little tricky," he said honestly, "but a couple of two-thousand-pound smart bombs in the mouth of the cave should do it nicely. If they don't bring the roof down, the overpressure should take care of anyone inside."

"Overpressure?"

When he saw the look on Katz's face, Hammer added, "I think you ground pounders call it 'blast effect.' In a confined place like a cave, you can get a much more powerful effect with a smaller explosion than you can out in the open. The cave will contain the blast so it isn't wasted, but the trick is to get the bombs in there."

"And what's the best way to do that?" Katz asked.

"That's easy," the pilot said, grinning. "A stealth fighter. It can come in from the west with a couple of GBU-27s and drive them right through the front door. If Striker can illuminate the target the same way he did for the STABO canister delivery, it'll be a piece of cake."

Katz looked at Hammer. His original intention in having the pilot temporarily assigned to the team was to keep him from letting anything slip about the Bosnian exercise. But since the pilot was on board, Katz might as well try to get more out of him than merely aeronautical advice. As always on Stony Man operations, the fewer people who knew what was actually going on, the better. Katz didn't want to get another aircrew involved unless he absolutely had to.

"Can you fly a stealth fighter?"

"Before I flew Night Owls, I was an Eagle driver, but I've been checked out on the F-117."

"Can you hit anything with their ordnance package?"

"I can put a GBU-27 smart bomb within three feet of the laser spot," he said with some pride. "We carried them on our Strike Eagles, too, and I got all good hits when I went Scud hunting in the Gulf."

"Good," Katz said as he reached for the phone. "Get ready to go flying while I see about rounding up a stealth fighter for you."

"That may be a little difficult," Hammer said. "The stealth jocks are a little particular about who they even let get close to their toys."

"I'll just ask the Man to have the blue-suiters loan us one."

These guys were always talking about "the Man" as if the words were all in caps and Hammer couldn't help but think that it was the President of the United States they were so casually referring to. "Who do you guys work for, anyway?" He couldn't stop himself from asking.

Katz smiled wolfishly. "I could tell you, Major, but then I'd have to kill you and I need you to fly for me."

"Never mind."

HAL BROGNOLA also had copies of the satellite photos of the Iranian camp that Katz had examined and he had also been thinking of an air strike. For something that big, there was no other way to take it out. Phoenix was good, but they weren't good enough to take on an entrenched battalion and suicide was not an option.

When Katz's request for the loan of a stealth fighter and two smart bombs came in, he got right on it. Since the nerve gas was on the top of the President's agenda, he immediately got to see him and made the necessary calls to the Chief of Staff of the Air Force from the Oval Office. There were some perks with his job.

TWO HOURS LATER, Katz called Hammer back in. "Get down to the flight line," he said, "and get suited up. I've got a stealth fighter standing by for you."

"Just like that?"

Katz grinned. "All you have to do is call the right people, and things happen."

Hammer shook his head in amazement. "I'm going to that cave site, right?"

"I'll give you the coordinates once you're in the air."

"Can I at least know where I'm going?"

"East, to Bosnia."

"Damn, I was hoping for the Riviera."

"They don't have any nerve-gas rockets there."

"I'm on the way."

As unlikely as it sounded, Hammer found that Katz was as good as his word. When he walked out of the ready room in his flight gear, he saw the wicked shape of a night-black F-117A stealth fighter waiting in the hangar for him, its twin GE F404 turbines humming at an idle.

"She's loaded up as directed, sir," the crew chief said, saluting as he reported. "You have two GBU-27s with laser-guidance heads."

The two-thousand-pound GBU-27, better known to the public as the smart bomb, had been the real star of Desert Storm. During the air-war phase of the Gulf War, the worldwide TV audience had sat in front of their screens mesmerized as they watched the bombs being guided into their targets with almost magical accuracy. The American TV audience had cheered when they watched smart bombs take out single trucks on the road or blast down the air shafts of command bunkers like a scene out of the *Star Wars* movies.

This had almost been video-arcade warfare, and the public had eaten it up. But they hadn't enjoyed it half as much as the pilots had. Until the advent of laser-guided weapons, delivering the bomb on the target had always been an art form, not a repeatable science. With the smart bombs, though, it had become a snap. They almost guaranteed first-round hits under any conditions.

"Thank you, Sergeant," Hammer replied, returning the salute before climbing into the plane's cockpit. "I'll take real good care of her for you."

"You'd better, sir," the crew chief warned. "I have my ass on the line because I have to personally report back to the Air Force chief of staff when you bring her back."

"I'll be careful."

Bosnia

"KATZ HAS ROUNDED UP a stealth fighter with a couple of smart bombs on board," David McCarter reported, "and it's on the way now. Hammer's driving, and he wants to know if we can illuminate the target for him."

"No problem," Bolan said. "Put Gary and T.J. on it again. They did a good job with the STABO canister."

Taking the target illuminator out of their rucks, the two commandos found a good place in the rocks and set up their equipment. If Hammer wanted it lit up, they could accommodate him.

LIKE HIS TR-3 Night Owl, the F-117A stealth fighter Major John Hammer was flying was subsonic. But for this kind of mission, speed was not of the essence. The opposition didn't have emplaced antiaircraft weapons, and there was no gauntlet of MiG fighters or SAMs that he would have to penetrate. And with the heat-diffusing exhausts of the fighter cooling his exhaust plume, the Strellas wouldn't be able to get a lock on him, either. This would be a milk run.

It *should* be a milk run, the pilot automatically corrected himself. As every combat pilot was all too aware, there was always the golden-BB factor to consider. A golden BB was any shot, even a rifle bullet, that was blindly aimed up into the sky, but that just happened to hit something essential as you flew by. It happened all the time in aerial warfare. Even the Red Baron had fallen to a golden BB. In his case, however, the something vital it had hit had been him.

But along with the rest of the long list of things that could end his career, Hammer was too busy to worry about it. He had a mission to fly and two tons of high explosive to deliver on the target. If he ran into a golden BB, he ran into it. Worse things could happen—he could miss the target completely.

Approaching the target area, he keyed his throat mike. "Striker, this is Hammer, over."

"Striker, go."

"This is Hammer, I am inbound vector two-eight-niner. What's the situation down there? Over."

"This is Striker," Bolan answered. "The target is as briefed. There are no flak guns and no SAMs, so you're free to do your thing. Over."

"Roger, copy target clear," he acknowledged.

''Just make sure that you're well out of range. These things make a big bang, over.''

''Roger, we're clear.''

''This is Hammer. Light it up, then.''

Hawkins and Manning were on the laser designator, and they had it aimed at the middle of the cave's entrance so all they had to do was switch it on. Unlike the red lasers that were featured in all of the action-adventure movies, this laser was invisible to the naked eye. It wouldn't do to have their targets see a big red dot appear on the ground right in front of them.

''The target's lit up,'' Hawkins radioed to Bolan on the comm link.

''The target's illuminated,'' Bolan radioed to Hammer.

''I got it,'' the pilot replied, seeing the pip appear on his target-designator screen. After locking the aiming point into his computer, Hammer waited until the readout told him that the signal had been accepted by the bomb's guidance units in the belly of his plane. When the red light came on, he banked the F-117A around to come in on his bomb run and opened the doors to the internal weapons bay.

''Look out, baby,'' he called out over the radio, '''cause here it comes.''

Coming out of the west, the aircraft was silent, as well as being invisible to radar. There was no thunder of jet engines to announce its presence and no smoke trail in the sky as was the case with so many conventional jet fighter bombers. Someone with real good eyes might have been able to spot the black speck in the sky, but would have had to know exactly where to look for it.

Because the dust that would be thrown up as soon as the first bomb hit would obscure the laser marker, Hammer salvoed his two weapons ten seconds apart. That way, the blast of the first smart bomb wouldn't affect the trajectory of the second, and it would already have its lock on the laser's aiming point so the dust wouldn't affect its approach.

With the fire-control computer controlling the weapons drop, Hammer didn't even have to punch the bombs off. At the right point, they were automatically released.

"They're on the way," he radioed as he pulled the fighter bomber into a tight turn. "And I'm out of here."

"Roger," Bolan replied. "Thanks, and we'll call in the BDA when it's over. Have a cold one on us."

At Bolan's signal, the rest of the team hugged the earth on the back side of the ridge. Four thousand pounds of HE wasn't the biggest explosion they had ever been close to, but it was more than enough to want to take cover from.

The first bomb went right through the mouth of the cave and detonated ten yards inside. The cave contained the blast of two thousand pounds of explosives like a giant cannon barrel. After banking off of the rear and side walls of the cave, the blast belched out the front, carrying bits and pieces of whatever had been in its path.

The second bomb hit a little farther out, but with even more destructive force. In its case, the blast ricocheted off the rock floor and smashed into the roof of the cave with stunning effect. For an instant, everything seemed to be normal. Then, with a groan that reverberated through the mountain, the roof collapsed. Chunks of rocks weighing tons rained down, finishing the destruction that the bombs had started.

When the roar of the rockfall echoed away, the silence was stunning. Then, the earth shook anew as more tons of rock slid down the mountainside into the void that had been left by the collapse of the roof.

"Jesus, Mary and Joseph," Encizo muttered as a cloud of smoke and dust boiled up into the air.

For several long minutes, the entire camp was obscured. Slowly the dust settled to reveal a scene of complete devastation. The cave was gone, hidden under a new face of the mountain. The rockfall had also sent huge boulders smashing through the camp, destroying everything in their path.

Stunned survivors staggered around not knowing what to do next. Most of their comrades had been in the cave and were buried under tons of rock. Their vehicles had been in the cave, as well, along with the majority of their supplies. These Iranians were finished as a fighting force.

"That should take care of that," Hawkins said.

"And I am locked and loaded for a little R and R in Italy before we have to go back."

"Better keep it in your pants, T.J.," James cautioned him. "Haven't you ever heard of a BDA?"

"Katz wouldn't do that to us, would he?" Hawkins wailed.

A Bomb Damage Assessment was a physical examination of the target area after the bomb run was over. Usually it was done to see how much damage the bombs had done to the target. This time, though, it was pretty obvious that walking around down there could be hazardous to one's health.

"Katz wouldn't order us to do a BDA," James agreed with him, and then paused. "But Hal Brognola might."

"Bummer!"

CHAPTER TWENTY-ONE

Stony Man Farm

As Air Force Major John Hammer was flying his stealth fighter into Bosnia to deliver its belly load of laser-guided HE, the primary Stony Man players gathered again in Aaron Kurtzman's computer room to watch the fireworks. The satellite video of the Iranian camp was crystal clear, and they could almost see the men on the ground right before the first smart bomb struck.

"All right!" Akira Tokaido yelled as he jumped up and high-fived the empty air over his keyboard when flame and smoke belched out of the cave mouth like a giant cannon. "Go get them Air Force!"

Even Hunt Wethers smiled when he saw the results of his having tracked the Toyota pickup trucks pay off big-time. He always tried to keep his emotions closely in check so as not to influence his rational thinking process. Good problem solving required that a man keep a cool mind at all times. But seeing these spectacular results of his work justified a sense of satisfaction for a job well done.

"That should pretty well take care of that." Hal Brognola wore a satisfied smile as he watched the thick, billowing cloud of smoke and dust rise in the air where the cave had been. "And it's about damned time, too. The President has been very concerned about this situation, and I'll be happy to be able to tell him that he can finally put this to rest."

"Wait a minute," Kurtzman said, breaking in on the round of mutual self-congratulation. "We may have a stray truck that didn't get rounded up with the rest.

"No," he added after a pause, "make that two strays."

The silence that followed was deafening.

The program that had put the satellite to tracking the Toyota pickups from the fortress to the camp by the cave hadn't been shut down and was still running. And since the dust that obscured the target area didn't impede its radar-mapping sensors, it was still tracking two of the trucks. The rest of the vehicles had entered the cave where not even the Keyhole sensors could see them, but these two trucks hadn't gone inside before the bombs stuck.

"What do you mean?" Brognola snapped.

Kurtzman pointed to the upper left-hand side of his monitor. "I've got two of the marked trucks moving out of the area. They were the last two to arrive, and it looks like they weren't taken out in the attack.''

Brognola felt like a prizefighter had punched him in the stomach. "Oh, no."

"Oh, yes," Kurtzman said. "And I don't think that's the worst of it."

"What do you mean?"

"I'll have to run the tape back to check and make sure, but I don't think that those particular two trucks off-loaded their cargoes before the bombs hit. If that's the case, we're back to square one again."

The big Fed found an empty chair and sat down. "Get Katz on the horn," he told Price, "and have him alert Striker about this immediately."

"I'm doing that right now," she replied.

Wethers's smile was gone now as he brought a detailed map of the area around the camp onto his screen and superimposed the icons marking the last two Toyotas. The cyber-chase was still on, and he wasn't going to let the terrorists get away from him.

Price saw him flick over to the map and asked, "What're they doing?"

"It looks like they're making for the road that runs through the valley north of the camp. When they reach that, they can go either west into Bosnia or try to escape to the east."

"They won't be going east," Kurtzman said. "That's the Serb Republic, and they don't much like Muslims, Iranian or not. They're going to continue west, and they're still going to try to use that nerve gas."

Brognola's hand went into his pocket and came up with two solitary, lint-covered antacid tabs. It was time for him to break into Price's stash before he flew back to report to the President.

Bosnia

AS HE DROVE AWAY from the blazing camp, Major Naslin knew that God had protected him from the Yankees yet again because his work still wasn't done. The nerve-gas attacks would have to be scaled back now, but they would take place nevertheless. He still had almost two dozen rockets in the two surviving Toyotas. He would have to change the target list and concentrate on hitting the largest towns and hope that panic among the infidels would do the rest.

There was still a good chance that when he was done, all of Bosnia would be Muslim once again.

He looked back at the sixteen survivors of his former hundred-man unit and realized that he was lucky to have even that many left. On the trip out from Asdik's fortress, each vehicle had carried only five or six men. But some of the other crews had been visiting with the crews of the two surviving trucks while their vehicles were in the cave being fitted with the rocket launchers.

Naslin saw their survival as being another sign of

God's favor. He had fewer men, true, but those who had been left were the toughest of the tough. They had been through the fire and had emerged only stronger in their faith and determination to bring God's vengeance on the infidels. With even only half a dozen men like these, he would still be able to do his duty to the future of Islam.

The modified Katusha rocket launchers he had intended to use to launch the gas rockets were gone, buried under tons of rubble along with the rest of their supplies and equipment. But he wasn't going to let that prevent him from carrying out his mission. There were other ways to launch rockets, but even if they couldn't be launched, the gas attacks could still be made because of his men.

As a last resort, Naslin vowed that he would send his men to detonate the rockets themselves. And he wouldn't hesitate if this time he had to die for the revolution, as well. Suicide as such was prohibited in the Koran, but freely giving up one's life in the conduct of a mission against the infidels was highly praised. The holy martyrs were welcomed into Paradise and sat on the right hand of God.

He hoped to live to see the glorious triumph of Islam in the West. But if it required his life to make it happen, he was more than ready to die as a martyr to the cause. As were, he was convinced, his men. If he told them that their only path to heaven was through martyrdom, he was confident that they would follow him to death.

The sudden attack had brought home to him the fact that he had seriously underestimated his enemies. Someone, somehow, had leaked information to the West, and the sudden attack was the result. His suspicions were that one of the few Bosnians who was in on the plan had been the traitor. If he survived the next few days, he would track this man down and make him pay for his betrayal.

For now, though, he had to make good his escape so he could deliver the rockets he had left to his enemies.

As THE DUST SETTLED, the Stony Man team could see the damage Hammer's bomb run had inflicted on the base camp. The cave had completely vanished; there wasn't even a trace of where it had been under the tons of rock. When the bomb had brought the roof down, the mountain had slid in to fill the void. There was no telling how many men had been buried in the collapse, but they would remain there for all time. The presence of the nerve-gas rockets under the debris made sure that no one would ever try to excavate the site.

"Are we going to go down there and finish them off?" Hawkins asked as he watched the dazed survivors try to figure out what had happened to them. From the way they were aimlessly staggering around down there, a decent Girl Scout troop could go in and mop them up.

Bolan shook his head. "No. We got what we came

for, and someone else can worry about what's left of them. We need to leave something for the UN to take care of after we get out of here.''

"We may not be finished yet, Striker," McCarter said as he took off the earphones of their satcom radio. "Katz says that Kurtzman's satellite is telling them that two of the trucks escaped and are heading west right now."

"Let me talk to him."

Katz was apologetic when he explained the situation to Bolan. "I'm sorry, Striker," he said, "but Hal wants you guys to keep after those trucks that got away. From what they can see, they appear to be carrying some of the rockets. He knows that you have been pushing the limits, but you're all that we have on the ground in the area. It's imperative that none of those rockets are launched anywhere in Bosnia."

Bolan saw the truth in what Katz was saying. He also knew that the Israeli wouldn't commit them unless there was no other option available. And like Katz, he had an abhorrence of chemical weapons. Even if there was only one nerve-gas rocket unaccounted for, he knew they had to go after it.

"Jack and Hammer are loading up the Black Hawk for another resupply run," Katz continued. "And they'll have atropine injectors, full protective suits and gas masks on board."

Bolan knew that if the nerve gas was used, the protective measures really wouldn't do them much good. The suits and masks worked okay if you were in a static position with medical backup and a decontamination unit close by. But the way this team operated, they were more than useless, particularly if the nerve gas involved was VX. With that particular agent, a single drop on the skin would kill. A small tear or leak in the suit would be as fatal as not having any protection at all. Their only hope to survive this was to make sure that the rockets weren't fired at all.

"Hold off on the resupply," Bolan said. "We have the chemical-detector unit you sent on the first run, and the suits won't do us any good. We're okay on everything else for the next three or four days, but I'll call you if we need anything."

"As you wish," Katz said before switching subjects. "You'll want to copy down the route they're taking."

"Send it."

As the Stony Man team drove away from the mountain overlooking what was left of the Iranian camp, McCarter had Hawkins give it a wide berth. Even buried under tons of rock, there was no telling if any of the gas had been released. Once they reached the main road to the north of the camp, Bolan checked in with Katz again to get an update.

"They're moving fast," Katz said, relaying the information on the Iranian trucks Wethers was tracking, "and they're still heading west."

"We'll head west, then."

THE FARTHER WEST the Stony Man team drove, the more populated the area became. Once they were out of the mountains, the land became rolling hills and valleys. Little villages and farms dotted the landscape, but too many of them proved to be destroyed and deserted when they got closer. The few people they saw in the distance stayed clear of them. They weren't in a gun jeep or an armored vehicle, but with the matte tan paint, the Toyota pickup had a decidedly military look to it. The locals couldn't tell which side they were on, but experience had taught them that any military unit could be dangerous.

Now that they were coming into the zones patrolled by the UN PROFOR, they had to keep an eye out for them, too, and this was where the Farm came in again. The same satellite that was tracking the Iranians was also keeping track of the PROFOR units and marking them, as well.

At midday, Katzenelenbogen called McCarter. "There's a French mech unit coming your way," he reported. "They're about six klicks to the north, and you need to clear the road to let them get past you."

"Give me their grid coordinates," the Phoenix Force Leader requested.

After marking his map, McCarter wasted no time telling Hawkins to get off the road and up into the wooded hills to get under cover.

Hiding from the good guys wasn't a new occurrence for the members of Phoenix Force. The clandestine nature of their work meant that they usually had to stay hidden from everyone. This time, though, they didn't have a cover story or false papers to let them go free. If they were surprised by a PROFOR unit, they would be disarmed and taken into custody. Katz would be able to free them, but probably not until it was too late.

With their Toyota well hidden in the trees, the commandos dismounted and watched the convoy of a dozen armored cars and personnel carriers rumble past on the road below. When the French unit had passed, McCarter let them get a mile or two down the road before giving the order to move out again.

MAJOR NASLIN WAS also keeping a sharp eye out for the PROFOR units. With as few men as he now had, he couldn't afford to get into a firefight. And since the Aviano air base hadn't been taken out of action as the plan had called for, he had to be alert against enemy aircraft, as well. Fortunately, though, the trucks that had escaped destruction had been carrying almost a dozen Strella missiles between them, so he could fight back if UN aircraft appeared.

The odds were against him as they had never been before, but a merciful God had seen him through this trial so far and the Iranian was confident that He wouldn't let him fail now. Not when he was so close to victory. He had been prepared to give his life for the revolution since he had been a child. Never had it been so close as it was now, and he was unafraid.

But his death would be so much sweeter if it came as the price of this victory he sought.

If he was successful, generations of schoolchildren would remember his name on Martyrs' Day. If he failed, even his family would curse his memory.

"WE'RE GOING to need to get some gas," Hawkins announced half an hour later, "and real soon."

"How much more do we have?" McCarter glanced over at the fuel gauge on the dashboard.

"I'd say about another ten miles or so."

"You should have let me know sooner."

"I was a little busy trying to keep us out of sight of the UN, remember."

"We need a gas station ASAP," McCarter radioed to Aviano. "Can you help us find one?"

"A gas station or just a source of fuel?" Katz asked.

"Just the fuel."

Katz studied the satellite video that was being sent directly to the CP and compared what he was seeing with the large-scale military map of the area on his desk.

"I have some kind of a garage on the edge of the village right over the hill in front of you, a place called Diminia. There's a couple of trucks parked around it and what looks like an above-ground fuel tank behind the building. I can't read any markings on the tank to see if it's gas or diesel, but it's worth a try."

"We're on it," McCarter said and signed off.

"What does he have?" Bolan asked.

"There's a village right down the road, and Katz says it has a gas station or a garage we might be able to use."

"We also need to try to find a couple more jerricans, too," Encizo commented. "We can't count on finding a gas station every time we need one."

The village looked deserted when the Stony Man team cautiously drove in. As Katz had told them, the garage was on the edge of town and there were trucks parked in front, but the place looked deserted, as well.

"What kind of village is this," Hawkins asked as he looked around, "Serb, Croat or Muslim? I don't know how to tell the difference between them."

"Are you going ethnic on us," Encizo asked, "and picking your targets by culture?"

"No," Hawkins replied, shaking his head, "I'm just trying to figure out the likelihood of someone shooting at us based on what flag they're saluting. It's strictly a rules-of-engagement kind of thing."

"The rules of engagement are 'If someone shoots at us, we will shoot back at them regardless of their religion, creed or political faction.'"

Hawkins grinned. "That's fair enough."

"That's the only way we ever work."

Luck was with them again, and the storage tank behind the garage still contained fifty or sixty gallons of gasoline. Rummaging around inside the garage, they found a hand pump to transfer the gas. While James and Manning filled the tank, Encizo and Hawkins scrounged three more serviceable jerricans to add to the one that had come with the truck.

As soon as the Toyota was refueled and the full gas cans had been stashed in the back, the Stony Man team was on the road again.

CHAPTER TWENTY-TWO

San Simone

From Able Team's observation point overlooking the Villa del Norte, Schwarz's acoustical scanner picked up the sound of a shot coming from inside the building. "Someone just fired a pistol in there," he announced.

"Just one shot?" Lyons asked.

Schwarz nodded.

"Maybe our man was expressing his dissatisfaction with one of his subordinates."

"Or maybe he was cleaning his pistol and had an accident."

"Someone's coming out the back of the house," Blancanales said. "Two men and they're carrying a body."

The two men took their burden to the kennel behind the house, opened the door in the chain-link fence and dumped it inside. In a flash, the dogs were on it, tearing and eating the flesh.

"God Almighty!" Schwarz muttered.

"Okay," Lyons said. "Now we have him cold. He's a hotheaded bastard and likes to feed the bodies of his men to his dogs. Nice guy."

"He's acting like a mafioso," Blancanales said, "not an Arab terrorist."

"Maybe he's been in Italy too long," Schwarz observed, "and the Mafia has rubbed off on him like a bad habit."

"Now that we have a good ID," Blancanales said, "and know that it's him, what are we going to do about it?"

Lyons was silent for a long moment. "Well," he said finally, "I guess that we can always go down there and bust his chops."

"Or?" Blancanales could hear an unspoken alternative still forming in Lyons's mind.

"Or we can just sit up here and see what plays out down there. We're on him now, so the ball's in our court."

Neither Blancanales nor Schwarz could believe what they had just heard. Carl "The Ironman" Lyons was recommending caution?

"Are you feeling okay, boss?" Schwarz asked.

"I've never felt better, Gadgets. I'm just trying to put myself into the mind of that bastard. He's got some kind of problem, and I'd like to know what it is. And I think he's just squirrelly enough that he'll slip up and let us know before too long. Remember, we don't just want him—we want everyone who's working for him, too. That will save someone else a lot of trouble later.''

"He has a problem other than the fact that every cop in Italy and hundreds of NATO security people are after him, you mean?''

"Actually, yes. If he's shooting his own people, he's panicking, and I'd like to see if we can work that into something we can use.''

"I thought that was my line,'' Blancanales said. "I'm the guy who's supposed to do all of the psyching out and playing mind games around here.''

"Just consider it cross training,'' Lyons replied.

"Does that mean that I'm going to have to start busting down doors, then?''

"Better get yourself some shoulder pads, Pol,'' Schwarz said, grinning, "or start taking steroids. You're not built for going through doors like the Ironman.''

ALI NADAL PICKED UP the phone and was surprised to hear the voice of his main Italian informant, the head of the Italian police's drug-interdiction unit, on the other end of the line. The Lebanese had other midlevel police informants, but this man was the most senior official he had in the Italian government.

"You have a problem,'' the police colonel said without identifying himself or passing pleasantries. "There is a top secret American counterterrorist unit operating against you. They are the ones who hit your safehouses, and they foiled your attack on the air base. They have also been able to break into your computer communications and have released information about you to the police and the UN.''

Nadal felt a chill shoot through him. ''How did they break into my computers?''

''I do not have that information,'' the colonel continued. ''I just know that they did. I also know that they have access to everything you had in your computer files. In short you have been compromised, and I recommend that you leave the country immediately. You are in danger every minute that you remain in Italy, and there's nothing I can do to protect you now. It's grown far too big, and I must protect myself. Once you are back in Tripoli, I will contact you through the usual channels, but I can no longer afford to have any contact with you here in Italy. Good luck.''

The line went dead, and Nadal put the handset back on the cradle. This couldn't have come at a worse time. There would never be a good time for him to hear that the network he had spent so much time building had been compromised. But with the decision about further attacks on Aviano still up in the air, this wasn't the time for him to abandon his operation and seek personal safety in Libya. His controllers would take that as a sign of cowardice, and the penalty for that was death.

He didn't doubt that the colonel's warning was true, but he couldn't go back to Libya now and still live. The only way he could survive was to turn this situation around. This special Yankee counterterrorist team had to be the men he had been curious about before. From the reports of his agents, there were only five of them, and one was believed to be a pilot. Surely he could come up with a plan to take out five men.

He hadn't forgotten that he had already tried to capture one these Americans on the base and had failed. It was clear to him now that he hadn't chosen the right man for that job. When he targeted them again, he would use every man he had to ensure that the hit was made properly. Then, when the Yankees were out of the way, he would see what he could do to put his organization back together. He wasn't about to stand by and watch while what he had worked so long to put in place was brought to ruin.

On his way back to the living room, Nadal put a stern, determined look on his face. He couldn't let his two remaining cell leaders know of the police colonel's warning. They were both good men, but they didn't burn with the same revolutionary zeal that fueled everything he did. If they learned that the organization had been compromised, they might try to run to save their lives. And that would be unfortunate, because then he would have to kill them, too.

"We have a new mission," he told them. "First, though, as soon as you get back to your cells, I want you to destroy all of your computers immediately. The enemy has found a way to break into them, and it is no longer safe to use them for communication."

"But everything we have planned is on our computers, as well as all of our contacts."

"Make printouts of the information if you have to, but destroy the computers.

"Then," he said, looking both of the men straight in the eye, "there is a small group of Americans based at the Aviano air base who must die as soon as possible. There are only five of them and you can use as many men as you have to to get the job done."

"Are these the same men that Jamal went after?" the Syrian asked cautiously. The failed assassination team had come from his cell, and the man in charge had been one of his best. Or so he had thought.

Nadal nodded. "Yes. And this time you cannot fail. They must be killed, all of them."

The Syrian locked eyes with his leader. "Now that the air-base security forces have been alerted against us, it will not be as easy for us to get weapons into the base as it was the first time."

"I know that." Nadal kept his voice neutral. He didn't want to have to kill this man, too. The cell structure of his organization required good subcommanders, and he didn't have anyone to replace him at this time. "But it has to be done anyway."

The Syrian dropped his gaze. "I will set my best men on it."

"Both of you will do that," Nadal said. "And you will lead them yourself."

He glanced at his watch. "Now, I want you to go

and ready your units. I will be in touch with you on the phone tomorrow to work out the details.''

"HEADS UP, GUYS," Schwarz sang out. "We have movement to our front."

In the glare of the security lights around the villa, they saw the front door open. This time, there were only two men who walked out and got into the white BMW sedan.

"You were right about him having been pissed at one of his own guys," Blancanales told Lyons. "He seems to have misplaced one of his visitors."

"He didn't misplace him," Schwarz said. "He invited him to be his dogs' dinner."

"Do we follow these guys?" Schwarz continued as he watched the two men start down the long driveway. After spending a day on the hill, a nice warm car ride would go well right now.

Lyons shook his head. "No, I got their mug shots and the plate number, so we can track them down later. Right now, I want the guy in the house."

"So we're going to follow him?"

"More or less," Lyons said.

"Dammit, Ironman!" Schwarz exploded. "How about letting us in on what's going down? I'm freezing my ass off up here and I'm hungry. If there's some purpose to this exercise, I'd really like to know what it is."

"Patience, Gadgets, patience. But since you're

burning with such a great desire to go into action, there is something you can do for the cause.''

"What's that?"

"Do you have any of your tracking beacons in your little bag of tricks?"

"Sure. I always have a couple."

"Good. Here's what I'd like you to do. I want you to sneak down there and—"

"Forget it," Schwarz broke in. "I'm not going anywhere near those man-eating dogs."

"They only eat you after you're dead."

"No way, Jack," Schwarz stated, shaking his head. "My telephone psychic told me to stay away from dogs this year."

Just then, Lyons's cellular phone rang. "Lyons," he answered.

"We have a problem," Katzenelenbogen told him. He hated to call Able Team off of the chase, but with the Bosnia mission going the way it was, he needed them at the CP in case they had to be sent to back up Bolan.

"The situation in Bosnia has turned serious," he explained. "The air strike didn't do the job, and the guys have had their mission extended. I need you guys back here to stand by in case they need backup."

"Damn!" Lyons said. "Things were just starting to get interesting around here."

"It can't be helped, Ironman. The guys have the priority this time."

"I copy," Lyons said. "We'll wrap up and head back."

"Make it sooner rather than later," Katz advised. "And if you get hung up, call and I'll send Jack after you."

"Will do."

"Katz wants us to break off here and get back to Aviano ASAP," Lyons told his teammates. "Apparently Striker's mission isn't going well."

Schwarz didn't wish the other team any bad luck, but getting off this cold hill sounded good to him. "I'll start packing our stuff up."

Lyons knew that Katz wanted them back ASAP, but now that they had tracked the Lebanese to his lair, a few more minutes one way or the other wouldn't make any real difference.

"Gadgets, did you get the phone number to this place when you were tracking the E-mail address?"

"Yeah."

"I want to give our man down there a call and see if I can get him to rabbit for us."

"I thought you said that Katz needed us back at the CP ASAP?"

"He does. But I still want to put a tag on that guy's car so we can find him later."

"I told you that I'm not going down there with those damned dogs, Carl. You can just forget it."

"But there won't be any dogs where I want you to go."

"What's the catch? Are you and Pol going to take the dogs out first?"

"Nope. I'm going to get our man to run, but I'm going to create a diversion so we can tag his car. I don't want to lose track of him."

"Why don't we just shoot the bastard while we have the chance and have done with it?"

"Because I want the rest of his people, too," Lyons replied, dropping the banter. "Leaving them in place only means that someone will have to chase all of them down later. And you know that I really hate to leave things half-done."

"What kind of diversion?"

"I'm going to have Pol take the Lancia down there and have a breakdown right at the end of the driveway. And then..."

WHEN ALI NADAL'S black BMW sports sedan approached the end of the driveway, he saw a silver gray Lancia sedan off the road blocking his way. The car's hood was up, and a man was leaning over as if he was working on the engine. Drivers often used his turnout to park, but he also knew a good ambush site when he saw one.

The phone call he had just received made an ambush a distinct possibility. The caller had said that he was an American tourist who had seen the villa on his way to San Simone and wanted to know if he could come and take pictures of it in the morning. Nadal declined the man's request, but the call made him realize that while the remote villa offered him security, it also isolated him as a target. If the call had been to check if he was home, it could be a setup.

The lights illuminated the Lancia, and the man came out from under the hood and waved. The terrorist stopped his car a dozen yards away, but left the lights on high. Reaching under the seat, he drew out his Beretta subgun and flicked it off safe before opening the door. Nadal slung the Model 12 at his side with the pistol grip ready at his right hand as he walked forward.

SCHWARZ LAY in the ditch well to the rear of the Lancia, his 9 mm Beretta in his right hand. In his left, he held two of the Farm's special vehicle-tracking bugs. They had been put together by the same company that made the SAR implants for the military, and they worked on the same principle. They activated only in response to a radio signal. That way, they couldn't be detected by a bug sweeper. Now, all he had to do was to get close enough to the terrorist's BMW to attach them.

Lyons was in position to the front of the Lancia, his Colt Python ready in his hand. As much as he wanted to police up all of the Lebanese's men, if the terrorist made a single wrong move, he would settle for just bagging him. A .357 Magnum slug in the right place would do a lot to make Italy a safer place to live.

"I am so sorry I am in your way," Blancanales said, gesturing expressively. "I will push my car out of the way so you can get past it."

THE MAN'S ACCENT and halting use of the language told Nadal that he was a foreigner. But it wasn't an American Italian accent, so he relaxed a little.

"I will help you," Nadal offered, making sure that the foreigner saw the Beretta.

"You're too kind."

While the Lebanese was helping Blancanales push the Lancia, Schwarz ducked out of his hiding place and dashed the few yards back to the BMW. Once he was safely behind the car, he reached up under the left rear fender to place the first bug. After making sure that the magnet was firmly attached, he slid around the side and put the other one under the right front fender before fading back into the dark.

"Thank you," Blancanales said when the Lancia was clear of the driveway. "Again, I am sorry for the inconvenience."

"It's nothing," Nadal said.

Getting back in his car, Nadal kept the Beretta ready in his right hand. He didn't put the weapon back under the seat until he was well out of range.

"DID YOU PLANT THEM, Gadgets?" Lyons asked as he watched the BMW's taillights fade in the distance.

"Yeah." Schwarz slapped at the mud coating his

night suit. "I planted the damned things and caught pneumonia in the process."

"We can stop and get you a little medicine on the way back, some of that brandy you were talking about."

"Right. Bribe me and figure that I'll forget all about laying in a muddy ditch for an hour."

"If you two are through," Blancanales said as he closed the hood of the Lancia, "we should probably hit the road. Katz is waiting for us."

CHAPTER TWENTY-THREE

Bosnia

Since leaving the bombed-out forest camp, Major Naslin had kept his drivers moving as fast as they possibly could, but it hadn't been fast enough. He wasn't covering as much ground as he needed to make the rendezvous on time. The roads in the region were the worst paved roads he had ever seen. Years of neglect, as well as war damage, had reduced them to little more than rutted tracks.

Worse than that were the numbers of bridges that had been destroyed. With the mountains to the west supplying snow melt, the region was crisscrossed with streams and rivers. There was a bridge every few miles, and most of them were down. The time it had taken them to find fording places had added hours to the driving time.

To make up for the lost time, they would have to drive through the night and run the risk of having their lights spotted. If the cave base camp hadn't been destroyed, his drivers would be equipped with night-vision goggles and the dark wouldn't be an obstacle. But the trucks that had escaped destruction hadn't been equipped before the bombs fell, and the night-vision goggles were buried under tons of rock.

Naslin was riding in the lead vehicle, doing the map navigating, when the Toyota crested a hill. Seeing a military convoy parked on the side of the road below, he quickly ordered his driver to back up and pull off behind the crest of the hill. After putting out security, Naslin went to the top of the hill and watched the vehicles. From the flags flying from their radio antennae, they were French and it was apparent that they were planning to spend the night down there.

The major couldn't believe that the PROFOR unit had chosen to stop where it had. The valley was narrow here, and the road followed the river that cut through it. A few hundred meters beyond the PROFOR laager, the road forked to turn north and that was the road he had to take. Without turning around and going back several miles, there was no way he could get past the UN troops. And to complicate the problem, it would soon be too dark to drive without using the truck's lights.

With the sun going down, the wind had picked up and was blowing from his back. When Naslin reached to turn up the collar of his jacket, he got an idea. It was a dangerous idea, but God always stood at the side of those who put themselves in danger to bring his revolution.

There was simply no way for him to get past the French unit without getting into a firefight, and there were too many troops down there for him to make a successful conventional attack against them. But with the wind blowing away from him, the chemical rockets in the truck could be used without even having to launch them.

The type of nerve gas in the rocket warheads was called a binary agent. The warhead contained two chambers holding the separate chemicals, each of which was harmless until combined with the other. But when the warhead detonated and the chemicals were mixed together by the explosion, they reacted and produced the deadly gas.

He would send a volunteer down there with one of the rockets, and the man would activate the fuse to detonate the warhead. The man would die a martyr's death, but it would eliminate the PROFOR unit completely.

When he went to ask the technical sergeant in his group about his idea, he learned the bad news.

"The rocket's fuse has a setback arming feature," the sergeant explained. "It has to undergo launch acceleration to overcome the setback and make the fuse active. It's designed that way for safety."

Naslin snorted. Safety during war was for women and Western unbelievers, not for God's faithful. Islam hadn't triumphed by trying to keep its holy warriors safe from harm by putting safety devices on their weapons; only God could do that.

"What will happen if you tie a grenade to the warhead and set it off? That will break the containers and spread the gas, will it not?"

"Setting off a grenade tied to the warhead will release the chemicals, and they will mix to form the gas," the sergeant admitted.

"Ready one of the rockets with a grenade and find me a volunteer who is willing to do this for the revolution."

"The volunteer will not be able to get far enough away in time to escape the effects of the gas," the sergeant observed.

"The martyr lives at the right hand of God," Naslin reminded him.

The sergeant dropped his eyes. "That is true."

The man returned in a few minutes with one of his soldiers at his side. This freedom fighter was one of the youngest men in his unit, but his eyes burned. The best martyrs were always the young, the ones with the most to lose by dying early. But Naslin wasn't reluctant to use him for this mission. The young were also filled with the fire of devotion to the cause.

"Do you understand what you are to do for our revolution?" the major asked him.

"Yes, Major." The young soldier stiffened to attention. "God is great."

"Yes, He is," Naslin agreed. "And He will take you into his Paradise tonight."

"As God wills."

The volunteer stripped off his field gear and left it with his assault rifle and grenades. The rocket warhead was the only weapon he would need in this, his final battle, and it would send many more of the unbelievers to hell than his AK ever could. After the youth covered his face and hands with mud, the sergeant handed him the prepared warhead. With a last salute, he started down the hill.

Naslin watched the French laager from the crest of the hill through his night field glasses. They weren't as good as using night-vision goggles, but with the starlight from a clear sky, they gave him a fairly good view. After watching the camp for a few minutes, he tried to spot his volunteer, but couldn't even find his track through the tall grass and that was good. If he couldn't see him from above, the French couldn't see him from where they were.

THE FRENCH mechanized company had put its armored personnel carriers and scout cars into a circular laager for the night. The command-and-control vehicle was in the middle of the circle, and the lights were burning inside as the officers took care of their daily after-action paperwork. Since the day's patrol had been as routine as always, the paperwork was minimal.

The French had put sentries out, but they weren't too far in front of their vehicles. Other guards kept watch from the gun turrets of the scout cars. The sentries wore night-vision goggles and they were alert, but it was peacetime alert. After months of endless patrolling without even a single shot having been fired at them, they weren't battlefield alert. Months of seeing nothing had taught them to expect more of the same—nothing.

The Iranian volunteer made his way through the tall grass flat on his belly. It was slow going, but time wasn't crucial this night—approaching the target unseen was. He knew that God was waiting to welcome him to Paradise, but he knew that he had to wait until he was close enough for the gas to be effective.

Raising his head slowly until only his eyes cleared the tops of the grass, he studied his objective. The sentries were close by their vehicles, and there didn't seem to be any other early-warning devices. Seeing that he was as close as the sergeant had told him to get, he reached for the pin on the grenade.

"God's great!" the young volunteer shouted in Farsi as he pulled the pin.

The flash of the detonation blinded him, and he gasped when red-hot grenade shrapnel sliced through him. He wasn't in pain very long, however. The explosion tore open the binary warhead of the rocket, and the gases instantly combined to produce the deadly gas.

Two quick breaths of it was all it took to paralyze his nervous system. He died seconds later.

Alarmed by the shout and the grenade's detonation, the French tried to react. But they didn't get to travel three steps before, twitching and shaking, they died in their tracks.

On the command-and-control vehicle, the automated chemical-attack alarm went off, sending its radio warning to the PROFOR headquarters. After the first three seconds, though, no one in the laager was alive to hear it.

FROM HIS POSITION overlooking the valley, Major Naslin saw the flash of the grenade. A second later, the sound of the muffled explosion reached him. There were a couple of shouts, but they were quickly choked off. Beyond that, he could see nothing changing in the laager. He knew, however, that men were dying down there.

He thought he smelled a sharp odor on the cool night air, but he knew it was only his imagination. The wind hadn't changed and was still blowing from his back. Were it not, he wouldn't have made the attack. Dying to further the revolution was one thing; dying by mistake was a betrayal of God's will.

Waiting impatiently, Naslin counted down the minutes until the gas could disperse and it would be safe to drive through the area. The sergeant had said that it would take at least an hour before all traces of the gas would be gone. He hated the delay, but it couldn't be helped. He would make up the time by driving with the lights on.

"Is it time now?" he finally asked the technical sergeant.

The man looked at his watch. "It should be clear. But we will still need to be careful. I will go ahead on foot with the gas detector to check."

"There is no need to do that," Naslin stated. "God will protect us. Tell the men to load up."

"As you command, Major."

Stony Man Farm

"BARBARA?" Aaron Kurtzman's familiar voice cut through Barbara Price's dreaming mind and awakened her. After encouraging the rest of the crew to get some rest when they could, she had taken her own advice. After a long hot shower, she had dressed in fresh clothes then lay down on her bed just to rest for an hour. Apparently she had fallen asleep.

Opening one eye, she hit the intercom button by the bed in her quarters. "Yes?"

"We just picked up a gas-attack alert from one of the PROFOR units."

"I'm coming down."

With everything focused on the chase of the two trucks still carrying the nerve-gas rockets, Kurtzman's people were going all out to cover the area of operation. And since the chase had moved into the regions patrolled by the UN, that also meant monitoring the PROFOR radio communications.

When Price walked into the computer room, the place was abuzz. "What happened?"

"We're not sure," Kurtzman admitted. "Most of

the PROFOR units are equipped with automatic chemical-detector alarms that broadcast a warning, and one of them sounded an alert just a few minutes ago over—'' he moved an arrow on the map into a valley with a river running through it ''—here.''

''Has there been anything since then?''

''No. The alarms are set to transmit for a few minutes and then reset themselves.''

''Is there any radio traffic from them?''

''No. Their headquarters keeps trying to call them, but no one is answering.''

''Do you think that they were attacked?''

''It sure as hell looks that way,'' he said. ''I've got the satellite scanning the area right now, but it doesn't show any movement. I'm getting stationary heat signatures from generators and commo vans, that kind of thing, but that's about all. I'm not picking up any moving warm bodies.''

''You'd better tell Striker what's going on,'' she decided. ''If it is a gas attack, I don't want them running into it. And, while you're doing that, I'll go wake up Hal and talk to him. The President is going to need to know about this. It may be time for us to pull out completely and hand this mess over to the UN.''

Kurtzman could hear the fatigue in her voice mixed with concern for the Stony Man commandos. She never liked to admit defeat, but there was only so much they could do even under the best of circumstances. And this situation had gone far beyond the call of duty. "I'll get the chopper pilot on the pad," he said.

"Do that."

BARBARA PRICE SAW that Hal Brognola was also sleeping fully clothed, but he hadn't bothered to change into fresh clothing before going to bed. He had been kept in the air so much lately that he hadn't even had a chance to set his dirty laundry out to be washed by the Farm support staff. She'd make a point of sending someone up to gather his laundry in the morning.

"Hal?"

Brognola muttered something incoherent and rolled over.

"Hal?" Price's voice was more insistent.

"Yeah," he said, finally awake, "what is it now?"

"Aaron thinks that one of the PROFOR units has been hit with a gas attack."

"Oh, shit!" Brognola sat up and swung his legs around to put his feet on the floor. "What happened?"

"We're not sure yet, but a French PROFOR convoy in a night laager just sounded a chemical-attack alarm. It was one of those automatic transmitter alerts, and Aaron picked it up on a routine communications intercept."

Brognola hoped against hope that it had been a malfunction of the equipment and, as unlikely as that was, he had to ask. "Has it been confirmed yet?"

"No," she replied, "but their own headquarters isn't able to get anyone to answer their calls."

"I assume that it's in an area that could have been reached by the missing Iranian trucks?"

"In fact the target trucks have been parked a couple of klicks away for some time now."

Brognola shook his head. "The President is getting tired of being awakened up and seeing my face the first thing in the morning. It might be different if I was bringing him good news at least once in a while."

"Well, that's why he makes the big bucks and gets to live in the White House. He's the Man, and he gets to make all the big decisions."

"Have you alerted Striker yet?"

"Aaron was calling Katz to pass on the word when I left to come up here."

"How far away from the French laager site are they?"

"About a two-hour drive during daylight hours."

"Have them move in to confirm the incident if they can," he ordered. "But tell them to be damned careful. They do have a chemical detector with them, don't they?"

She nodded.

"Good. Tell them that I do not want them to take any unnecessary risks."

She refrained from commenting that the only way to be completely safe around chemical weapons was to not be anywhere near them.

the PKC belt through and took out the remains with the forceps. The gas was still in a layer in the hole above him, so he had left the shaft alone. He knew it wouldn't rise into the hole to fill the vacancy with fresh air; like any mass, it would go straight down.

It had only taken him a couple of minutes to get behind a heavy ledge—no telling where it might have come from way up there—but once that job done, he felt protected enough to go down. He needed to get into the lower part of the valley, the layers of air below the tree-line.

CHAPTER TWENTY-FOUR

Bosnia

At first light the next morning, David McCarter drove into the valley toward the French laager with only the gas detector riding on the seat next to him. Checking to see if there had actually been a nerve-gas attack as the Farm thought was a one-man job, and no one was better suited to do it than him. Both Manning and Hawkins had argued about his going, saying that since he was the Phoenix Force leader, he couldn't be spared if the gas was still present.

But, as far as McCarter was concerned, the job was his precisely because he was the leader. His SAS-trained concept of leadership was that the head man got paid the big bucks to lead, not to send men into danger in his place. Plus Kurtzman had assured him that since the nerve gas involved was likely to have been manufactured to the Russian formula, it would have dissipated in an hour or so and would be completely gone by now.

He stopped the truck a quarter of a mile away from

the PROFOR laager and took another reading with the detector. The air was still clean. Picking up his field glasses, he scanned the silent camp. The French armored vehicles had been parked in a circle with their machine gun and autocannon turrets facing outward.

It had been a good move and would have worked against almost anything they could have expected to come up against in Bosnia. But guns and armored vehicles were no protection against deadly nerve gas. Putting the Toyota in gear, he drove the rest of the way in, keeping one eye on the detector all the way.

The first bodies he came to were right outside the ring of vehicles and would have been the sentries. The bodies bore no visible signs of the cause of death. There were no bullet holes and no blood. Their sprawled postures told of their having died in midstride as it were.

The only sign that they had died unnaturally was that most of the faces were in a grimace of death that told of their nervous systems having been attacked. The gas hit so fast that the poor bastards probably hadn't even known what was killing them.

Inside the laager, one of the officers in the command vehicle, a captain by the stripes on his rank straps, had died with a radio microphone in his hand. Another officer lay where he had fallen halfway out the back door. Some of the troops were in their sleeping bags under their vehicles, sleeping the long sleep.

McCarter hadn't been a stranger to war for more

years than he liked to count. He was well acquainted with violent death and had seen every way that a human could possibly die. But there was always something obscene about the victims of gas attacks, either military or civilian.

These men had been soldiers, and putting their lives on the line in combat was part of their job description. But they hadn't been killed in combat like soldiers. They had been slaughtered like so many sheep without even having had a chance to defend themselves.

After making a count of the bodies, McCarter turned the Toyota around and was driving back to rejoin his teammates when he passed a single body beyond the ring of sentries. This man was wearing desert camouflage instead of the olive drab battle dress of the French. Stopping the truck, he got out and rolled the corpse over with his boot. The soldier wasn't French unless he was of Algerian extraction, and the uniform was a dead giveaway. The Iranians at the fortress had worn this kind of desert camouflage.

Close to the Iranian's corpse was what looked like a half-exploded round of some kind. Moving in closer to look at it, McCarter thought he caught a faint bitter smell and jerked back. He felt silly because if there was gas present, he would already be dead. But he went back to the truck to get the chemical detector to check this round anyway.

When the detector showed that the air didn't contain any lingering traces of nerve gas, he looked closer at what he had found. The thin-walled round appeared to be a chemical rocket warhead, but the nose fuse was still intact and hadn't exploded. Seeing the safety pin of the grenade by the corpse's hand, he realized what had happened.

This had been a suicide attack. This Iranian had sneaked up close to the French laager and had detonated some kind of explosive device to rupture the gas warhead.

Suicide bombers weren't as common in Islamic national armies as they were in terrorist bands, but they weren't unknown, either. The lure of immediate entrance into Paradise was strong and enticed many men to martyr themselves.

Leaving the evidence where it lay for the UN to find, he got back into the truck and drove to where he had left Bolan with the rest of the team.

"They've raised the ante," he informed Bolan as he stepped down. "The French were gassed."

Hearing the expected, Bolan reached for the radio to make his report to Katz.

Stony Man Farm

"McCarter found the bodies." Yakov Katzenelenbogen's face on the Farm's video screen showed his concern. "It was a French patrol, platoon size, thirty-eight men, and they're all dead. There was another body close by that David thinks was an Iranian who had a chemical-rocket warhead with him, so it looks like it was a suicide attack. The Iranian got in close to the laager site and detonated the warhead.''

"Poor bastards," Kurtzman muttered.

"Have the French headquarters been notified?'' Barbara Price asked.

"They had choppers in the air at first light looking for the unit because they lost communication with them last night. They were approaching the site right as our team was pulling out of the area. I told them to move out so they wouldn't get hung up with the UN.''

"Good call," Brognola said.

"What are your instructions at this point?'' Katz asked formally. He was the Farm's tactical adviser, but the ultimate decisions were on Brognola's shoulders. Particularly a decision of such magnitude.

This was the first time that war gases had been used in Europe since the end of World War I, and it was an important escalation of the long Bosnian crisis. The decisions that would be made could have a dramatic effect on the future of Europe, and he didn't want to be the one who had to make the call.

"I'll be damned if I know," Brognola answered. "Until I can get a conference with the President and see what he wants to do, have the guys continue tracking the bastards and hope that they can make contact before any more of the rockets are used.''

"Striker and the team are closing in on them,''

Hunt Wethers commented. "I have them no more than an hour or so behind the targets at this time."

Since Wethers had set up the tracking program that was tagging the Iranians' trucks, he was keeping watch over the progress of the long-distance chase.

"Can we vector in a NATO gunship to destroy those trucks now?" Katz asked. "This is a serious enough incident that it should be enough to cut through the usual bullshit to get some prompt action."

Brognola thought for a moment. "This has upped the threat," he agreed. "There's no doubt about that, and I'll argue for an immediate air strike, but I can't even begin to guess what he'll say."

"Urge him to take quick action, Hal," Katz said. "Since we've seen that they are more than willing to use the gas, the team is in danger, as well."

"I'll try my best," Brognola replied, knowing full well that he had little chance of success. Anything that was linked to the UN in any way defied quick action. "But I don't want to pull the guys off them yet. I want them to keep trying to get within striking range. And tell them that if they can attack, I want them to do it immediately. They're the last, best chance we have of putting a quick end to this."

"Will do," Katz said. "But you have to give them warning if you can get an air strike authorized. A bomb blast hitting those rockets would be even more dangerous than launching them, and I don't want our people to be caught in the open."

"I understand." Brognola read between the lines of what Katz had explained. An air strike would release the deadly gas, and nerve gas didn't care whom it killed.

He turned to the bank of printers against the wall and reached for the satellite photos of the French laager that were coming out of the photo printer. "The President will want to see these."

Aviano Air Base, Italy

WHILE KATZENELENBOGEN waited to hear back from Stony Man Farm, he mulled over the report McCarter had made about the gas attack. One thing stuck in his mind that he didn't understand. Why had the Iranians made a suicide attack instead of launching the rocket the usual way?

It was true that the trade-off had been good—one Iranian KIA for thirty-eight French. That was a good combat equation, but this hadn't been real combat. Considering that the Iranians had taken a beating in the bombing at the camp, they had to be short on men. Even if those two pickups were packed to the sides of the bed, they couldn't have many more than two dozen men all told.

Maybe there was a simpler explanation. Maybe a suicide bomber had been sent in to take the French out because the Iranians didn't have a launcher with them to fire the rocket from.

Katz was well aware that a rocket launcher wasn't

a big deal—a chunk of sewage pipe would work if it was big enough. He even knew that the Viet Cong had often launched Russian 120mm rockets by resting them on crossed sticks stuck in the ground. Using the proper launcher, however, did give a better guarantee of hitting what you were aiming at. But that was only important when you were dealing with conventional HE rocket warheads. With an HE round, if you couldn't hit it, you couldn't blow it up.

With chemical rockets, however, accuracy wasn't really important. What was important was making sure that you were upwind from the target. Dropping the rocket almost anywhere upwind from the intended target would do the trick when the gas was released. And if he assumed that the Iranians didn't have a launcher, he could narrow down the number of possible targets. If that was in fact the case, the best target would be anyplace where people were gathered in large numbers.

His mind flashed to something Brognola had said about the importance of getting Richard Lacy back in American hands in time for an important meeting. Had it been something about an election? Or was it so he could take part in the renewed peace talks?

Grabbing the phone, he hit the key to activate the video hookup and called the Farm. "I need you to help me with something," he told Aaron Kurtzman.

"What's that?"

"Tell me again what was so important about our getting Richard Lacy back on time."

"Katz, that's old news. You're supposed to be chasing after a shipment of nerve-gas rockets, remember."

"To be a little more precise," Katz replied, "I'm supposed to be chasing nerve-gas rockets so they won't be used. And part of solving that puzzle is figuring out who they are going to be used against. I think that your man Lacy might be a key to solving that puzzle."

"I'll bite—how?"

"I think that the Iranians may not have a launcher for those rockets. That would go a long ways to explain why they used a suicide attacker to take out the French when they're low on men. My thought is that if they have to use up a man every time they pop one of those rockets, they'll want to make sure that they get their money's worth. They're going to want to hit a large target."

Kurtzman was silent for a moment. "The elections. They're having another round of regional elections in the Serb and Croatian sections of Bosnia. The Bosnian Muslims have gotten their stuff together as far as choosing their own leaders, but the Serbs and Croats are still working on it. The elections are scheduled to start—" he glanced at the calendar "—in the cities on the day after tomorrow."

"Which cities?"

"Let me find out and get back to you," Kurtzman said. "I know that not all of the cities were chosen as election sites. There was some concern about fraud, and the UN wants to oversee the vote this time, so the elections have been consolidated. People from the outlying districts and smaller towns will have to travel to cast their ballots, and that's why it's a two-day vote.''

"That could be it," Katz said. "A bunch of people gathered to vote would be a perfect target for a suicide bomber armed with a nerve-gas rocket.''

Kurtzman had worked with Katz long enough to recognize that particular tone in his voice. It meant that he had just put two and two together and come up with twenty two instead of merely four. "I'll get right on that.''

Now THAT HE HAD a likely target, Katz put his battle-trained mind to work to ensure that the attacks weren't carried out. According to McCarter's report, a single man had been responsible for the attack on the French, and it was possible that they would try that tactic again.

A single-man attack had a lot going for it. One man could hide better than a rocket-launching team, and the warhead could be easily concealed. However, considering that the attackers were more than likely Iranians, they probably wouldn't speak the local language. That and cultural differences would make a lone Iranian bomber vulnerable to the security measures that he knew the UN PROFOR monitors would have put in place to protect the election.

Two men would have a better chance, particularly

if they came in from different directions. Better yet, two men coming in under the cover of a diversion. If the main body of Iranians attacked a PROFOR outpost, they could draw the UN to that area and reduce the security somewhere else. That was how he would do it, and he couldn't make the mistake of underestimating the enemy commander. So far, he had done a very good job and couldn't be counted on to make a mistake.

The Iranians had pulled off some very skilled terrorist attacks over the years, and while this was being done under the guise of military action, it was a terrorist attack nonetheless. To Katz's mind, any time that a state of war hadn't been declared and the primary targets were civilians, even the actions of soldiers was terrorism pure and simple. He didn't buy the story that any action was justified as long as it got the desired results.

He had sympathy for the Bosnian Muslims. They had been the victims of brutal Serb and Croatian aggression ever since the Turks had pulled out of the region. During the Bosnian War, they had taken the most serious casualties both on the battlefield and in the so-called ethnic cleansing that the Serbs had conducted.

The mountains of Bosnian Muslim dead called out for justice, but this wasn't the way to get it for them. Killing other civilians wouldn't bring back the dead. Further, justice in Bosnia wasn't going to be promoted by anything the Iranians were likely to do. The

Western concept of justice wasn't part of their thinking in any way. If they were involved, it was for their own reasons and would benefit the Bosnians only as an afterthought.

The key to solving any tactical problem was to find what was in it for the attackers. If he could figure out what the imams of Tehran had to gain by getting involved in Bosnia, he would know how to counter their moves.

CHAPTER TWENTY-FIVE

Bosnia

Major Naslin approached the appointed meeting with
the Bosnian Muslims with extreme caution. Dragan
Asdik had set up the rendezvous, but that didn't ease
the major's mind. Though Naslin had worked closely
with Asdik for months, he still didn't completely
trust the man. In fact he trusted very few of the Bosnian Muslims he had encountered since arriving in
the country, even the ones he was meeting today—
and they were the reason he had embarked on the
plan.

Though the Bosnian Muslims were followers of
the Prophet, they weren't Arab. Being an Iranian,
Naslin wasn't exactly an Arab, either, but Arabic cul-
ture and thought was the bedrock of Middle Eastern
Islam. Having been cut off from the motherland of
Islamic thought for so many centuries, the Bosnian
Muslims thought and acted too much like their Chris-
tian European neighbors for Naslin's tastes. In par-

ticular, they were prone to changing their minds when the going got too tough.

That was why the Iranian felt it was so important for his mission to succeed. As soon as the new Bosnian Muslim government was recognized by the other revolutionary Islamic states, it would be reinforced by thousands of troops from several Islamic nations. Iran, Syria and Libya were just three of the Islamic states that had offered arms and men to the Bosnians to help them defend their new state.

Once the new nation was secure and well established, even more Islamic people would come, civilians this time. In effect they would colonize Bosnia and make the country over in the image of the Middle East. The native Bosnian Muslims wouldn't be pushed off their lands like the Serbs and Croats had tried to do to them. Nor would they be imprisoned or restricted in any way. But within a very few years, they would be blended into the new population and would become proper revolutionary Muslims.

Naslin knew that the transition wouldn't be easy, especially once strict Islamic law was imposed. But if it could be done successfully in a nation as corrupt as prerevolutionary Iran, it would work in Bosnia, as well.

The major and the four soldiers with him found the Bosnians at the appointed place. The leader of the Bosnian National Rebirth Party, Hukan Rezak, was a typical Bosnian mountain man, as Naslin called them—a big, bearded, scowling man who, like so many Bosnians, had the light-colored eyes of a demon, not the dark eyes of a proper human. His greeting was short, and he got right down to the business at hand.

"I was told that you would have a dozen trucks and a hundred men with you," Rezak said in good but accented Arabic, "but I only see two trucks and a handful of troops."

"The Yankees bombed our camp," Naslin explained, "and these are all the men I have left."

"And the rockets?"

"I have enough for several attacks if you can get me a Katusha launcher."

"Exactly how many rockets do you have?" Rezak sounded suspicious. The plan that would put him and his party in power depended upon the mass slaughter of his opponents, and that required having enough of the nerve-gas rockets to make this great killing all on one day.

"I have eighteen, no seventeen, left. I had to use one of them on a PROFOR unit that was blocking my route."

Rezak frowned—attacking PROFOR troops wasn't a wise move. The UN might be a bumbling, uncoordinated entity, but even so, like an elephant, it was to be feared. So far, he had been able to keep his organization a secret from the UN. No one in the PROFOR had any idea that the National Rebirth Party even existed, and he wanted to keep it that way until he took over the country.

"Did you leave any survivors behind?" Rezak asked. "The last thing I need right now is for PRO-FOR to connect that with me."

Naslin wanted to laugh at this slow-thinking man. "Of course there were no survivors. Anyone who gets even a whiff of the gas dies. Nothing was left behind to point to either you or me." Except, of course, for the body of the martyr who had detonated the warhead. But Naslin was confident that there was no way to get information from a dead man.

Rezak heard the unvoiced contempt in Naslin's answer and frowned. Like Dragan Asdik, he had no love for the Iranians, but he welcomed their arms and supplies. His group wasn't a part of the Bosnian national army. In fact it was an outlawed party, so there was no way that he could draw supplies from them. Were it not for the Iranian connection, his men wouldn't even have small arms, to say nothing of the rockets that would be his springboard to power.

The plan to use the nerve-gas rockets to free his country had originated with Rezak. The way he saw it, in the aftermath of freeing Bosnia from everyone who wasn't Muslim, he would be positioned well to become the leader of the new regime. Now, though, Naslin was telling him that his plan couldn't be carried out as he had envisioned it.

"How is it that the Americans learned about your camp?" he asked. "I was told that it was a secret."

"I do not know." Naslin didn't feel like going into the story of Richard Lacy and the capture of the Yankee pilot. "All I know is that they attacked us without warning with one of their stealth fighters."

The mention of the almost mythical, radar-invisible plane was enough to calm the Bosnian's fears of Iranian incompetence. Though no one in Bosnia had ever seen a stealth fighter, the stories of their unimpeded sorties over Baghdad during the Gulf War were legendary. If the entire armed might of Iraq hadn't been able to even damage one of them, there was no hope that a small Iranian unit could defend itself from one of them.

"But," Naslin continued, "with the rockets I have left, we can still carry out the plan. It is true that it will be more difficult. We will have to choose the targets more carefully and may not get the results we originally planned. But it is still possible to free your country from Serbian and Croatian domination as you want."

"With so few rockets, we will have to attack the Serbs first and eliminate them. They are the main enemy. The Croats can live a little while longer."

Serbs or Croatians—Naslin could hardly tell the two of them apart. Both groups, though, were enemies of Islam and would have to be exterminated sooner or later. For now, though, he was willing to allow the Bosnian to pick the targets for his rockets, and killing the Serbs first was fine with him. Since there were fewer Croats, they could be easily taken care of later—if need be, with AKs.

"Agreed," Naslin said. "Now, to ensure success,

can you get me a Katusha launcher? I need one of the single-barrel types, or if that is not possible, a three-barrel launcher.''

"That may be difficult." Rezak frowned. "I do not have one available right now. The authorities confiscated all of our heavy weapons and put them in holding areas.''

"Can these holding areas be attacked? Is there any way we can free a launcher?"

Rezak thought for a moment. "There is one of the UN artillery parks not too far from here. And the garrison is not very large.''

"Take me to it.''

BOLAN AND McCARTER were both studying the map while Hawkins and James refueled the truck from another deserted gas station. Encizo and Manning stood guard, but again the village seemed to be completely empty. They knew, though, that they were being watched by the frightened eyes of those who had gone into hiding at their approach.

"It looks like they're headed for Spivak," McCarter said as he plotted the latest locations of the Iranian vehicles he had just received from Aviano.

"That's as good a bet as any," Bolan replied.

Katz was sending them updates every half hour, and they were slowly closing the gap. But since they were in the same kind of truck that the Iranians were driving, they didn't have any advantage over them.

Not even with Hawkins taking care of most of the driving chores.

McCarter was convinced that if he looked into the Southerner's background, he would find that Hawkins had a misspent youth making white-lightning runs through the back country of Georgia or Kentucky. Either that or he'd grown up around a NASCAR track. McCarter was an accomplished race car driver himself, but Hawkins had a real flair for rough-road driving.

Even so, they were still behind their prey and time was running out. "Catch up with them," McCarter told him as soon as they were refueled.

"I'm on it, boss."

THE UN ARTILLERY PARK had been established at what had been a Yugoslavian police barracks back in the good old days before the breakup of Yugoslavia. When the PROFOR came in, heavy weapons ranging from T-64 tanks to artillery and rocket launchers had been taken from the warring factions and stored for the duration. Neither the extent of that duration nor the final disposition of the weapons had yet been decided. But as long as the UN PROFOR units were patrolling Bosnia, the weapons would be kept under guard.

The guards, however, weren't keen about the job they had been given. For one thing, the troops were Spanish, and they weren't experienced combat soldiers. And there was only one platoon—forty men—

stationed there at any one time. The rest of their company, another three platoons, was nearby. But if an emergency was to occur, it would take the reinforcements at least half an hour to respond.

As Major Naslin scanned the artillery park with his field glasses, he considered using another one of his rockets to wipe out the troops guarding it. In one way, that would be the quick solution, but then he would have to wait two hours for the gas to dissipate before he could get the launcher he needed. It was better to save the rocket for the civilians and take this place with his AKs and RPGs.

"The troops guarding this site are Spanish, you say?" he asked the Bosnian leader.

"That is what I have been told." Rezak shrugged. "I do not recognize their national flag, but all foreign flags look the same to me."

"I am going to go down there with a truck full of my men," Naslin said, "and pretend to be a UN officer from Algeria. While I am talking to them, I want you to come in and surround them so no one gets away."

THE YOUNG SPANISH lieutenant in charge of the garrison at the depot was new to the assignment and wasn't aware that there were no Algerian PROFOR units in his sector. He also was young enough that he didn't want to check with his headquarters before letting the truck full of armed men inside the main gate.

These were common mistakes that any inexperienced officer could make, but the Spanish lieutenant wouldn't get a chance to grow any older or wiser.

With a gun to his head, the lieutenant was quick to order his men to surrender. A quick radio call to Rezak brought the Bosnians in, as well, and the depot was secured. While the Spanish troops were put under guard, Naslin went with his technical sergeant to find a suitable rocket launcher.

The heavy weapons had all been tagged as to which faction they had been taken from, then separated into types. All of the rocket launchers were in one place, and Naslin immediately spotted one of the Yugoslavian-made, three-barreled Katusha launchers. These lightweight weapons were mounted on wheeled carriages that could be towed behind the Toyota pickups with no difficulty.

"What do you want to do with them?" Naslin asked Rezak as he hooked a thumb in the direction of the disarmed Spaniards. "I do not have men to spare to guard them."

"I do not, either," the Bosnian answered. "And they are infidels anyway."

Naslin called his sergeant to his side and, when the man reported, gave his orders. "Kill the prisoners."

The sergeant paused for a moment. "They are UN troops, Major."

"I know that, you fool!" Naslin exploded. "I want them dead."

"As you command, Major."

None of the Spaniards spoke Arabic, but they didn't have to understand what was being said to know what was in store for them. In any language, a firing squad being formed was easily recognizable. Several of them tried to make a run for it and were gunned down. Others fell on their knees and begged for mercy, but there was no mercy to be found in the old police barracks that day.

When the last shots echoed away, the air reeked with burned cordite and the smell of slaughter. The Spanish lay in piles, leaking their blood into the ever thirsty soil of Bosnia.

Naslin surveyed the results of his handiwork and smiled. More infidels had been sent to hell. It was a good warm-up for what would happen in the morning.

"Get the men mounted up," he told his sergeant. "We have a long ways to go yet."

"As you command, Major."

Stony Man Farm

"I THINK we've got a problem," Hunt Wethers told Aaron Kurtzman. "I think the Iranians just raided a UN weapons depot."

Kurtzman closed his eyes for a brief moment. When was this ever going to end? "What happened?"

Wethers quickly explained that the two target vehicles had stopped next to the UN compound and drove on after an hour. Since the depot was manned by UN troops, they wouldn't have gone there without a good reason, and they wouldn't have been able to not go in shooting.

"There's a possibility that they were looking for a launcher to fire their rockets," he concluded.

Kurtzman hit the uplink for the satcom. "I'll tell Katz. You talk to Barbara."

Bosnia

KATZENELENBOGEN'S CALL to McCarter came as the Stony Man warriors were driving down a road a few miles and one ridgeline away from the artillery park. The Phoenix Force commander didn't want to break off the pursuit, but he knew that they had no choice. "We'll check it out," he said.

Half an hour later, they drove through the deserted main gate of the compound. One look at the pile of bodies, and it was all too apparent what had happened. The small garrison guarding the depot had been taken by surprise and had surrendered. This wasn't the first time that a UN PROFOR unit had laid their weapons down and stuck their hands in the air rather than get into a firefight with one of the Bosnian factions. Usually these incidents ended with the UN making threatening noises while granting concessions and the hostages were released.

This time, though, the surrender hadn't gone according to the accepted UN game plan. Rather than being turned loose as further proof of the UN's inability to deal effectively with armed opponents, the soldiers had been gunned down to keep them from talking about what had happened.

"There's no way to tell if they took anything," Encizo stated, "but my bet is that they came here to get something to launch those rockets from. There are some Yugoslav Katusha launchers in the park, and they're small enough to tow. They could have hooked one up to their trucks."

"Get everyone loaded up," McCarter said as he reached for the radio. "I don't want us to get caught anywhere around this place."

WHEN THE COMPANY commander of the Spanish unit at the artillery park couldn't get anyone to answer his calls, he got his driver and drove the five miles to their compound. As they rounded the bend in the road and approached the old police barracks, he noticed a tan Toyota pickup truck heading the other direction. The vehicle wasn't wearing the UN PROFOR insignia on the door and he didn't know of any of the UN contingents that painted their vehicles that color.

As he drove up to the main gate, the red-and-gold flag of Spain was flying, but the sentries weren't at their posts. Drawing the Astra pistol from his holster, he stopped his jeep and walked through the gate. Though the day wasn't yet warm, the smell hit him like a hammer blow. Unlike most of his troops, the captain had been in combat and he knew well the smell of blood and cordite.

Death had come to this outpost today.

CHAPTER TWENTY-SIX

Aviano Air Base, Italy

Now that Able Team was back at Aviano, Yakov Katzenelenbogen was having second thoughts about having called the trio in from the field. With Jack Grimaldi and the Air Force major hanging around, as well, the small building was getting crowded. As always, Lyons was the most restless with the forced inactivity. He was pacing the floor and staring out the window, driving Katz nuts.

Katz made a mental note that if the Farm ever sent Able Team with him to another CP, he'd make sure that he brought a cage to keep the Ironman in when he didn't have anything to keep him busy.

At least Kurtzman had sent him a list of the towns that were due to hold elections tomorrow, so he had something useful to do. Looking at the map, he saw that three of the cities were arranged in an arc around the location of the artillery park that had been raided. Considering how close they were to the last known location of the Iranians, they were the most likely targets.

He had no idea how many rocket launchers the Iranians had taken from the artillery park after massacring the Spanish garrison. What was worse, there was no way for him to find out what was missing until the UN made its investigation of the incident. Knowing the UN as he did, however, he knew that it would be weeks before they were finished. And that was time the Stony Man team didn't have. If he was right, and he had to think that he was, the attacks would take place tomorrow on election day.

That meant that he had to choose between the three towns and decide which one to send the commandos to, and he didn't have a clue as to which one of them would be the target. Then it hit him; it had to be the Serbian town of Spivak. According to the information the Farm sent, the other two places had a mixed Serb and Croatian population, but Spivak was solely in Serb hands.

Of the Bosnian Muslims' two enemies, the Serbs were the strongest and had caused them the most problems since the breakup of the former Yugoslav republic. In fact the Muslims had even briefly allied themselves with the Croats against their common enemy. If the Muslims wanted to strike the strongest blow, it would be against the Serbs first.

When he made contact with the Farm, Kurtzman's face came on the video screen. "It's Spivak," Katz stated. "They're going to hit Spivak."

"How do you know?" Kurtzman asked. "The satellite doesn't show that yet."

"I applied a little reason and logic, and that's how it came out. It's going to be Spivak because that's a Serb town and the Muslims hate the Serbs more than they do the Croats. They're going to want to get the most bang for their buck, and that's where they'll get it."

"Okay," Kurtzman stated. "We'll watch for the satellite indicators and get back to you."

Stony Man Farm

THE GAS ATTACK on the French laager and the massacre of the Spanish troops at the artillery park had ratcheted the already tense Bosnian situation up yet another notch. Now the UN PROFOR was aware that the rockets were present in their area of operation. But rather than this being a help to the Stony Man team's efforts to stop a major tragedy from taking place, it was only making their situation more dangerous. The PROFOR command had put every available troop they had in the field looking for an enemy force moving in tan vehicles, and that put Bolan and Phoenix Force in their sights, as well.

After getting the latest update from Katz, Barbara Price went out to the helipad to greet Hal Brognola as he returned from his latest flight north to update the President.

"Hal, the mission has been compromised and I

want to bring the guys home before something else goes wrong. With the gas attack and the massacre of the Spanish troops, this situation isn't any kind of secret anymore. PROFOR has every troop under its command looking for terrorists. And with all those trigger-happy UN grunts racing around looking for nerve-gas rockets, they're going to get shot up as soon as someone spots them in that tan Toyota."

"That was what I was thinking, too," he admitted as he keyed the lock on the door, "and I discussed mission closure with the President."

"And?"

"And he said it's a no go. He thinks that since the guys have been in on it since the beginning and are still closing in on the Iranians, they're still the best bet for stopping them in time."

Like it or not, Price knew that Brognola was right. "Okay, then," she said, "since the cat is out of the bag, as it were, I want to go all out. We're blown and it's just a matter of time now before someone scopes our people out and shoots them up. So, since we're compromised, there's no need to maintain our secrecy, and I want to pull out all the stops."

"What else can we do that we aren't already doing?"

"We can send Grimaldi in with a gunship to give them some aerial mobility and fire support. The elections are tomorrow, and they don't have much time left. Going aerial may be our last chance to catch up with them in time."

"Do it," he said.

"I've got an armed Black Hawk on standby at Aviano. With it, Grimaldi can carry them to the contact and then provide a little air support, as well."

Brognola sighed. Once more Barbara was second-guessing him, but he also knew that there was nothing he could do to get her to stop doing it. After all, that's why she had been chosen to be the Stony Man mission controller.

"Just do it and I'll worry about the political fallout later."

Price clicked in her comm link. "Aaron, tell Jack to launch."

Aviano Air Base, Italy

"I WISH I WAS GOING with you this time," Hammer said as he walked out of the ready room beside Grimaldi.

"I know. But like Katz said, this has gone well beyond what we normally do on our missions. We'll be facing the PROFOR guys now, as well as those Iranians. It's going to get nasty, and he doesn't want you to have to answer the same questions we're going to have to answer when this is all over. It won't be a good career move if you know what I mean. Plus you're still our ace in the hole, son. If I get a Strella up the ass, you'll get to fly in and pick up what's left."

"Nonetheless," Hammer replied, "I feel like I'm not holding up my end of the stick."

"You've done a lot for us already," Grimaldi said. "And it's all been things you didn't sign on to do when you took up wearing the blue suit. If you hadn't made that bombing run for us, the guys would be facing several times the number of bad guys that they are now."

"I still wish I was going with you."

The UH-60 Black Hawk Grimaldi strapped himself into this time was another loan from Aviano special operations squadron. It was painted matte black and looked like it had had a nose job. In this case, though, it had been a nose extension and not a reduction.

In fact the nose-gun package from a AH-64 Apache gunship had been grafted onto the Black Hawk to give it more firepower. And the 25 mm chain gun packed a lot of firepower in a small package. With the chain gun and the 7.62 mm Minigun on the door mount, he could work his way through almost anything short of heavy armor. Since the Iranians were driving Toyota pickups, he shouldn't have any problem putting them out of action as soon as he could get them in his sights.

Hammer watched until the Black Hawk was out of sight before getting back into the jeep and driving back to the CP. Like Grimaldi had said, there was still a chance that he'd get into the game.

GRIMALDI'S MODIFIED Black Hawk chopper also had up-rated turbines to go along with the extra armament and equipment. And since he was flying without a strike team in the back, he made record time across the Adriatic. As he approached the coast of Bosnia, he flipped the switch to the IR-emission units mounted on both the belly and the back of his machine. They emitted strobe-light-like bursts of high-energy infrared radiation and were designed to burn out heat-seeking-missile guidance systems. It was a passive defense, but every little bit helped.

Then, to try to keep off of anyone's radar screens, he activated the chopper's ECM suite. The chopper's Electronic Counter-Measures weren't as good as the ones on bigger aircraft, but he felt more comfortable with the unit turned on.

Lastly he armed the chain gun in the nose turret and selected the armor-piercing ammunition feed. The 25 mm bullets would chew through most anything he might encounter.

With everything set to rock and roll, the pilot tightened the fingers of his flying gloves before flipping on the TFR navigation system. The Terrain-Following Radar would let him get right down in the dirt for a nap-of-the-earth flight, which was another way of saying that he'd be flying closer to the ground than most of the local bumblebees. No big deal, though. If he had to, he'd roll in on the chopper's landing-gear wheels. Anything to keep him out of the sight of the Strellas.

As he nudged forward on the cyclic to drop the Black Hawk's nose, he keyed his throat mike to let the boys know that he was on the way. "Stony Man, this is Flyboy. I'm inbound to your location, over."

"Flyboy," McCarter's voice came over his earphones, "this is Phoenix One, copy inbound. Welcome to the party. What's your ETA? Over."

Grimaldi glanced at his nav screen and his airspeed indicator. "I'd say a little under an hour, over."

"Roger. We'll keep on trucking until we can find a good Lima Zulu. Over."

"Roger, I'll be looking for you."

Italy

ALI NADAL NEVER THOUGHT that it would come down to this. Since that day of death in Beirut, he had seen himself as a holy warrior, killing the enemies of Islam wherever he found them. He had always assumed that he would die somewhere along the way as did all the best holy warriors. He only feared death because it would take him away from his quest for vengeance. A dozen or more Westerners had died in the attack at Aviano, but that wasn't enough blood to even begin to pay for the deaths of his family. The blood of a hundred Americans wouldn't be enough to pay.

But he had never thought that he would ever have to offer himself to God this way, as a human bomb.

He knew the stories of other freedom fighters who had strapped explosives to their bodies and then walked up to Israeli patrols before detonating them. It was a tactic that had worked particularly well with young female suicide bombers before the Israelis learned to fear Muslim women, as well as the men.

The call he had been expecting from Tripoli had finally come in, and he had been ordered to eliminate that secret American team at Aviano at all costs. And he hadn't been given the option of failure this time. When he explained that he had come to the same conclusion and was already moving against the Yankees, his superiors wanted to know how he intended to attack them. But when he explained his plan to smuggle in small arms, it had been turned down cold.

Tripoli wanted a bigger attack, something that wouldn't only take care of the American special unit, but that would do more damage to the base itself. A suicide-bomb attack had been ordered, and he had been told to lead it himself. Tripoli couldn't afford to take any more chances.

The explosive strapped to his body was RDX, Rapid-Detonating Explosive, and was several times more powerful than an equal amount of C-4 plastique. To increase the fragmentation effect, the RDX had been studded with small pieces of hardened steel rod. When the RDX detonated, the steel rods would fly out in all directions like a thousand machine-gun bullets. But, being square-tipped rods instead of pointed bullets, they would do more damage when they hit, tearing through flesh and bone instead of punching a hole.

The system had been extensively field-tested against the Israelis and it worked well. Anyone within twenty yards of the blast would die, shredded by the projectiles. He would die in the blast, as well, but it would be a death well spent if he could take the Yankees with him.

When he stepped out of his black BMW, he left the keys in the ignition. It had been a great car, but the booby trap under the seat now made it yet another weapon against the West. Whoever tried to drive it from the parking lot would become another victory for the revolution.

Walking across the parking lot, he got into the waiting ambulance.

Stony Man Farm

WHEN HUNT WETHERS checked his satellite-orbit monitor, he saw that he had another satellite coming up on a pass over Italy. Thinking that he would get a jump on what he knew Lyons would be asking him to do before too much longer, he programmed it to activate the position trackers Gadgets Schwarz had planted on the terrorist's car.

No sooner had he told the satellite to send the activating signal than he got a return. Flashing the map up on the monitor, he saw that the icon marking the bugs was motionless in what looked like a parking lot on the western side of the Aviano air-base perimeter.

He uplinked the satcom video connection, and Katzenelenbogen's face immediately appeared.

"Katz," Wethers said, "you may have a problem. I don't know what to make of something I just came up with here."

"What's that?"

"I punched in the code for those trackers Schwarz put on the Lebanese's car and it came back that it's parked right outside the air base."

Katz didn't need to hear any more; neither did Lyons.

"Gadgets," Lyons snapped, "Get your locator and see if you can pick up your trackers. The Farm says that we have company coming."

"What is it this time?" Hammer asked. Since Grimaldi's departure, the Air Force pilot had been monitoring his progress to pick up the Stony Man team.

"I think we have a hit team coming after us."

"But that's impossible," Hammer said. "This base is closed tighter than a nun's knickers. There's no way that any Iranians or Libyans are going to get in here."

"Electrons don't lie," Schwarz said as he watched the directional needle of his bug locator swing. "They're here or they're going to be real soon."

He looked over at Katz. "You want me to notify base security?"

The Israeli smiled. "Let's not do that this time.

Since they've decided to come all this way just to visit us, I think we should get ready to give them a nice warm welcome.''

"You guys are completely nuts!" Hammer exploded. "You've got a terrorist hit team coming, and you're acting like they're invited houseguests."

"But they are, Major Hammer, they are," Katz said soothingly. "Lyons and the gang have been looking for them for a long time now. And since they've decided to come to us, they've saved us a trip to see them later and we should be properly grateful."

"Jesus, save me from these people."

"You can sit this one out if you want," Lyons offered. "I don't think we'll be very long."

"Oh, no, you don't," the pilot replied as he turned to dig his AK out from under his bunk. "My mama always told me never to let people shoot at me unless I had something to shoot back with."

"Smart mom," Schwarz said. "It's a good thing that you listened to her."

"Obviously I didn't listen to her well enough or I wouldn't be here with you maniacs."

Just then, a thundering explosion shook their small frame building.

"Show time," Lyons said, smiling.

The second blast only emphasized the obvious.

CHAPTER TWENTY-SEVEN

Aviano Air Base

Ali Nadal repressed a smile as a roiling fireball rose over what had been the pilots' ready room at the Aviano base's main hangar. More unbelievers had just been sent to hell, and before the hour was out even more would join them. Despite the air base's security having been so dramatically increased, it had been almost child's play to get the bombs in. Not even a highly motivated security guard wanted to search a reeking sewage-pumping truck too closely.

Since the terrorist's contacts included several key men in the companies that provided facility maintenance for the base's buildings, it had been easy for Nadal to arrange for the truck to come in. He didn't even have to forge the work order or pass that explained the presence of the vehicle to the gate guards. The smell of the contents of the tank on the truck had done all the rest.

When a second explosion sounded by the base vehicle-dispatch office, it was time for Nadal to make his move. After making sure that his medic's white coat was buttoned over the blocks of explosives strapped to his body, he started his vehicle and pulled out of the parking lot. With the ambulance's sirens wailing and lights flashing, he drove up to the air base's main gate and screeched to a stop in front of the barricade.

"Do you need medical help?" he asked the Italian sergeant in charge of the security detail at the gate.

"You guys sure got here fast enough," the sergeant said when he saw the Aviano hospital logo on the ambulance.

"We were just driving by empty when we saw the explosion." Nadal shrugged. "It was just good luck."

"Not for those poor bastards in the hangar," the sergeant answered as he hit the button to raise the barrier. "Go on in and see if you can help."

"Will do."

As soon as the barrier was out of the way, Nadal stomped on the gas pedal and the ambulance shot forward. Once he was out of sight of the main gate, he killed the lights and siren and turned down the street leading to the building housing the American special unit. He knew God was guiding his footsteps today and nothing could go wrong.

Reaching behind his head, he slid open the window that opened into the rear of the ambulance. "Get ready to go," he told the eight men sitting in the back. "We are almost there. When I crash the truck into the fence, get out and go to the glory that awaits you.''

''God is great.'' One of the men raised his fist in a defiant salute.

The other suicide bombers weren't dressed as medics. Instead, they wore battle dress and carried AKs, as well as the bundles of explosives strapped around their waists. Even a man willing to die a martyr's death liked to have a little something in his hands when he went out.

''God is great,'' Nadal answered, and he was surprised at how calm he felt.

LYONS, BLANCANALES, Schwarz and Hammer had all taken cover around the windows and door on the front side of the building. The thin walls wouldn't provide much protection, but it was better than nothing. Katz had his Uzi covering the two windows in back.

Over the wailing of the alert sirens and the clamor of emergency vehicles rushing to aid the wounded, they heard the roar of an engine rapidly approaching. ''Company's coming,'' Lyons called out.

Schwarz flicked his M-16/M-203 combo off safe and prepared to open the party with a little long-range fire. The M-203's 40 mm round was antipersonnel, but it also did wonders against thin-skinned vehicles. If the terrorists showed up in an armored car, though, they'd be in trouble.

When a red-and-white vehicle rounded the corner

a hundred yards away, he smiled as he drew down on it.

"For Christ's sake," Hammer shouted, "don't shoot. It's an ambulance!"

Schwarz ignored him and triggered the M-203 anyway. They hadn't requested medical assistance, and there was no reason for an ambulance to be racing toward them. If it did turn out to be legitimate, the U.S. government could always buy the hospital a new one. Right now, though, ambulance or not, he didn't feel like taking any chances with it.

The 40 mm grenade arched out and connected with the middle of the vehicle's grille. The explosion blasted the radiator to fragments and blew the hood up, covering the windshield. Though unable to see, the driver kept on coming.

Sliding the breech of his grenade launcher open, Schwarz loaded another round, snapped it shut and had the weapon raised in an instant. This time, he sent the grenade into the right front tire.

The explosion shredded the tire. The rubber remnants rolled off the rim and dropped the vehicle down onto the steel wheel. This jerked the ambulance to the right, and the wheel smashed into the curb, bending it and dropping the vehicle onto its frame. The ambulance came to a skidding halt well short of the chain-link fence.

Before the vehicle stopped rolling, the back doors were flung open and half a dozen men stormed out,

AKs and Beretta subguns blazing in their hands as they charged the fence.

As Schwarz ducked to escape the storm of fire, he thumbed the selector switch on his M-16 back to full-auto and sent a short burst into the center body mass of the lead gunman. To his complete surprise, the terrorist vanished in a blinding flash and a puff of dirty black smoke and red spray.

Schwarz instinctively ducked, and the shrapnel passed over his head. "They're suicide bombers!" he shouted.

Hearing the warning, Lyons shifted his point of aim to send his .357 Magnum slug into his target's belly. The best way to stop bombers was to detonate their explosive packages far enough away to keep out of the blast radius.

Lyons's heavy slug connected, and the gunman disappeared. Unfortunately a large section of the chain-link fence diasappeared along with him as one of the fence posts was blown over. Seeing the gap in the fence, the remaining terrorists raced toward it.

From his window position, Hammer was snapping out 3-round bursts from his captured AK. Right after one of his bursts cut the legs out from under one of the terrorists, the bolt of his AK locked back on an empty magazine. When he ducked to change magazines, the man escaped by crawling for cover behind the team's Lancia sedan.

When the Air Force major got into his firing position, he found himself trading bursts with the man behind the car. When neither one of them could score on the other from cover, the terrorist struggled up to get a better shot. Hammer hit him with a long burst that ended with another detonation. Fortunately, most of the shrapnel was absorbed by the Lancia.

A frustrated Nadal watched his assault quickly falling apart. He had expected the Yankees to run for their lives from his human bombs. But that wasn't what they were doing. They were fighting like men possessed and not quailing like the cowards he knew them to be.

To make things worse, since the ambulance hadn't been able to crash through the fence, his men were being forced to try to fight their way into the compound through only two entrances—the gate and the one hole that had been blown in the wire.

Only two of his men were on their feet when Nadal made his decision that the time had come for him to kill the Yankees himself. Yelling for the two gunmen to rush the hole in the fence, he jumped out from behind the fender of the ambulance and dashed for the gate.

With his left hand holding the detonator and his right wrapped around the pistol grip of his Beretta subgun, he raced across the open ground screaming "God is great!"

As he ran, he saw a big blond man step out into the open door of the building with a pistol in his hand. The Yankee showed no fear as he sighted the pistol. The calmness of his enemy infuriated Nadal, and he screamed his defiance right as the Yankee fired.

The .357 round took him in the face, on the right side of his nose, and blew his brains out the back of his skull. A twitch of dying nerves pressed his hand against the detonator and the ten pounds of RDX detonated with a bright pink-tinged flash.

Nadal hadn't even made it to the gate, and he didn't hear the other two explosions that marked the deaths of the last of his suicide squad.

"IS EVERYONE OKAY?" Katz asked.

"Nothing major," Lyons said as he examined a couple of minor shrapnel hits. Even slowed by the fence, some of the fragments had still had the power to cut.

"I hope we've seen the last of these guys," Schwarz said as he looked over at the wreckage of the team's Lancia. "Look what they did to our car. I was really beginning to like that thing. We'll have to see if we can get another one."

"We've seen the last of them in human form at least," Lyons declared. "Bits and chunks of meat and things aren't likely to cause us much more trouble."

"Unless they don't get this mess cleaned up quickly enough," Blancanales added. "It gets a little too warm around here for this to lay in the sun very long."

Hammer looked a little green around the gills.

Shooting people was one thing; seeing them explode was another. "Can I be excused now, guys?" he asked plaintively. "I think I've enjoyed just about all of this that I can stand. I feel a distinct urge to vomit."

"Go ahead." Blancanales sounded sincerely sympathetic. "We understand. It happens to all of us at first. You'll get used to it."

"Jesus, I sure hope not."

"Heads up, guys!" Schwarz shouted when he caught the sound of more vehicles racing toward them.

Rounding the corner came three jeeps of Air Police, their weapons at the ready.

"Not those clowns again," Schwarz moaned when he recognized who they were. "I'm in no mood to sit in their jail again until the Farm can spring me."

"That's not going to be a problem this time." Katzenelenbogen sounded determined. "Ground your weapons, and I'll talk to whoever's in charge."

Katz walked out through the blasted hole in the chain-link fence and stepped over the remains of a suicide bomber to meet the security vehicles. As he had expected, the officer in charge was none other than Colonel Waters, the senior U.S. officer at Aviano. As a professional chair-borne warrior, the Air Force colonel wasn't well prepared to deal with the realities of combat he was facing.

The ground in front of the CP building looked like someone had driven a couple of cows into a spinning airplane propeller. Most of the bleeding chunks of meat weren't even recognizable as having ever been human. The odd dismembered arm with a hand still attached to it was a dead giveaway, however.

"I see that they hit you, too," Waters said, his eyes avoiding the pool of blood at his feet. "Obviously this was a diversion attack designed to keep us from—"

"We were the real target," Katz cut him off abruptly. "Not the air base. The bombs at your hangars were a diversion so your security force would let the ambulance inside the perimeter without searching it."

The colonel realized where this conversation was going and tried to recover. "But it was a real emergency," he bleated. "We had causalities that needed immediate medical assistance. No one ever thought that the terrorists would use an ambulance to get through the gate."

"Did you think that they were going to drive up in armored vehicles flying the Palestinian flag?"

"But," Waters repeated, "they were in an ambulance."

"You might want to have a talk with your chief security officer about your vehicle-admission procedures before someone from the White House does."

The colonel blanched. "Yes, sir," he said.

"And now, if you're through here, Colonel, I need to file my report on this incident."

"Of course, sir."

On the way back to his vehicle, Colonel Waters was very careful about where he put his feet.

Stony Man Farm

FOR A CHANGE, the entire staff of the computer room was on duty when Katzenelenbogen called in to report the suicide attack on the CP. They had all caught up on their sleep and wanted to be in on what they hoped would be the final hours of the mission.

"Are you all okay?" Barbara Price asked after Katz gave his report.

"The Ironman and Pol picked up a few shrapnel nicks," Katz reported, "but nothing serious, and we can take care of it here."

"That's good news."

"The best news," Katz said, "is that I think that's the end of the Lebanese's operation. If he had to resort to using suicide bombers, that tells me that he didn't have anything left to use against us. Now we can devote all of our energy to supporting the Stony Man team."

"Are you still functional, then?" Price asked.

"We've got a bunch of new holes in the walls, and the windows will never be the same, but it appears that none of our comm gear was damaged. We can still coordinate the operation from here."

Knowing that the CP was still in operation, Price switched subjects. The second Aviano attack had just become old business. "What's the status on the air option?"

Katz glanced at his watch. "Jack's approaching the LZ, and the guys should be on board within the next ten minutes or so."

"Good," she said. "Hunt has a new location where the Iranians have stopped, and they should get on it as soon as they can."

"Great," Katz replied. "I'll pass that on as soon as they're in the air. Maybe we can actually get this thing wrapped up today."

"Cross your fingers."

"I've got everything but my ears crossed."

"Just as long as it's not your wires that you have crossed."

"Never happen." Katz laughed at her pun. Laughs had been hard to come by lately and he liked how it felt.

Bosnia

AFTER A GROUND-HUGGING, tree-hopping flight across half of Bosnia, Grimaldi was vectored into the landing zone by radio. The pilot spotted Hawkins standing in a clearing beside a road and clicked in his throat mike. "Got your Lima Zulu," he radioed.

"Bring it on down," McCarter answered.

Grimaldi flared out and brought the chopper down, but kept the rotors spinning. "Come on, guys, come on!" he radioed. "We don't have all day."

"Keep calm, Flyboy," McCarter sent back. "We have to grab our gear."

"Katz is on the horn for you." Grimaldi held out a headset when Bolan entered the cockpit.

"Hunt has come up with a location you need to check out," Katz said. "The satellite shows that the target trucks have been parked there for some time now."

"Send it."

Bolan marked the coordinates on his map and passed it over to Grimaldi. "Here's the target this time."

McCarter slid into the copilot's seat and entered the coordinates into the navigation computer. "Let's do it."

CHAPTER TWENTY-EIGHT

Spivak, Bosnia

Major Naslin was glad to have finally reached his destination—the hills overlooking the Serb-held town of Spivak. Though the town was less than sixty miles from the artillery park, it had taken him hours to get into position. One reason for the delay was that the area was crawling with PROFOR units, and they had been forced to use the back roads and forest trails to reach their position unseen.

Then, on Hukan Rezak's recommendation, he had abandoned the Toyotas he had driven since leaving the bombed-out camp for half a dozen ex-Yugoslavian army Mercedes Unimog trucks. As the Bosnian had pointed out, the Unimogs were painted olive drab like the PROFOR vehicles and wouldn't be as noticeable as the desert tan pickups. Now, back under the trees of the wooded hillside, they were well camouflaged and impossible to spot from either the air or the ground.

As he watched the town below, Naslin went over

the plan in his mind. Rezak's information was that there would be some fifty or sixty thousand people in Spivak in the morning. That would make a good first killing for what would become known as the Day of Death. Of the seventeen rockets, he would send eight of them screaming down on Spivak, spreading their yellow death.

As soon as he had launched the rockets at Spivak, he would hitch up the Katusha launcher and tow it to Daniva, where another twenty or thirty thousand people would be gathered. Two volleys of three rockets should take care of them. Then, the last volley of three would be fired at Zubor and another twenty thousand Serbs or so would die.

By noon, well over a hundred thousand Serbs and Croats would be dead, not counting their children, and Bosnia would be well on its way to becoming an Islamic state.

When word of the fate of these towns spread, and the agents of Rezak's party were prepared to see that the word did get out quickly, the ensuing panic would clean thousands more of the infidels out of Bosnia. Fear of more chemical attacks would send Serb and Croatian refugees stampeding out of Bosnia back to their national homelands.

Naslin would rather simply kill them now and have done with it, but that wasn't possible with so few rockets. He knew that every able-bodied man who fled to the Serbian or Croatian territories would one day come back with an AK in his hand to try to retake Bosnia. But by the time they returned, the Islamic troops would be in place to protect the Muslims and they would die then.

Even with all he'd had to overcome since leaving Asdik's fortress, the plan would still work. All he had to do to bring this to pass was to keep out of sight of the UN patrols until the morning. He had been informed that UN aircraft would be less of a problem because another attack had been launched against Aviano that would cripple their ability to send ground-attack fighters over Bosnia.

Even so, Naslin had been told before that the air base would be shut down, and it hadn't happened. And since he still had several Strella missiles, he ordered that they be sent out to the sentries with instructions that they keep watch for any aircraft flying too close to their hideout.

McCARTER WAS FLYING in Grimaldi's copilot's seat and manning the weapons in the nose turret as they approached the location Hunt Wethers had vectored them into. In the back, Hawkins was on the door-mounted Minigun while the others searched the ground below for their targets.

Bolan was on the radio to Aviano, where Katzenelenbogen was forwarding the latest tracking coordinates from the Farm's borrowed satellite. "The Farm says they haven't moved."

"Damn," Grimaldi said as he nosed the Black Hawk even lower so he could look into the edges of the tree line. "They've got to be somewhere down there." The forest was thick here, and flying over it wasn't cutting it.

"There they are!" McCarter stated. "Two o'clock, fifty meters inside the wood line!"

Stomping on the rudder pedal, Grimaldi snapped the gunship around to face the trucks. McCarter's hands were on the firing controls for the 25 mm chain gun, but he couldn't find a target. Nothing was moving in the wood line, and no one was firing at them.

"Set it down," Bolan told Grimaldi, "and we'll go in on foot."

"You sure?"

Bolan nodded.

Going into a low hover, the pilot bled off his lift until the landing-gear wheels scraped the dirt. The instant he touched down, the Stony Man team, minus Hawkins, exited the chopper in an assault mode.

Grimaldi pulled the chopper back up in the air and kept both the nose turret and Hawkins's Minigun covering the trucks as the team fanned out. When no one shot at them, James and Manning ran toward the trucks. Once inside the wood, they found that the Toyotas had been abandoned.

"We've been suckered." James sounded disgusted over the comm link. "No one's here."

The trampled earth and tire tracks around the two tan Toyota pickups told the story. The Iranians had met up with someone and had transferred the chemical rockets to other vehicles. And since the satellite's computer hadn't been told to be on the alert for a switch, it wasn't tracking the new trucks.

"Now what in the hell do we do?" James asked. That question was on everyone's mind, and he had just been the first to voice it.

McCarter's jaw was set. "I'll be bloody well damned to hell and back if I know. Unless the Bear can pull another one of his bloody rabbits out of his bloody hat, we're bloody well screwed."

Bolan was on the horn to the Aviano CP and gave Katz the bad news. After talking for a moment, he pulled out his map and turned to McCarter. "Katz says that he thinks they're going to hit three towns not too far from here."

"Show me."

Bolan's finger traced an arc covering the three potential targets. "He's saying that it's going to be Spivak first."

"That's his hunch?" McCarter asked.

Bolan nodded.

With the exception of Hawkins, who was the new kid on the block, all of the Phoenix Force commandos had worked off of Katzenelenbogen's hunches for years and knew that they were usually better than hard intel.

"You want to go with it?" McCarter asked again.

"I can be there in twenty minutes or so," Grimaldi said, cutting into the conversation as he glanced at his nav screen.

"Let's do it," Bolan said.

The team was loaded back on the Black Hawk and headed west as fast as the beating rotors could carry it.

Stony Man Farm

HUNT WETHERS was working overtime trying to find what had happened to the Iranians. The vehicle switch had taken him completely by surprise, and he wasn't a man who liked surprises.

Operating on Katzenelenbogen's hunch, he was focusing on the area within a twenty-mile radius of the town of Spivak as the primary target. It was a gamble to put all of his efforts in just that one area, and if Katz was wrong about his prediction of the target, a lot of people would die. But there were those times when you had to go with a hunch, and this was one of them.

Using the borrowed satellite yet again, as quickly as he could identify them, he was marking the vehicles of the PROFOR units. Then, by telling the satellite to ignore all of the marked vehicles and only show him the ones he hadn't yet tagged, he was working his way through all of the traffic in the search area. He wasn't sure exactly what he was looking for, but he knew that he'd recognize it when it flashed on his monitor.

After tagging all the PROFOR units he could find, he marked all the buses and trucks in the belief that it would be unlikely for the Iranians to want to drive to their targets in something big and clumsy. They would want four-wheel-drive rigs if possible, or at least something that had good cross-country mobility.

With that done, he started to look for anything he had missed on the first go-around. He passed on single vehicles, figuring that since the Iranians had stayed together since leaving the camp, they'd be doing that now. It was an assumption, but in this business assumptions had to be made or nothing would ever be done.

The satellite's radar showed him a group of vehicles that was registering as being Mercedes Unimog trucks. The versatile four-wheel-drive German trucks were used all over Europe by both the military and civilians. There was no way for him to tell if these were from a UN unit or a group of civilians. Their location, however, was suspicious. According to the radar, they were clustered in a tight group inside the tree line of a hill overlooking the town.

When that was all he could come up with, he uplinked to Katzenelenbogen in Aviano.

"I've got a group of vehicles that look out of place," he reported. "According to the computer, they're Mercedes Unimogs, but I can't tell if they're military or civilian. Anyway, they're hiding under the trees, and I had to use the radar to find them."

"Even in Bosnia," Katz replied, "vehicles usually don't hide under the trees unless they're trying to hide from somebody. It might be a long shot, but they're hiding in the right area, so they're worth taking a closer look at. I'll pass this on to the team.''

''And I'll keep on looking,'' Wethers said as he signed off.

Bosnia

MAJOR NASLIN HEARD the sound of the Black Hawk's rotors long before the chopper appeared. Any helicopter flying over Spivak was his enemy, and this close to his victory, he wasn't going to let anything stand in his way.

''Use the missiles!'' he shouted. ''Bring that helicopter down!''

Fearing that the chopper might have radioed his position to other UN forces, Naslin raced for the Unimog that had the Katusha launcher hitched to the rear.

''Start the truck!'' he yelled to his sergeant.

He knew that there would be even more Serbs in Spivak when the polls opened in the morning, but the town was already packed with them as it was. He wanted the greatest kill he could get. But as it was said in the holy Koran, God didn't promise any man tomorrow, so the time to do his work was always today.

''What are you doing?'' Hukan Rezak shouted. ''They will see you if you drive out there.''

''I am going to kill Serbs for you.''

EVEN THOUGH the previous target had been a dry run, Grimaldi was taking no chances as he came up on the new target Katz had just called in to them. He came in along the back side of the wooded area, fast and low.

"Keep a sharp eye out, guys," he called to the team in the back.

From his observation post in the rear of the chopper, Gary Manning saw the puff of smoke as the Strella was launched from the wood line.

"Missile!" he shouted over the comm link. "Coming in from our six!"

Grimaldi shoved forward on the cyclic and aimed the Black Hawk for the ground. If he had been in a jet fighter, he would have zoomed up toward the sun to use the solar glare to confuse the heat-seeking warhead. As close to the ground as he was, though, that tactic wouldn't work. Their only chance to survive this was for him to get the chopper in the dirt and present a tail-on, jinking target to the Strellas as he was fleeing the area.

In the back of the chopper, the Stony Man commandos braced for an impact, but the missile was thrown off by the high-energy IR-emission units. After passing by a little too close for Grimaldi's tastes, it impacted on the hillside and detonated harmlessly.

"We have another one coming in from starboard!" McCarter yelled.

"Another one on our six!" James reported.

With two Strellas coming in from different directions at once, Grimaldi had to stop running and go into missile-evasion maneuvers, but he made his move a microsecond too late.

The Strella coming in from the side missed them completely. But though the heat seeker of the missile coming in from the rear was thrown off by the IR emitters, its nose grazed the top of the Black Hawk's tail fin and detonated.

The hardened-steel triangular fragments embedded in the warhead's explosive charge sliced through the chopper's skin as if it were tinfoil. Some of the fragments slammed into one of the U-joints on the tail rotor's driveshaft and kept it from rotating properly. Under the driving power of the turbine, the spinning torque shaft flexed against the immovable U-joint and snapped.

"Oh, shit," Grimaldi muttered when he felt the tail rotor give way. "We've lost the tail rotor."

Bolan keyed the mike to call Aviano.

"We're going down," Bolan said calmly. "You might want to inform the UN boys and tell them to come and collect the pieces."

"Good luck," Katzenelenbogen replied. "I'll make the call."

Katz knew that Hal Brognola had been trying to keep the UN out of this because the President wanted it that way. But the time had come to get some outside help, and he wasn't going to bounce the idea off the Farm. This was his call, and he was making it.

Even so, he also wasn't going to involve the European PROFOR units unless he had to. There were American PROFOR units in the Spivak area, and he knew what buttons to push to get them involved. Reaching for the phone, he tapped in a number at the PROFOR headquarters on the other side of the base.

"U.S. PROFOR," the operator said after picking up on the first ring. "How can I help you?"

"This is Mr. Brown," Katz said, "and I'm calling on a Code Aurora Three Zero priority. Let me speak to the U.S. commander."

"Wait one moment, sir."

"This is General Tucker," a gruff voice said seconds later. "Whoever you are, mister, you're taking my time and I'm a busy man. So who the hell are you and what do you want?"

Katz smiled. After dealing with the wishy-washy Colonel Waters, it was refreshing to talk to a man who knew how to get to the point.

"My name is Brown," Katz said. "As in boot. Code word is Falling Star. I need to have one of your units in Bosnia do me a favor."

"You've got the right buzz words, Mr. Brown," Tucker replied, "but there'd better be a damned good reason for this call. If you haven't heard, we're up to our collective asses in alligators right now."

"I know, General," Katz said soothingly, "and that's why I'm talking to you. I'm the man who can drain the swamp and make the alligators go away."

"I'm listening."

CHAPTER TWENTY-NINE

Aviano Air base, Italy

When Katzenelenbogen put down the phone, he turned to John Hammer. "I know you're not a chopper pilot, but I'd like you to get down to the flight line and get another Black Hawk cranked up. I'll have a rotary-wing pilot standing by to fly it, but I want you in command of the aircraft."

"Are they still alive?"

"I don't know," Katz said bluntly. "You'll find out when you get there."

Hammer took a deep breath. If Grimaldi had run afoul of those Strellas, *he* could be shot down, too. But going in was the least he could do for the men who had risked their lives to rescue him. "I'm on the way."

"I'm going with you," Lyons said. "You'll need someone on the door guns."

"Bring them back here, Ironman."

"One way or the other," Lyons vowed.

He didn't have to add that he meant he'd return with them dead or alive.

JACK GRIMALDI HAD BEEN able to keep the stricken Black Hawk under some control almost all the way down. With the tail rotor disabled, the torque of the turbine shaft wasn't being counteracted, and it made the ship's fuselage want to turn against the rotation of the main rotor. As long as he kept his airspeed up, he could do what was called slip stream. That meant using the pressure of the air streaming past the fuselage to keep it aligned with his flight path. But he had to kill his speed so he didn't crumple the Black Hawk into a ball when it hit.

The instant he came off the throttles, the fuselage started to turn, sending the ship into a slow, flat spiral. Feeling that he was losing control, he yelled out, "Hang on, we're going down!" and dumped pitch to the main rotors.

The Black Hawk fell out of the sky like a stone. At the last possible moment, Grimaldi hauled up on the collective, pulling full pitch to the still spinning main rotor. The blades caught the air and cushioned the impact.

The abrupt stop jammed the landing gear legs up through the bottom of the fuselage and tipped the chopper over onto its side. Grimaldi killed the fuel feed, but the spinning rotor tips slammed into the ground and snapped off at the hubs. The Stony Man team could only hold on while the machine beat itself to death.

By some miracle, when the chopper came to a rest, the fuselage was right side up.

Dazed by the impact, Hawkins pulled himself up to his feet by grabbing on to the Minigun mount. Looking out the open door, he saw the winking of muzzle-flashes in the wood line 150 yards in front of him. Then he heard the pings of AK rounds punching through the chopper's skin.

Getting shot down and crashing was bad enough, but to have someone shooting at him when he was down really angered him. Checking the ammo feed for the Mini, he saw that the indicator light for the gun's power source showed that it was still on.

Settling his hands on the butterfly grips, he smiled as he depressed the trigger. Shoot at him, would they? He'd show them what it felt like to be shot at!

The Mini growled and whined as a solid stream of 7.62 mm tracers reached out and savaged the wood line like a laser beam. The slugs tore through everything in their path, animal, mineral or vegetable.

HUKAN REZAK'S Bosnians, Naslin's Iranians and trees alike suffered under the hail of lead. At first, the Bosnians didn't know what was happening to them; they had never experienced the raw fury a Minigun could unleash. The eerie, whining howl of the motor driving the gun barrels echoed inside the hollow fuselage, adding a frightening note to the ripping roar of the steady muzzle blast.

The stream of fire went from one end of the enemy line to the other and back again, as if the man in the fallen helicopter were holding a water hose. Unlike a stream of water, however, this fiery stream brought sudden death. After watching their comrades instantly chewed to death as dozens and dozens of 7.62 mm slugs tore into them, the fainthearted broke and tried to save their lives.

One of the first to run was Hukan Rezak. The Bosnian had once been a soldier, but the slow poison of Balkan politics had leached all traces of courage from his character along with his humanity. The man who had planned to murder tens of thousands of his fellow citizens didn't make it even three steps before Hawkins saw a flash of movement and gave him a short squirt.

At six thousand rounds per minute, even a short burst from a Minigun meant complete destruction. After the stream of fire passed over him, the Bosnian was no more than ragged chunks of bleeding meat.

With Rezek gone to bloody ruin, there was no reason for anyone else to stay. As fast as they could run, Iranians and Bosnians dropped their weapons and fled.

Suddenly the Mini fell silent except for the whine of the electric motor spinning the barrels, and Hawkins released the trigger. "Yeeee-haaa!" Hawkins yelled over the comm link. The adrenaline racing through his veins made his voice shrill as he sounded the battle cry of his ancestors, the rebel yell.

Waves of heat shimmered above the overheated Mini, and the barrels glowed dull red. He had just delivered some twenty thousand 7.62 mm rounds on target, and he felt fine. In fact he would have liked to have another twenty or thirty thousand to give the bastards. Shoot at him, would they?

With Hawkins's masterful work on the Mini keeping the enemy's heads down, the other Stony Man warriors were able to get out of the wreckage and take cover.

''T.J.,'' McCarter called on the comm link, ''if you're done screwing around in there, we still have work to do.''

''I'm coming, boss.''

NASLIN HAD PAUSED just long enough to watch the Black Hawk fall out of the sky and destroy itself when it hit the ground. He had been on the verge of congratulating himself for having sent the Strellas out with the sentries when he heard the eerie, howling growl of the Minigun.

Panicked that the Yankees would turn their guns on him, he stomped on the gas. With his attention focused on the downed Black Hawk, he hit a boulder that sharply slewed the vehicle sideways to the steep slope of the hill. The Unimog simply rolled over onto its side and skidded to a halt. The swivel hitch tow-ing the Katusha launcher turned far enough to keep the weapon from overturning, as well.

Jumping out of the truck, Naslin saw that the launcher was still usable. "Help me with the Katusha," he shouted to his sergeant.

He was at the extreme range of the rockets. But even so, they would reach the edge of the town and the wind would carry the gas as far as he needed it to go. The Serbs would die. "Hurry," he snapped, "before the Yankees can get here."

The two men quickly unhitched the launcher, spread the trail legs and locked them into position. Each rocket had to be loaded in the breeches of the launcher and the firing contacts lined up. When the third round had been loaded, Naslin cranked the elevation screw wheel to give the rockets maximum range. A half crank of the traverse wheel aimed the rockets at the middle of the town.

Jumping out of the launcher's back-blast area, Naslin shouted, "Fire!"

The technical sergeant was reaching for the launcher's firing button when his head snapped back and he crumpled to the ground.

Looking back at the crashed helicopter, he saw one of the Yankees with a long rifle in his hands, a sniper.

Screaming his rage, the Iranian backed away from the launcher as the sergeant took another hit where he lay. Pulling his pistol, he aimed at one of the nerve-gas rockets that had been laid out for the second volley and fired.

In his haste, his first shot missed. He never got a chance to take a second one.

Manning's sniper rifle spoke again, and the 7.62 mm NATO round crossed the four hundred yards to his target in a heartbeat and drilled through the center of Naslin's chest.

The Iranian staggered from the impact and tried to aim his pistol again. Manning's second round took him in the throat, and he went down.

Not being in a mood to take any chances, the sniper sent a third round into his head as the major lay on the ground.

"Target down," he called over the comm link.

"IS THAT THING INTACT?" Hawkins anxiously asked as he and Encizo approached Naslin's body and saw the rocket round on the ground beside him. It was an unnecessary question because if the warhead had ruptured, they would all be dead. But it was one of those questions you asked just to reassure yourself that what your brain was telling you was true.

"It's okay," Encizo said with obvious relief. "The safety pin on the fuse is still in place, and he didn't hit it."

"Thank you, Jesus," Hawkins muttered softly. Suddenly he was tired. Like everyone else, he had been running on adrenaline for longer than he could remember, and all he wanted to do was to take a long nap. The long-overdue shower could wait.

"Heads up, lads," McCarter called out on the comm link. "We have company coming up on our six. This may not be over yet."

Bolan turned around and was relieved to see the good old Stars and Stripes flying from the antenna masts of the PROFOR vehicles charging up the hill from Spivak toward them. At least American forces would treat them well until Brognola could get them released from wherever they would be incarcerated.

"It's okay," he said. "It's the U.S. Cavalry."

"'Bout damned time they showed up," James growled.

When the vehicles stopped, Bolan saw that the officer in command was an infantry major. Normally a lieutenant would command such a unit, so this was an indication that Katz had gotten through to someone and explained the seriousness of the situation. He stepped forward to meet the major.

"Are you Belasko?" the major asked as he jumped down from his Hummer.

Bolan nodded. "I'm Mike Belasko, yes."

"I'm Major James Worthington, American contingent, sir. I have a message from my command to take you and your men into protective custody and to secure a chopper LZ for your immediate extraction."

Bolan repressed a smile. Once more the Farm had been handed a lemon, but had made lemonade out of it. He didn't like handing over his weapons, even to U.S. troops, but it beat falling into the hands of the UN.

"We're certainly ready to leave here, Major," Bolan replied. "Where do you want us to put our weapons?"

"You're to keep your weapons, sir." The major seemed to be surprised at Bolan's question. "We're just here to reinforce you and to provide security until your extraction. Let me make the call now, because your chopper is already in the air."

"Does your headquarters have access to a chemical-decon unit?" Bolan asked.

"I think so, sir. Why?"

"You might also want to notify them that there's a truckload of Iranian nerve-gas rockets over there." He pointed to the overturned Mercedes Unimog. "They might want to get some security on them, as well."

The American major blanched. "I'll do that immediately, sir."

"And if you don't mind, let's find an LZ upwind, as well."

"That's most affirm, sir."

THE NEXT MORNING, hundreds of thousands of Serbians and Croatians stood in front of their designated polling places to cast their ballots for the future of their war-torn nation. Old men and women, families with children and young adults all waited patiently for the chance to take the power of the vote in their hands. It was a solemn moment, but one filled with joy because they saw their voting as a sign that the long war was finally over and they could live without fear.

While the Bosnians waited in line, in Italy a small group of men also waited. But they waited to board their C-141 Starlifter for the long flight back to Andrews Air Force Base. Like the Bosnians they, too, were joyful. Once more they had put their lives on the line to make the world a better place for ordinary people to live. Once more they had gone into the pit and had come out alive, leaving the bodies of their enemies behind them.

That was the way it should always be.

Preying on the helpless…

DON PENDLETON's

MACK BOLAN®

INITIATION

A doomsday cult known as the Millennial Truth preys on the fears of millions as the year 2000 approaches. But this cult goes far beyond speeches and letters…it is comprised of brilliant hackers, trained commandos and a charismatic leader—clearly a recipe for disaster.

Mack Bolan goes undercover in the cult, looking to stem the tide of Millennial fever.

Book #1 in the Four Horsemen Trilogy, three books that chronicle Mack Bolan's efforts to thwart the plans of a radical doomsday cult to bring about a real-life Armageddon—to take place, of course, in the year 2000.

Available in February 1999 at your favorite retail outlet.

In the badlands, there is only survival....

JAMES AXLER

DEATHLANDS®

Crucible of Time

A connection to his past awaits Ryan Cawdor as the group takes a mat-trans jump to the remnants of California. Brother Joshua Wolfe is the leader of the Children of the Rock—a cult that has left a trail of barbarism and hate across the ravaged California countryside. Far from welcoming the group with open arms, the cult forces them into a deadly battle-ritual—which is only their first taste of combat....

James Axler

OUTLANDERS™

ICEBLOOD

Kane and his companions race to find a piece of the Chintamanti Stone, which they believe to have power over the collective mind of the evil Archons. Their journey sees them foiled by a Russian mystic named Zakat in Manhattan, and there is another dangerous encounter waiting for them in the Kun Lun mountains of China.

One man's quest for power unleashes a cataclysm in America's wastelands.

Bolan takes up arms on a personal mission of vengeance....

DON PENDLETON's

MACK BOLAN®

RETRIBUTION

A vendetta spanning generations places Bolan's friend Yakov Katzenelenbogen and his daughter in grave danger. Ulric Zhandov has vowed to avenge his half brother's death at the hands of Katz's father, aiming to eliminate the family name altogether.

Katz and Bolan have to team up again—to save Katz's daughter from Ulric's minions and to end Ulric's evil vendetta once and for all.

Available in December 1998 at your favorite retail outlet.

The dawn of the Fourth Reich...

THE Destroyer™

#114 Failing Marks
The Fatherland Files Book III

Created by
WARREN MURPHY
and RICHARD SAPIR

From the mountains of Argentina the losers of World War II are making plans for the Fourth Reich. But when the Destroyer's brain is downloaded, he almost puts an end to the idea. Adolf Kluge plans to save the dream with a centuries-old treasure. But then, the Master of Sinanju may have different plans....

The third in The Fatherland Files, a miniseries based on a secret fascist organization's attempts to regain the glory of the Third Reich.

Available in February 1999 at your favorite retail outlet.